Nelda's Homecoming

Agnes Alexander

Nelda's Homecoming

The next thing she heard was the clomp of his boots as he climbed the stairs to their apartment. She felt paralyzed. What could she do now? She took a deep breath and bit her lip. She knew she had tried, but it was no use to attempt to escape him any longer. She'd just have to face him and get it over with. She jerked open the door at the top of the stairs and glared at him.

He smiled at her.

Bucking up her courage and using as unemotionally charged voice as she could, she asked, "What do you want, Spencer?"

He didn't answer until he got to the top of the steps and reached for her. She backed away and he dropped his hands to his side. "I want to talk to you, Nelda."

His voice was low and soft, and she had to look away. Why, after all he'd done, did his voice make her feel weak inside? She should hate him. Instead she wanted to reach out and grab him around the neck and pretend he'd done nothing to warrant her leaving him. She managed to fight off those feelings. "Then talk fast. I have to get back to work."

He came into the sitting room and closed the door behind him. "I don't want anyone to hear what I've got to say."

She tossed back her head and a lock of her sandy brown hair fell out of the twist. "Of course, you don't. If I were trying to sweet talk somebody with lies, I'd want privacy, too."

"You really are upset with me, aren't you, darling?"

"Don't you think I have a right to be?"

"I believe you think you have the right but if you knew the whole story, you'd think differently."

"I know the story and I don't believe you."

"To be honest, I didn't think you'd believe me."

"Then why are you here?"

"I'm here because I love you, Nelda. I loved you the first time I came through Settlers Ridge and laid eyes on you. I loved you when I was finally able to convince you to marry me. I love you now and I'll always love you. That will never change."

Oh, how she wanted to believe him. Though they'd been married almost two years, his presence still thrilled her. She loved this man so much. She knew if she would open her arms to him, he'd love her with his body, if not his heart and mind. But his actions belied his pretty speech. He didn't love her, no matter what his mouth said. He'd proven that the day she saw him standing on the porch of that house in Denver with that pretty blonde Antoinette pressed against him with her arms around his neck.

What They Are Saying About
Nelda's Homecoming

Scoundrels, working girls, royalty, and murder! *Nelda's Homecoming* delivers a taste of the old West with cowboys and lawmen along with frontier women who are quick to take matters into their own hands. Agnes Alexander shines again with another trademark western, this time adding a mystery layer complete with a lurking killer. A lot of western, some romance, and some mystery put *Nelda's Homecoming* in the can't-put-it-down category.

—Lynn Chandler Willis
Award-winning author of *Tell Me No Secrets*,
Tell Me You Love Me, and Shamus Award finalist

Nelda Gentry Barrington was married to the love of her life, Major Spencer Barrington. She trusted her husband and cared for him deeply and loved the life they were building. Then the gossip started and stories about another woman. She didn't want to believe what she was hearing but proof made it hard to ignore. But a more menacing secret lay between them, a secret that could not only destroy her marriage and take away the man she loved, but if Nelda discovered the real truth, she could lose everything, including her life.

—Karen Fritz author of *Crossroads* and *Blind Vision*

Nelda's Homecoming

Agnes Alexander

A Wings ePress, Inc.
Romance Novel

Wings ePress, Inc.

Edited by: Jeanne Smith
Copy Edited by: Lynn Hanson
Executive Editor: Jeanne Smith
Cover Artist: Trisha FitzGerald-Jung

All rights reserved

Wings ePress Books
www.wingsepress.com

Copyright © 2019 by: Agnes Alexander
ISBN 978-1-61309-605-5

Published In the United States Of America

Wings ePress Inc.
3000 N. Rock Road
Newton, KS 67114

Dedication

Dedicated to the memory of
my dear friend, Katherine Fisher
who loaned me her daughter's name,
Nelda

One

Fort Delling, Colorado 1879 - 1880

Nelda Gentry Barrington thought she heard her husband's name mentioned as she bent to pick up the letter that had blown out of her hand and into the <u>alley</u> beside the fort's commissary. Though she was out of sight of the boardwalk, a woman's voice had floated to her. She immediately recognized the speaker as Layla DeLay, the wife of Gilbert DeLay, Fort Delling's commanding officer. The woman who answered was Sarah Nostrum, wife of Captain Seth Nostrum.

Moving closer to the side of the commissary so she would stay out of sight, Nelda paused and listened. Were the women talking about her husband? No, she told herself. There had to be a mistake. There was no way Spencer would do such a thing as they were accusing him. He wouldn't do it to her again.

She and Spencer had been happily married for almost two years and the union was growing stronger and happier all the time. How could Layla say such a thing? Mrs. DeLay had to be wrong.

Moving further back into the shadow of the building, Nelda bit her lip and listened as Layla DeLay, the fort's biggest gossip spoke again. "It's the truth, Sarah. Gilbert told me all about it when he came in from maneuvers yesterday."

"But I saw Nelda last night. She said Spencer had told her he'd be taking a couple of the men on a special patrol and that they'd be home in three or four days after the others arrived back at the fort." Sarah voice was much softer than Mrs. DeLay's.

"I know, dear. That's what Gilbert sent one of the enlisted men to tell her. He said he wanted to spare the woman as much embarrassment as he could."

"So, you're telling me that Major Spencer Barrington has a mistress in Denver, even after he promised his wife he'd never see the woman again?"

"That's exactly what I'm saying. He still visits the woman frequently. Gilbert said Nelda found out about the woman when she found a note in the jacket a few months ago. Major Barrington confessed, but swore to Nelda he'd broken it off with the woman."

"And now you're telling me he's still seeing her?"

"Yes, Sarah, I am. Gilbert said Spencer set his lover up in a nice new house on Maplewood Street in Denver after

Nelda found the old address. Almost every time the soldiers leave here for a few days, the major spends time with her."

"Do you mean he actually spends time in the woman's bed?"

"Of course he does. Why else would he visit her so often?"

"And he's still able to keep all this from Nelda?"

"Well, you know she was only about seventeen or eighteen when she married him and followed him here from somewhere in Wyoming. I'm not sure where."

"I'm so sorry. I really like Nelda, and she's a lovely young woman."

"I know. She's grown a lot since she's been here." Layla De Lay let out a sigh. "I'm not sure why he married her so young, but I'm guessing it was because his mistress isn't the kind a man marries. I think she's French or something and with a name like Antoinette, I'm sure she isn't the kind he wanted to introduce to his fellow officers."

"French, you say?"

Layla laughed, but it sounded more like a snort. "Yes, French. I guess it goes to show that any man is likely to stray when some beautiful foreign woman struts her stuff in front of him."

"I feel so bad for Nelda. Is there anything we can do?" Sarah sounded as if she really cared, but Nelda figured she was enjoying the gossip.

"Of course there is. We'll still be her friend. Poor little thing. We'll make sure none of this talk gets to the enlisted men's wives, but I felt all the officers' spouses should know. That way, we can look out for her when he decides to go to Denver for a few days. We'll keep her so involved with our teas and things she'll never notice."

"You're right, Layla. We should do that. We should also keep her busy when he's away from the fort."

"I plan to visit her tomorrow. Why don't you go see her the next day if he's not back?"

"I'll do that."

Their voices began to fade as Nelda moved deeper into the alley separating the trading post from the barber shop. When she was sure she wouldn't be seen, she ran behind the buildings until she came out near the house she called home. Making sure no one was watching, she rushed inside, closed the door and stumbled to her bedroom.

Only then did she let out the disappointment and hurt she felt as she dissolved into tears. She fell across the bed she shared with Major Spencer Barrington. The man she loved and who she thought loved her. Oh, how she wished he'd given up his career in the military when they'd first married. He'd told her then that his plan was to stay in service for another five or ten years, then move to some small town and set up a law practice or go into some business such as banking. His father was a lawyer turned newspaper man and besides being a soldier, that would be the career Spencer had said he might want to delve into someday. He said that, since he'd be thirty-five in five years, he'd still be young enough to have a second career. But now that career would never happen. Not with her as his wife, anyway.

When the tears began to subside, she sat up and her emotions jumped from one feeling to another. Anger gripped her and she made a quick decision about what she should do. She didn't think it would be hard to pull off. And if what the gossips said were true, Major Barrington would have to deal with the consequences when he returned.

The next morning, Nelda said a quick good-by to a surprised Layla DeLay when she came by for the promised chat.

"I'm sure you'll tell Spencer where I've gone," she said to the general's wife. "I'm sure he'll understand it's important I visit Aunt Susan in Cheyenne since she's so sick." She picked up the carpetbag she'd packed and indicated the private was to bring her trunk to the stage stop.

It didn't bother her that a confused Layla watched as she pulled her cape tighter around her and boarded the stagecoach. Nelda didn't explain to her or anyone else that before going to Wyoming she was going to make a stop in Denver.

~ * ~

A few days later, Spencer was glad when he saw Fort Delling looming before him in the darkness. He stifled a yawn as he and his patrol rode through the gate. He was tired. The maneuvers had been longer and more strenuous than usual and several of the men were out of sorts since they didn't find the outlaws who had raided the trading post out on the prairie and killed the owner. Then Spencer had chosen to add three days to go by Denver. He was exhausted and was glad to be home with Nelda and to get back into his daily routine. Leaving his horse with the private at the Fort livery, he walked to the edge of the compound and headed toward the house that served at his quarters.

Stepping on the porch, he expected Nelda to open the door and greet him with a warm smile on this chilly evening as she always did when he'd been away for several days.

The front door remained closed and there was no light inside. He frowned as he opened the door and realized the house was empty. "Nelda must still be out somewhere. I only hope she's not still mad at me."

He thought they'd overcome the fight. After all, the day he'd left with the troops, she told him she'd always love him. He knew she was looking at him strangely when she said it, but he didn't dwell on it. Nelda was the love of his life and he was sure he was the same to her. Just because she'd somehow found out about Antoinette a few weeks earlier didn't mean he didn't love Nelda and always would.

He thought she'd finally accepted his apologies and believed him when he lied to her and said he'd never visit Antoinette again. He'd almost meant that promise because he didn't want to lose Nelda. Besides, Antoinette was becoming more and more of a problem and that wasn't part of the bargain he'd made with those in power. Though he intended to honor his pledge to his country, he didn't want to lose his wife over the debt or the promise he'd made to the government when they approached him to spearhead the secret assignment to see to Antoinette's safety. He'd made the arrangement before meeting Nelda, and he now wished he'd refused to get involved, but he couldn't get out of the situation.

He couldn't help remembering when he met Nelda. That beautiful young woman with the flashing blue eyes and soft brown hair had stolen his heart the first time he looked at her. But he knew if it came to it, he'd try to make another arrangement with Antoinette. He wasn't going to lose Nelda.

Entering the parlor, he looked for a note. When his wife went to visit one of the other officers' wives, she always left him one, but maybe she didn't expect him to come home that night. Not finding anything, he headed to the kitchen, then the bedroom.

There wasn't a note anywhere.

Shaking his head, Spencer unbuttoned his uniform jacket and slipped his arms out. Sitting on the side of the bed, he removed his boots, then the rest of his outer clothes. When he was down to his drawers, he poured water from the pitcher on the dressing table and washed off. Though he was hungry, he decided to lie back and rest for a bit. When Nelda came in, she'd surely be agreeable to fixing him a bite to eat. He just hoped she wouldn't be too late.

He didn't like her walking around the fort in the darkness. Though none of his men would think of accosting the major's wife, there were often cowboys, miners, drifters and a few Indians around. He knew they wouldn't think twice about taking advantage of any woman who was out alone. And one as pretty as Nelda was especially venerable.

Before he could think about it any longer, he had fallen asleep.

~ * ~

Three weeks later, the afternoon stage stopped in front of the Sheriff Lance Gentry's office in Settlers Ridge, Wyoming. It was three o'clock. The driver jumped down, opened the door and offered his hand to his only passenger.

"Thank you for bringing me right to my brother's door, Mr. Wilson."

"There's no need to thank me. It's a pleasure to have you back in Settlers Ridge, even if it's just for a visit, Miss Gentry. Or should I call you Miz Barrington?"

"Gentry is fine. I intend to take the name back soon." She smiled at him and shook some of the dust off her rose-colored velvet traveling suit. Though the weather was turning cooler, the dust was still abundant in the area.

Wilson looked puzzled, but didn't ask why she might take her maiden name back after she'd been married to Major Spencer Barrington for two years. He simply shook his head and took her valise from the top of the coach and sat it at her feet. Turning, he untied her trunk from the back and hoisted it to his shoulder. "I'll put this on the boardwalk for you."

"Thank you, Mr. Wilson."

He set the trunk near the edge and called out, "Hey, Sheriff. Got a surprise visitor out here for ye." He came back to her and took the valise from her hand and put it beside the trunk.

The door to the jail opened and Lance stepped outside. "I don't believe this." A smile spread across his face. "What in the world are you doing here, Nelda?"

Nelda put her hands on her hips. "Well, isn't that a fine welcome from my big brother?"

Lance shook his head and came down the steps toward her. "Of course, I welcome you, little sister. I'm just surprised to see you so soon after you were here for my wedding six months ago."

"Well, it's me." She reached out to hug him, as he did her. "And it's good to see you, too."

"Are you alone or is Spencer coming?"

"Spencer's not coming." She frowned at him and added, "Now how about taking my trunk to your house?"

"Yes, my dear." Lance looked at Mr. Wilson. "I hope she wasn't this bossy with you on her ride here."

Wilson grinned. "No, sir. She said she was anxious to visit her brother, so I drove fast. She was too busy bouncing around in the stagecoach to complain."

"Good for you. She needs a good shaking every now and then."

"Lance!"

Lance squeezed her shoulder and turned back to the stage driver. "Thanks for bringing her right to the jail, Wilson."

"No problem, Sheriff. I hope you two have a good visit." He climbed back on his bench seat and headed down the street.

"Well, little sister, my house is not very far behind the jail. Are you up for a short walk carrying your valise?" He picked up her trunk.

"Don't you want me to go to the hotel?"

"Of course not. We'll be happy for you to stay with us while you're here."

"I know you won't mind, but how about Grace? She might not want another woman in her house since you've only been married a few months."

"I'm sure Grace will be delighted to have you. Now, are you going to pick up that valise or do you want me to carry it as well as your trunk?"

"I'll carry it. I'll even carry the trunk if you want me to." She made a face at him and grabbed her bag.

He chuckled. "Still think you can do anything your big brother can, don't you?"

"Of course." She turned her head and gave him an innocent smile.

They were on the street behind the jail when he said, "Is there a reason you decided to visit without Spencer?"

"Yes."

"I still can't get over you coming alone." Again, he said, "You know it hasn't been that long since you and he were here for my wedding." When she said no more, he went on, "Are you going to tell me why you're alone or is it a secret?"

"Maybe I'll tell you later. Not now."

"I thought from your last visit that you couldn't stand to be away from the major for any length of time. Now you show up alone."

She didn't answer.

"Still not going to tell me?"

"Don't push it, Lance. I don't want to talk about it now."

"So, what *do* you want to talk about now?"

"How's my friend, Amelia and her family? Even after seeing them at your wedding I'm still amazed she married Jed Wainwright and they're so deliriously happy. She's always been so fancy, and he was a rough and tough half-breed bounty hunter."

Lance chuckled again. "If they were any happier you couldn't stand to be around them. They were in town the other day with little Aaron. You should have seen big tall Jed carrying that baby while his tiny little wife looked up at him as if he was some Greek god or something."

Nelda shook her head. "How about Wilma? Is she still working at Brown's Mercantile?"

"For the time being, she is."

"What do you mean by that?"

"Brown's is for sale. Stanley is moving back to Chicago with his mother as soon as they sell the store."

"Is Wilma going with them?"

"She says not."

"Then I guess I better go see her tomorrow and find out what's going on."

"I'm sure she'll be happy to see you."

They reached the house. Lance followed her up the steps and waited until she opened the unlocked door. She stepped inside and asked, "Is Grace here?"

"No. Mrs. Olsen had a pretty severe burn in the hotel kitchen last week and Grace volunteered to help Effie out with the cooking and serving until she's better."

She gave him a quizzical look. "Should she be doing that?"

He raised an eyebrow. "Why shouldn't she?"

"Lance, don't be coy with me. Grace wrote me that she thought she might be with child. I'm excited about it. I'll be its aunt, you know."

"I might have known that her friends would know almost as soon as I did." He chuckled. "I guess I might as well tell you...we're sure now. Your brother will be a father in early spring."

"Oh, Lance, that's wonderful. Let's get my luggage inside so I can give my big brother a big hug." She turned and looked at him. "Which room will be mine?"

"The one on the right belongs to Grace and me. I decided we'd use that one because I thought I could keep a better eye on the street from there. You can have either of those two on the left."

She entered the first room on the left and dropped her valise on the bed. Lance put her trunk at the foot. She turned and threw her arms around his neck. "Congratulations, Brother. I can't wait to be an aunt."

Laughing he hugged her back. "I'm kind of anxious about being a father myself, but according to Doc Wagoner, we're going to have to wait another six months or so."

"I bet you're hoping for a son."

"Doesn't really matter. I just want it to be healthy and Grace to be all right."

"Good. I'll hope for that, too." She released him and went to the window in the back wall. She pulled aside the pink flowered curtain and smiled. "This is nice. You can look at the woods where the leaves are beginning to fall. There's a good view of the stream. I like it."

"It's a prettier view than ours and I'm glad you like it." He took a deep breath. "Make yourself at home because I'd better get back to the jail. Had to lock Kemp Newton up last night and it's about time to let him out,"

"Is that man still getting drunk and disturbing the peace?"

"He sure is."

"I guess some things never change."

"You're right about that." He grinned at her. "You rest up and we'll go to Olsen's Hotel for supper when my day is through."

"Or I might cook for you if I can find enough in your kitchen."

"No need of that. Grace made a deal with the Olsens. She and I will take our meals at the hotel as long as she is working there. That way she wouldn't have to come home and fix anything. They thought it was a good idea and they even let us use the dining area in the apartment she lived in there before we were married. It's been nice having the privacy when I'm eating with her."

"Maybe she won't like me horning in on your private suppers."

"Then we'll make you eat in the dining room." He winked at her. "Now get yourself unpacked and I'll be back in a little while."

She followed him to the front door. "I don't want to cause you and Grace any problems, Lance. I don't know how long I'll be here, but I'll try to stay out of your way."

"Don't worry about it. I'm glad to have you and I know Grace will be, too." He stepped out on the porch and looked back at her standing in the doorway.

Without warning, Nelda blurted, "I've left Spencer, Lance. I'll be seeing Mr. Cramer about getting a divorce as soon as I can."

Before the stunned man could say anything, she closed the door.

~ * ~

As soon as Lance and Nelda entered the hotel dining room, Grace spotted them and came across the room as quickly as the limp she'd had since childhood when a limb fell from a tree during a thunderstorm and almost severed her foot, would let her. Throwing her arms around her friend, she said, "Oh, Nelda. It's so good to see you. I didn't know you were coming home for a visit."

"She surprised me, too," Lance said.

"When did you get here?"

"I came in on the stage today."

"Is Spencer with you?" Grace laughed then answered her own question. "Of course, he's not. He'd be here to eat if he was."

"That's right." Nelda smiled at her friend.

"What are we having tonight, honey?"

"Fried chicken, potatoes, gravy and green beans, and just for you, Effie made an apple cobbler. She said it probably wouldn't be as good as Henrietta's, but she hoped you'd like it."

"I'm sure I will. Tell her I appreciate it."

"I'll do that. I'll bring plenty so Nelda can eat in the room with us." She put her hand on her husband's shoulder and said, "Why don't you and Nelda go on to the room? As soon as I think Sophie can handle the dining room, I'll be right in with the food."

"That sounds good to me." Lance smiled at her and his voice fell to a whisper. "Hurry along. I'm anxious to take my wife in my arms and kiss her hello."

Grace blushed. "I'll come as quickly as I can." She turned and headed to the kitchen.

As soon as they reached the room where a table and chairs had been set up, Nelda looked around. "This really is private, isn't it?"

"This is the old apartment Grace lived in before we were married. After we were hitched, we lived here until our house was ready to move into."

"Not bad at all." Nelda's mind was whirling, but she didn't voice her thoughts at the time. Instead, she took a seat at the table and said, "Spencer deceived me, Lance."

He eyed her. "How?"

"He did something unforgivable."

"Unforgivable enough that you feel you must divorce him?"

"I think so."

"Do you want to tell me about it?"

"Maybe I'll tell you later. I don't want to talk about it yet."

"I understand." He started toward the door. "Why don't you relax, and I'll go see if I can help Grace bring the food? I don't much like her carrying the heavy tray. Effie Vaughn always piles it high for us."

Nelda nodded and watched her brother leave the room. She didn't want him to guess that she was already planning to move out of his house. Though they probably wouldn't want her to leave, they'd just have to understand that being around such a happily married couple was almost more than she thought she could handle for any length of time. Especially now that she was the most miserable she'd been since she first learned of Spencer's unfaithfulness.

Two

"Major Barrington, I'm telling you everything Nelda told me before she left. She said she had an aunt in Cheyenne who was ill, and she felt she had to visit her. Then she got on the Cheyenne stage and left." Layla DeLay stood on the front porch with her hands in the pockets of her long blue skirt. She didn't want to tell him that if he didn't hear from Nelda it was his own fault.

"But it's been three weeks, and I haven't heard a word from her."

"I'm sure it's because she has her hands full with the patient. Nelda is a responsible person. She'll get in touch with you whenever she can." Layla glanced at the door, hoping her husband would hurry up with his mail and come outside.

"Do you happen to know the aunt's name she went to see?"

"She didn't tell me her name."

"This is so exasperating. I don't know where to start looking for her."

"I wouldn't know either. I've never been to Cheyenne." Again, Layla Delay looked at the door.

"But..."

General Gilbert DeLay came out onto the porch. "Sorry to keep you waiting, Spencer. I had a couple of letters to finish and get out before we leave."

"That's fine, sir. It gave me a chance to have a chat with your charming wife."

Layla blushed. "Major Barrington, you sure have a way with words."

"Now, don't you get carried away by his pretty words, my dear. The major already has a lovely wife and I'm sure he's only being nice to you as he is to all women." Gilbert put on his hat. "I left the letters on my desk. Please be sure they go out in today's mail."

"Yes, Gilbert. I will."

As the general went down the steps and walked to his waiting horse, he said, "We should be back today, but it may be late."

She watched as he and Spencer rode their horses to where a dozen soldiers sat on their mounts, waiting. As soon as the leaders were mounted, the troops fell in line behind the officers and they headed out the gates of the fort.

Layla returned to the house and took a deep breath. In one way she felt sorry for Spencer Barrington because she could tell he was distressed about his wife. In another way, she felt he deserved just what he was getting. Though she liked Nelda, and missed her being at the fort, she hoped the woman would stay gone long enough to teach her wayward husband a good lesson.

~ * ~

The Wildcat Saloon was extra busy and the working women were trying to keep the men happy. Meggie and Liza had attended to the needs of their special customers. Pearl and Hessie were running back and forth to the gambling tables with drinks. It seemed every miner in the hills had decided to come into Settlers Ridge to play cards and to spend their money on liquor or a woman tonight.

Regular customer, Rolo Pullman, reached for the bottle Hessie used to serve drinks. "Give me that, honey child, and after I win this hand, you can take old Rolo upstairs and we'll celebrate."

"Now, Rolo, you know I'm working hard selling drinks tonight. It may be a while before I can go upstairs with you."

"I know that, sugar, but you know I ain't leaving here until you let me celebrate with you in the way you and I have been celebrating for more years than I can count."

"I guess that's why I like you so much, Rolo. You always have nice things to say to me."

"That's the truth, Hessie my love. If'en we was twenty or thirty years younger, you and me would get married and get away from this place."

She laughed. "That would be wonderful, old man. But unfortunately, we ain't young anymore and it's too late to think about getting married for either of us."

"We might be too old to marry, but we ain't too old for other things, are we?" He reached over and patted her ample behind. "Specially on a cool night like this."

She gave his hands a playful swat. "Watch where you put your hands, old man."

"Ah, don't start your complaining. You know you like it. Besides, if you act nice to me, I'll let you have your choice of the buttons off my shirt."

"Don't look to me like you got many buttons left."

"Maybe not, but I got at least one. That's enough for you to add to your collection tonight."

"We'll talk about that later." Hessie cocked her head, winked at him and moved away.

"What's buttons got to do with anything, Rolo?" a young miner who had come with the group for the first time, asked.

The rest of the men laughed and Rolo said, "I guess I better enlighten you just in case you ever get the chance to take Hessie to her room. When a man takes Hessie upstairs, he's got to be willing to give up a button. For some reason the old gal has collected buttons from all her customers ever since she started working. She's got a bunch of jugs plumb full."

The boy frowned. "Why buttons?"

"Who knows. Maybe cause she can't spend them like she does her pay." Rolo let out a hearty laugh. "If'en you're ever entertained by her, ask her to see her Rolo Pullman collection. She keeps them in a jar all to their self. I'd say they's as many from me as from all the other fellows she's known put together."

"Why would you want to take her upstairs when the other women here are much younger and a lot prettier?"

"You may think so, but Hessie's special. She knows just how to make me happy. Can't none of them younger whippersnappers compare to her." Rolo poured a drink and set the bottle down. "Now that's enough talk about Hessie and her buttons. Let's get this game over so I can go upstairs with her. I'm getting' anxious just talking about it.

~ * ~

Nelda walked into Brown's Mercantile the following morning. She decided not to interrupt her friend, Wilma, who was behind the counter waiting on a pretty woman who looked to be in her late twenties or early thirties.

As she walked slowly forward, she overheard the woman saying, "Yes, Wilma, we've settled into a wonderful family in the eight months we've been married, and we can't wait for the new family member to get here. I'm so thankful I decided to come to work here as Sheldon's nurse."

"I'm glad, too, Esther. You've made him a happy man and he seems very pleased that your children are calling him Papa."

"I'm glad they have taken to him so well. You know how their father was never in their lives except to knock them around, so they really do love Sheldon. He's taken to them, too, and treats them as his own. They even want to change their last names to Wagner."

"Are you going to let them?"

"I am."

"I think..." Wilma looked up. "Nelda! It is really you?"

Nelda laughed. "Yes, Wilma, it's me."

Wilma ran around the counter and threw her arms around her friend. "I'm so glad to see you. When did you get here?"

"I came yesterday. I thought I'd drop by to say hello and see how things are going with you." She smiled at Esther. "Wilma and I have been friends since childhood. I'm sorry to interrupt your conversation."

"Oh, that's no problem. Wilma was the first person I met in Settlers Ridge and I often pop in here to chat with her."

"I'm sorry, Esther. I was so excited to see Nelda I was rude. I'd like to introduce you to Nelda Barrington. And Nelda, this is Esther Wagner. I don't know if you learned that she and Doc Wagner are married when you were here for Grace's wedding. They were wed a couple of months before Lance and Grace."

"I didn't know, but that's good news. Doc is a wonderful man and needed a good woman in his life. I hope you'll be very happy with him."

"As I was telling Wilma, I think we've blended into a nice family. I have two children and Sheldon is really good with them. They love being with him just as much."

"That's wonderful. May I offer you my late congratulations?"

"Thank you, Nelda." Esther picked up her purchase from the counter. "I'll be on my way and let you two have a nice chat."

"I was happy to meet you, Esther."

"And I was delighted to meet you, too." Esther smiled at the two of them and hurried out the door.

"Now that we're alone, tell me what you're doing here, Nelda. Not that I'm not glad to see you, because I am, but I was just surprised since you were here only a few months ago."

"I just wanted to get away from the fort for the winter. Spencer is gone a lot this time of year and I get lonely. I decided it was a good time to come spend some time in Settlers Ridge." She hoped her friend wouldn't ask any more questions.

Wilma only said, "I'm so glad. I bet Lance and Grace are happy you're here, too."

"They've been very welcoming, but I feel like an intruder since they're still practically newlyweds."

"I'm sure they wouldn't want you to feel that way."

"You're probably right, and I've decided I'm going to see about getting a room at Olsen's Hotel. I thought maybe I could get Grace's old apartment."

"Will you be here that long?"

"Yes. I plan to stay the entire winter. I also thought I would need something to do while I'm here. I might see if I can get Grace's old job working in the hotel dining room."

"I think since their daughter, Sophie, is almost grown, she took up the slack when Grace left. They didn't seem to need anyone else until Mrs. Olsen burned her arm, then Grace volunteered to help them until Henrietta was able to get back to work."

If she couldn't work in the hotel, Nelda wondered if there was somewhere else in town she might find employment. Before she could ask, the bell over the door jangled and a family of four walked in. The man turned to his wife and said, "I'll be back in about half an hour. It shouldn't take the blacksmith longer than that to fix the wagon wheel."

"I'll be ready by then."

"Can I go with you, Pa?" the little boy asked. "I don't want to stay here with all these women."

He laughed. "I understand that, son. Come along."

Nelda knew Wilma would be busy for a while, so she said, "I'm going to the hotel to meet Lance and Grace for dinner. I'll drop back by later, Wilma."

"We close at six today. I put a stew on to cook for supper. Come back then and we'll have a meal together."

"I'll do that." Nelda nodded to the woman and her daughter and slipped out the door.

On the boardwalk, she paused and looked down the street. Settlers Ridge hadn't changed much. There were a couple of new shops, one of which was a sweet shop. She planned to visit it soon because she loved pastries and they weren't her strong point in the kitchen. Other than the new businesses, things still looked as they had when she left almost two years earlier. Her eyes were then drawn to the Miss Purdy's Dress Shop sign hanging from the roof overhang in front of the store. It still had the swirled fancy letters in the printing.

Nelda couldn't help smiling as she remembered Lillian Purdy coming to her mother and asking Kathrine Gentry to help her design the print for a new sign. Since Kathrine was a school teacher, Nelda guessed Lillian thought she would know about fancy lettering.

She made a mental note to drop in and visit with Miss Purdy after meeting Lance for dinner. Then she might go by Browns again and pick up a few groceries, so she could prepare some of her own meals. That way she wouldn't be horning in on Lance and Grace every time mealtime came around.

~ * ~

Lance had a busy day. He and his deputy, Bryce Langston, had to break up a couple of fights in the street. In the scuffle, Lance got punched in the nose and it was still sore. He had to walk out on his dinner with his sister because one of the ranchers to the south of Settlers Ridge had come rushing in saying somebody was rustling his cows and he wanted his neighbor arrested. Since Bryce had gone out to check on another rancher, there was nothing Lance could do but go with the man to check out the situation.

Now it was supper time and he was anxious to have a quiet evening meal with his wife. He probably should feel guilty that Nelda was joining Wilma instead of them for supper, but he didn't. He was glad to have a chance to be alone with Grace.

He stepped through the back door into the hotel kitchen and said, "Hello, all. Boy, am I hungry."

"I bet so," Effie Vaughn, the hotel's long time cook, said. "You ran out of here before finishing your dinner."

"Couldn't help it, Effie. When somebody needs my help, they don't care whether I've eaten or not."

"That's what makes you such a fine sheriff."

"Thanks, sweet lady."

Effie blushed, and after having dealt with the public for years, it took a lot to make Effie blush. But she had always had a soft spot for Lance.

Grace smiled at him and said, "I have the tray of food ready. Is Nelda in the dining room?"

"She's eating with Wilma tonight."

"Then we're going to have way too much food. Maybe I should put some of it back."

Effie shook her head. "Take it on, Grace. If he's as hungry as he says, Lance will need the extra food."

Lance picked up the tray and winked at her. "She's right. Let's go."

Grace picked up the coffee pot. "I'll be right behind you."

When they reached the room, he put the tray on the table and she set the coffee pot beside it. "You must be awfully hungry because you seemed to be in a hurry to get in here."

He reached for her and pulled her close to him. "I am hungry, but I'm more anxious to take my wife in my arms and tell her how much I love her."

"Oh, Lance. You know how much I love you." She turned her face to him as he leaned to kiss her. As they parted, she whispered, "I probably should feel guilty, but I'm glad Nelda decided to eat with Wilma tonight."

"Don't feel guilty, sweetheart, because if you feel that way, I'll have to share the guilt because I feel the same way. To be honest, I think she was glad to be away from us, too. It's probably because she's not used to her friend being married to her brother. She probably thinks it's strange seeing us together."

"I wonder if you're right." Grace frowned. "You don't think she doesn't like us being together, do you?"

"Not at all. It's more that she sees how happy we are and since she's unhappy with Spencer at the moment, it makes her feel awkward."

Grace began taking the food from the tray and filling their plates. "What do you mean, she's not happy with Spencer?"

"Has she told you anything about why she returned to town?"

"Just that Spencer was gone a lot and she didn't want to stay at the fort alone this winter. Is there more to it than that?" She added, "Food's ready. Have a seat."

He held a chair for her then sat in the chair opposite her. "There is more, but I guess it should be her place to tell you."

"I gather from what you said she's having some problems in her marriage, but I won't question you about it."

"Thanks for being so thoughtful, honey." He took a bite of his meat. "This steak is great. Cooked just the way I like it. Effie may be right. I might eat a second one."

~ * ~

Spencer pushed his chair back from the table in the general's dining room. "That was a wonderful meal, Mrs. DeLay. Thank you so much for inviting me to supper."

"It was my pleasure, Major Barrington. I was sure you were ready for a home cooked meal since your wife has gone to help her aunt."

"You were right about that. I really miss Nelda's wonderful cooking."

"Have you heard from your wife, Major?"

"No, General, I haven't, and I'm really getting anxious about her. Nelda should have at least written me by now. I just can't figure out why she hasn't."

"Maybe caring for her aunt is taking all of her time," Layla DeLay muttered.

Spencer shook his head. "I have a feeling something else is keeping her from getting in touch with me."

Lyla dropped her head and didn't say anymore.

Gilbert DeLay cleared his throat. "Why don't we retire to my study and have a brandy and a cigar, Major?"

"Thank-you, sir. I'd like that."

The two men excused themselves and left the dining room.

Once General DeLay had poured the snifters of brandy and held out the box of cigars for Spencer to select one, they took their seats.

Gilbert broke the silence. "I didn't want to say anything about this in front of my wife, Spencer, but do you suppose your wife found out about that woman in Denver?"

Spencer frowned. "How do you know about her?"

"When you were assigned to this fort, they told me you must be allowed to go to Denver whenever necessary. I figured you must have met her while you were there on business."

"So, some of the troops think I have a woman in Denver?"

"You know you can't keep a secret like that around a place like this, Major. Most of the men seem to be aware of her. It stands to reason the married officers and enlisted men have probably talked to their wives about her."

"I don't appreciate the people in the fort discussing my private affairs."

"I know that, but there's no way you can stop it." Gilbert sipped his brandy. "My wife asked me if I thought that was why your wife hasn't contacted you since she's been gone. I know the other officers' wives are aware of the lady. Somehow Mrs. Barrington could have learned about her through some of the gossip going around."

"I sure hope she hasn't."

"I know, but it's something you should think about. You know if she found out, she'd be so crushed and wouldn't want to get in touch with you."

Spencer downed the rest of his brandy and glared at his superior. "General, I need to take a leave. I need to go find Nelda."

The general nodded. "I've been expecting you to ask for one and I think I should grant it. Come by my office in the morning and I'll have the papers ready."

"I can't sign them tonight?"

"No, Spencer. We have to do this by the book. I don't want any questions of why you're leaving the fort alone. I'll put down that you're on a special mission."

"That won't be a lie. My mission will be to get my wife to come home."

The general chuckled. "I don't think I should state it that way."

Spencer couldn't help smiling. "No, I guess you shouldn't."

"Don't worry. I'll word it so nobody will suspect a thing. We don't want Mrs. Barrington coming back to ridicule and gossip if we can avoid it."

"I appreciate that, sir."

"Of course, you know there's no way I can stop people from thinking you're taking advantage of your wife's absence to go to Denver."

Spencer was irritated. "I never dreamed people were so interested in what I do and where I go."

"Look Spencer, you're the second in command here. People are going to scrutinize everything you do and everything you say. Especially the wives. You know they have a fairly confined life in the fort. Gossip is one way they cope with the loneliness they feel and the dreary days they live with only each other for company when we're out on maneuvers."

"I guess I never thought of it that way, sir."

"I hadn't either until Layla pointed it out to me. She said the troops are gone sometimes for weeks, leaving the women without anyone except a skeleton crew for protection and each other for company."

"I'm guess that's why they rely on gossip."

"You're right." He laid his cigar in a crystal dish on his desk.

"Then if you'll excuse me, General, I'm going home and pack. I just wish I know where to start looking for Nelda."

"Does your wife have any family in the west?"

"Yes, sir. She's from Wyoming. She has a brother there. In fact, we were in the town of Settlers Ridge about six months ago for his wedding."

"Is she close to her brother?"

"Very. They are the only two members left in their family."

"Then I suggest you get in touch with her brother. Since she hasn't contacted you, she has probably gotten in touch with him."

"I'm sure you're right, General. I'll go straight to Settlers Ridge."

After thanking Lyla again for having him for supper, he hurried to his quarters and packed for a trip to Wyoming. If Antoinette were the reason Nelda had left, he just hoped he could explain the woman's place in his life to his wife's satisfaction, though he knew he couldn't tell her the truth. But some way, he had to make Nelda understand. He had to. He couldn't give her up, no matter what.

~ * ~

Nelda looked around the apartment above Brown's Mercantile where Wilma lived. "This is a nice place, my friend."

"It's convenient. I only have to go downstairs to work."

"There's much more room than I thought there would be in here."

"When the first Mr. Brown came to Settlers Ridge and established the store, this is where his family lived. There are two nice sized bedrooms, the kitchen with this dining area, and a cozy parlor. It's as large as some homes."

"Did Stanley's folks live here, too?"

"When Mr. Brown came back from Chicago with his new wife, they did for a while. But after Stanley and Andy were born and began to grow, they decided to build that pretty house on the street beside the store. They then used this place for storage until I came to work here last year. I asked to be able to live here as part of my pay. Mr. Brown said he was glad to have someone living in the apartment again. I think he had happy memories of when he lived here as a child."

"I remember him as a nice man when I would come here to shop with Mama."

"He was nice. I think most everyone liked him."

"How did he die, Wilma? Was it during the measles outbreak last year?"

"Everyone thought so at first, but it was his heart. Doc said it just gave out on him."

"Why does Mrs. Brown want to go back to Chicago to live?"

Wilma sighed. "She said she only stayed here because she loved her husband and he wanted to live here and run the store. She has been homesick for Chicago for more than twenty-five years and Stanley has decided to take her home."

"What will become of the store?"

"It's for sale, but as far as I know they haven't had an offer on it yet."

Nelda grinned. "If I had the money, I'd buy it. I've always thought I'd like to own a store,"

"Me, too." Wilma's spoon full of chocolate pudding stopped in midair. "Nelda, I have a great idea."

"What's that?"

"I know you and I can't buy this place, but what if I convince Stanley's mother that we could run it until it was sold? If they would agree, she could move to Chicago before they sell the place."

"Do you think they'd trust us to run it the way they would want it run?"

"Stanley might have doubts. He's a man, and like most men, he thinks women aren't as smart as the male species. But his mother might look at it differently. If she were to like the plan, she'd convince him. She has a lot of influence over him."

"How would we set things up?"

"I keep the books now, so they know how meticulous I am about making sure each sale is recorded. They also know I'm good about writing up orders for items we're low on and on things we don't have in stock that more than one customer has asked for. They also know I keep good records that show what turns a profit and what causes a loss. I'd assure them we'd send the profits to them each month or each quarter. Whatever they desire."

"This all sounds interesting. I was wondering how to get a job now that I'm back in Settlers Ridge. I want to get my own place and quit intruding on Lance and Grace. Since they haven't been married that long, I feel as if I'm in the way."

"I'm sure they don't mind you being there, but if you want to move out, there's no reason why you can't move in here with me. As you can see, there's plenty of room and if you were here, we could cover for each other when something came up and one of us had to be out of the store for some reason."

"You've sold me on the idea, Wilma. Now, how do we go about approaching the Browns with this super plan?"

"We'll finish our supper, wash our dishes and go see them as soon as we're done."

Nelda laughed. "You're just like you were when we were younger. When you get an idea, you sure don't waste any time putting it into action, do you?"

"Of course not. I guess that's one thing I inherited from my mother. A lot of people think she's just bossy, but she's managed to get a lot of things she wanted by demanding it. It didn't take her long to move the family to Texas as soon as she inherited that ranch."

"Amelia wrote me when that happened. She said you went with them. That was one reason I was surprised to see you when I came back to Settlers Ridge."

"Mama took a train to Texas and I was traveling with my brother and father on the wagons. I managed to talk my dad into letting me come back here. Of course, at the time I thought I was returning because I wanted to pursue a relationship with Stanley."

"What became of that? Amelia had written and told me you had your heart set on winning his love."

Wilma shrugged. "I was enamored with him at first, but that didn't last. When I came to work here, I began to see the real Stanley. He's a nice man, but he's too much of a mama's boy for me. I guess I'm like most women. I want a strong man when I get married. I want all his attention and Stanley would never put me first, married or not."

"I think you're smart." Nelda couldn't stop herself from adding, "The only other thing that you should make sure you see in your man is faithfulness."

"You sound like you're speaking from experience."

Nelda's face took on a stern look. "I am. I came back to Settlers Ridge because I learned Spencer has a mistress."

"Surely he'll—"

"No, Wilma. The first time I learned about her was some weeks ago. He begged me to forgive him and he promised to give her up and never see her again." She sighed. "He lied to me. He only moved her to another address and he still sees her as often as he gets a chance, which is almost every time he leaves the fort."

"Oh, Nelda, I'm sorry. No wife should have to put up with that."

"You're right and I don't intend to. I deserve more from a husband. That's why I'm going to see Mr. Cramer about drawing up divorce papers for me, then I'm going to mail them to him to sign."

"Do you think he'll protest the divorce?"

"If he does, he'll have a fight on his hands. I don't intend to live with a man I have to share with another woman." She stood. "Now, let's get these dishes washed and go see Mrs. Brown."

"I see you go after what you want, too, Nelda Barrington."

"That's going to be Nelda Gentry soon, so you might as well start calling me that now."

"Yes, ma'am." Wilma laughed and stood to take the dirty plates to the dishpan.

Three

Lance came through the back door into the stockroom, then carried his sister's trunk up the stairs to the apartment over the mercantile.

"I'm sure glad Stanley has already brought up most of the furniture and you don't have a lot more to move, little sister."

Nelda laughed. "You've always told me how strong you are. Now stop complaining and put that in the room on the left. Wilma uses the other one."

"Where is Wilma?"

"She had supper plans with the Browns."

"I see." He put the trunk under the window. "You're already made your bed up in that fancy spread. I remember Mama used to have a hard time getting you to keep your bed made."

"I've been making my bed for a long time now, big brother, and Mrs. Brown gave me the fancy spread. She said it went well with the bedroom suit they sent for me to use. I think it's pretty, too."

"Well, I have to admit it's nice here, but you had a nice room at our house."

"I know I did, Lance, and I appreciate the wonderful welcome you and Grace gave me. But I'm a big girl now and I needed to find a place of my own. I feel like this is perfect and I'm sure Wilma and I will get along wonderfully. We've been friends too long not to."

"You're still determined to make a new life for yourself, aren't you?"

Nelda sat on the bed. "It's either that or continue living with a man I'll never trust again."

Lance figured she wanted to talk so he took a seat in the only chair in the bedroom. His voice turned serious. "Are you sure about this, Nelda? I can't help but believe Spencer loves you. If he didn't, I don't think he would have acted as if he did when you were here for my wedding."

She ignored his statement and said, "If I ask you something, will you be honest with me, Lance?"

"I've always tried to be honest with you, Nelda, and I will this time."

"Do you love Grace as much as you seem to?"

He nodded. "I never thought I'd be saying this, but yes, I love her with all my heart. As a matter of fact, I love her more than I ever thought it was possible to love a woman. There's nothing I wouldn't do for her if it was in my power to do it."

"Now that you're married, would you ever take a mistress?"

He frowned at her. "Absolutely not. I don't see how any man who loves his wife could do that."

She sighed. "That's exactly what Spencer has done to me."

Lance looked shocked. "That's hard to believe."

"Well, it's the truth."

"Are you sure, Nelda?"

"Yes, I'm sure. I've seen her."

"How could you do that?"

"Let me start at the beginning." He nodded, and she went on. "When we got home from your wedding, I was putting away our clothes and I accidently found a letter she had written my husband. When I confronted him, he didn't deny that she existed, but he promised he'd give her up and never see her again."

"If he told you that, I'm sure he did."

"No, he didn't, Lance. He simply moved her to a different house in Denver. He visits her every time he goes out on maneuvers or any other time he's away from the fort."

"Are you sure?"

She nodded. "I believed him when he said he'd give her up and we were working things out, or I thought we were. Then one day I heard the general's wife and another woman discussing Spencer's French-speaking mistress. Most of the troops had come back to the fort, but he was still out. I heard them say he was probably visiting Antoinette. I decided that day to come back here to live, but before I did, I made a trip to Denver. I found the house where she lives and while I was spying on it, Spencer came out the front door. She followed him onto the porch and threw her arms around his neck. His back was turned, but he leaned over and I know he was kissing her. I got away before they saw me. As far as I'm concerned, that was the day my marriage to that cheating major ended."

Lance stood and moved to the bed to set beside his sister. Putting his arm around her shoulder, he whispered, "I'm so sorry this happened to you, Nelda. It makes me want to beat that man within an inch of his life."

"No, I wouldn't want you to do that, big brother, but thank you for still wanting to protect me."

"I'll always try to do that, Nelda. And thank you for sharing your pain with me. Now I understand why you feel you must build a new life for yourself here in Settlers Ridge with your friends and family and all the people who love you."

"I knew you'd understand, Lance. It's just hard for me to talk about it."

"I'm sure it is, and I promise I won't say a word to anybody. It's your place to tell people what you want them to know."

"Thank you, brother, but I'll understand if you want to tell Grace. I'm sure she'll be as supportive as you are."

"Yes, she will, and I'll mention it to her, but I'll leave the telling of the details up to you." He squeezed her shoulder then added, "Now, what else can I do to help you move into your new home?"

She stood and smiled. "How about taking me to supper with you and Grace? As I said earlier, Wilma will be eating with the Browns, and I don't want to cook for myself on a Saturday night."

"I'd love to take you for supper." He stood beside her. "Do you have a key to lock the mercantile when we leave?"

"I do, but the front door is already locked and I latched the stockroom door when we came in. We'll go out the back door here. There are two entrances to this place. The door into the parlor goes down the stairs into the store room of the mercantile and is only for Wilma and me to use. When we have company, they're to come up the stairs from the alley. It leads into the kitchen. We'll use that one this evening."

"I know about this kitchen door. I want you to make sure you always lock it when you go in and out. I don't want something happening to my little sister."

"Don't worry. Wilma says it mostly stays locked and to make sure, we're to lock it behind us every time we use it or someone leaves that has visited us."

He tweaked her nose. "Good. I don't want anyone sneaking in on you ladies."

She gave him a good-natured punch on the arm. "You don't have to worry about your little sister. She's a grown woman now, but of course a little worry is always appreciated."

He laughed and followed her out the back door.

~ * ~

On Sunday, Nelda slipped into the church pew beside Grace and Lance. Grace reached over and squeezed her hand. Nelda squeezed back. She knew Lance must have told his wife about her martial problem because Grace looked at her with a sympathetic smile. She was glad. Now she wouldn't have to be careful about what she said in front of her sister-in-law.

Someone touched her shoulder and leaned over her. She looked up to see Amelia Wainwright smiling at her. "Great to see you, Nelda. We must get together while you're here."

This was another person Nelda knew she'd have to tell about her impending divorce, but this wasn't the time. She simply returned Amelia's smile and said, "I'd like that."

"We'll talk after church." Amelia turned to her husband, Jed, who held their son in his arm. He nodded to Nelda and moved with his wife to a pew in front of them.

Nelda looked around and recognized several of the women in the congregation and though there were some men in the audience, many women were alone. She saw Luella Baldwin, the mayor's wife. That was if he was still mayor, but she had no reason to think he wasn't. She also saw Esther Wagner with a young girl who she figured must be her daughter. She wondered if the doctor was out on a call since he wasn't with them. Miss Purdy was there, as were the Cramers. Their daughter Juliette was with them. Grace had told her how Juliette Cramer had tried to win Lance's heart when she returned from school and how selfish the once shy woman had become. Nelda was glad Lance had sense enough to fall in love with Grace and not a twit like Juliette.

As she thought about the Cramer family, she made a mental note to visit his law office that week. She wanted to get the paperwork started so she could free herself of her cheating husband. Then she'd be able to start building a new life.

Other friends spoke or waved to her and it made Nelda feel good to know that some of the people who remembered her were glad to see her back. She only hoped that when they learned she planned to divorce her husband they would still want to be friends. Divorce was a rarity in that day and time, and especially in a town like Settlers Ridge.

But she refused to think about that. She wanted to relax and enjoy a message from the preacher she'd never heard preach, but had met when Lance and Grace were married. Wilma told her he was well liked in the community. She did remember one of her friends writing her soon after she'd moved away and telling her Reverend Eli Ellsworth and his wife had come to town to replace the aging minister who had moved back to Virginia because of his wife's health. She supposed the woman sitting on the front pew on the left holding a little girl, who looked to be about the same age as Amelia's son, was the preacher's wife. She had no idea who the older woman beside her was. Probably either his or her mother, or maybe an aged aunt.

A tall young man walked in with a man who had to be his brother. He was too young to be the boy's father. Nelda wondered who they were because she was sure she'd never seen them. She did notice that the younger man grinned at Sophie Olsen and she grinned right back at him. *Ah, young innocent love.*

The preacher, a man of average height and with sandy brown hair, moved to the front of the congregation and asked everyone to stand. His smile was infectious as he the announced the hymn they were to sing to open the service. The rustle of skirts and the movement of bodies filled the sanctuary as the people began to stand. Before the piano played or the congregation began to sing, the group was stunned into silence when several shots rang out in the church yard.

Lance didn't hesitate. He moved into the aisle and ran out of the church before anyone could ask what was going on.

Jed Wainwright handed their son to Amelia and followed him. As did the man who had come in with the tall, younger boy.

When the shooting continued, Nelda grabbed Grace's hand and whispered. "What's happening?"

"I don't know."

"Folks, let's try to calm down," Reverend Ellsworth said. "I'm sure you're safe here in the church. Our sheriff will let us know what's going on as soon as he knows."

The older woman beside the preacher's wife left her pew and came over to Amelia. Nelda heard her say, "Dear, let me have Aaron. I know you and Grace want to check on your husbands, but please stay in the entry. It might be dangerous to go outside until we know what's happening."

"Thank you, Mrs. Ellsworth." She turned to Grace. "Let's go. You come, too, Nelda. I'm sure you want to make sure your brother is safe." She then motioned for the young man to follow them.

When they got to the entry in the back of the church, Amelia pushed the door open a crack and the shots became louder. "I see them. They look as if they've all taken cover in front of the hotel. Whatever is going on must be taking place there. I figure the outlaws are inside."

Grace looked out the crack from the other side. "Oh, thank God. I see Lance. He's behind that wagon in front of the hotel. He's all right, Nelda."

"Do you see Virgil Danforth?" The young cowboy's voice shook a little.

"No...wait. Yes, I do. Look there behind that water trough down below the gun shop. He's fine, too."

"I see him now. Oh, thank You, God." The boy's voice still shook.

"Do you have any idea what's happening?" Nelda asked.

"Best I can tell, somebody is shooting up the hotel," Amelia said.

"Oh, no," Grace cried. "Mr. Olsen is working the desk. He lets Mr. Drake have every other Sunday off, so he can bring his mother to church. I saw them inside, but Sophie's the only one of the Olsen family I've seen here today."

"Look, Grace. Somebody just ran up and is helping Lance."

"That's Bryce Langston, his deputy. He and Bryce have the same deal. They switch Sundays. Today it was Lance's turn to come to church. I saw Bryce's wife inside. Should I tell her he's involved?"

"I'm right here, Grace." Lettie Langston said. "Is Bryce all right?"

"Yes. He and Lance are hunkered down behind that wagon near the hotel. It looks like they're discussing something. Probably some kind of plan. Jed and Virgil are working their way around to the side."

Amelia took a deep breath. "I'm not taking this anymore. I'm too young to be a widow."

"What are you going to do?" Nelda asked.

"Watch me and you'll see." Amelia marched back into the church and said in a loud voice, interrupting the preacher. "Excuse me, Reverend Ellsworth, but I have something to say."

Everyone in the church got quiet and the preacher looked surprised. Amelia went on, "My husband, the sheriff, the deputy and another brave man are out there risking their lives and the rest of you men are sitting here doing nothing. If you're that afraid, let us wives have your guns.

We're not going to stand by and watch four good men die because you're too yellow to go out there and help them."

In a matter of minutes, three more men left the church with their guns drawn.

"Why did you have to say that, Amelia?" somebody yelled. "My husband is too old to get involved in a gunfight."

"Yes. I don't want my husband to get shot," another said.

"Do you think I want my husband shot or killed?" Amelia snapped back.

"But he's an Indian," someone said, then shut up.

Amelia's eyes blazed. "Indians bleed, too."

"Please, ladies. Let's calm down. I'm sure your husbands will be fine. Why don't we have a prayer for them right now?" Eli said.

Mrs. Gertrude Ellsworth stood. "Before you do that, son, I have something to say."

He looked shocked, but asked, "What's that, Mother?"

Gertrude handed the baby she had to another woman and moved to the front. Her voice was clear when she said, "Most of you think I moved here from Savannah, Georgia, to be with my son and his wife because Margo was about to have my first grandchild. That is only partly true. Yes, I wanted to be with them for the birth of their baby, but I also wanted to get out of Savannah because my life had changed completely. I had been living with my sister. The poor woman died, and I was left all alone. My sister and I had been through so much together that I didn't want to live there without her.

"Many of you were blessed not to have to live with people coming into your town and shooting anyone who crossed their paths as we in the South did back in the war. I was a young woman then. I had a husband who died in Gettysburg. I watched as women grieved and many went crazy because they lost their men. But there were others who said we won't allow those soldiers to come in here to completely destroy Savannah. We took up guns. We supported the troops who were able to come home with wounds and we hid them from the enemy. When someone's house was confiscated, we took the families in and took care of them and their children if they had them. If they were aged, we made sure they were taken care of, too. When the enemy took our food, we made sure our neighbors didn't starve, if at all possible. We shared what we had.

"I'm telling you folks this because I don't understand your mentality. When the shooting started outside, Sheriff Gentry, Mr. Wainwright and Mr. Danforth didn't hesitate. They went out to defend their town. Their wives rushed to make sure they were safe. Then when Mrs. Wainwright asked for help, many of you blamed her for bullying a few of your husbands into action. Actions they should have taken on their own.

"My question is, what's wrong with you women? This would have never happened when Savannah was being attacked. If those ladies were here, they would've asked a few of the women to keep all the children in here and the rest of the men and women would get whatever weapon they could get their hands on and go out there and take back the town. There is no reason whatsoever why you folks can't do the same thing. You can pick up a rock from the ground, you can use a gun or even a hat pin. Anything you can do damage with could be used, but instead you're sitting here waiting for someone else to do the job for you. Now that's all

I've got to say. You can do what you please, but I'm going to go out there and help my friends."

She started for the door.

"Come back here, Mother," the preacher said.

She ignored him and continued toward door.

"Wait," Grace said. "If you want to help, I know how we can go out the back door here and work our way around to the back of the hotel. That way nobody will be seen or hurt, since the shooting is all coming from the front."

"That's a good idea, dear." Mrs. Ellsworth turned around. "Let's go out the back. Do you want to lead the way, Grace?"

"Yes." She took Nelda's hand and several of the people including Miss Purdy, Luella Baldwin and Margret Cramer left the pews and followed them. At her mother's insistence, Juliette stayed to help with the children.

"Do you think this is a wise thing to do?" the preacher asked.

"Son, either come with us and help or please move out of our way. The Lord has given us a mission and we're going to heed Him.'"

Nelda noticed he picked up something from the back of his pulpit and yelled to his wife. "Margo, you help with the children. I'll take care of Mother."

A few women besides Juliette Cramer elected to stay in the church with the children.

The aisle filled with more people who were grabbing anything they could find. Without any more discussion, they followed the preacher's mother, Grace Gentry, Amelia Wainwright, Lettie Langston, Shawn Parnell and Nelda Gentry Barrington out the back door.

~ * ~

Lance frowned when he saw a group of ladies and a few older men edging through the trees growing in back of and on the side of the church. He almost cursed when he realized Grace and Nelda were among the women. *What are they thinking? Don't they know they could get killed and they have the preacher's mother with them, of all people?*

He almost stood and yelled for them to go back, but he was afraid it'd only draw the outlaws' attention to them and one or more of them could get hurt. Before he could make up his mind what to do, a bullet whizzed by his head and he crouched lower. He knew it was time to concentrate on what he had to do, and that was to defuse the situation before anything worse happened.

He didn't return the fire because he didn't know the location of the Olsen family, or even if they were in the hotel at all. He knew only Sophie was at church because he'd seen Mr. Drake and his mother there. Frank Olsen must be working, and he supposed his wife was helping Effie cook dinner for the crowd who often ate there after the church services were over. Though he hadn't seen him, he hoped their young son, Teddy, was with his friends, either at the fishing hole down by the creek or hiding so they wouldn't have to attend church. He couldn't help hoping fishing was the answer because he knew how much Teddy like fishing with his friend Joel. He didn't remember seeing Joel or his stepfather, Doc Wagner at church, though they could have been there or could have come in after he and Grace were seated.

Glancing to the right of the hotel, he saw Jed and Virgil had made their way to the end of the boardwalk. He didn't want the men to put themselves in danger, but he knew there was no way to stop them. He was too far away. Like everyone else in town, he knew Jed Wainwright wasn't afraid to take a chance. He wasn't sure he could face Amelia if anything happened to her husband, and Shawn Parnell would haunt him forever if anything happened to his brother, Virgil Danforth.

He knew he had to make a decision about what to do, and he had to make it fast. Since other church members had joined him and the men who first left the church, he couldn't let them down and he certainly didn't want any of them to be hurt by stray bullets.

Four

Gertrude Ellsworth convinced the group it would be best they not talk once they reached the hotel. "Our deeds must be done secretly and in silence. That's the way we did it during the war. It worked then, and it'll work now."

They all agreed, though her son looked as if he wouldn't go along with it, but must have changed his mind when she added, "And not a word of protest out of you, Eli."

Nelda watched as Grace tried the back door. It was locked. She slipped her key in the keyhole and it made an unusually loud click as she turned it, or at least Nelda thought it was extra loud.

The women froze. There was no reaction from inside, so in a minute, Grace pushed the door open. There was nobody in the kitchen and she motioned for the women, the preacher and the other men to follow her. Once they entered the kitchen, Nelda couldn't help smiling as Gertrude Ellsworth sprang into action.

She rushed to the corner and grabbed a broom and motioned for the other women and men to get something to use as a weapon. Nelda couldn't believe how quiet the women were as they armed themselves with knives, cast iron frying pans, long handled wooden spoons and any other selection of kitchen equipment they could grab. Gertrude motioned for them to follow her.

As quietly as their swishing dresses would allow, they entered the dining room. A man dressed all in black, stood there with a drawn gun in his right hand. His back was to them and he was peering out a window.

Mrs. Ellsworth motioned for the group to stand still.

Reverend Ellsworth started to say something, but she pointed her finger at him and he didn't continue.

Gertrude eased through the dining room and though her skirt swept the floor, she made no sound. When she was close enough to the man, she rammed the broom handle in his back and whispered, "Don't say a word and don't turn around. Reach behind yourself and hand me that gun. When you've done that, you may put your hands in the air."

Startled, he started to turn, but she jabbed at his back and warned him again. This time he did as he was told. He reached behind himself with his gun hand.

She grabbed it. "Now, up in the air with your hands."

When she had the weapon in her hand, she motioned for the women to come forward. "Somebody put a gag on his mouth, so he can't make a sound," she whispered. "Then find something to tie him up. We've got to find the Olsens and make sure they're all right."

Lettie Langston took the scarf from around her neck and gagged him. It was then he was permitted to turn around.

Shocked covered his face and his eyes flared with surprise when he saw he'd been subdued by a group of mostly women and a few older men. Then he saw the broomstick Gertrude had used to disarm him, and his eyes blazed even wider, this time with anger, as he started to reach for the gag.

Gertrude rammed the gun in his side. "Should have tied his arms behind him before he saw the army that captured him."

Nelda moved forward and tied his hands with a towel she'd picked up in the kitchen.

"Mother," Eli whispered. "I think you should wait here and let me check out the lobby."

She shook her head and nodded toward the door into the lobby. "I started this and I'll finish it, son. Besides I'm enjoying it. You just stay close in case I need you. You stay close, too, ladies." Pushing the door open a crack, she looked out, nodded then closed it and said, "Someone guard the prisoner, and when I fling this door open, I want the rest of you to come rushing out screaming and yelling as loud as a band of marauding Indians." They nodded. The two outlaws in the lobby didn't seem to know what to do when the group came in brandishing their selection of weapons and screaming at the top of their voices. At first, the criminals looked like they were going to shoot, but in an instant, they were surrounded by women hitting them with pans and spoons and a variety of other things.

In a matter of minutes, the two were gagged and tied.

Grace smiled at their leader. "Mrs. Ellsworth, don't you think we should find out what these unscrupulous men have done with the Olsens?"

"You're right about that, dear. I think I want to ask that man we first captured. He's probably the boss."

"Two women are guarding him in the dining room, Mother. I'll get them to bring him in here."

"Before you do that, son, get the sheriff's attention and tell him to come in here. I'm sure he'll want to take over now."

"Let me get Lance, Reverend, and you can go for the man and the ladies that are holding him," Grace said.

When Eli returned with the man. Gertrude reached up and jerked the man's gag off. "What have you done with the Olsen family?"

He glared at her. "I can't believe you made me give up my gun and you only had a broom."

"I guess that proves I'm smarter than you are. Now where are the Olsens?"

"Look, you old woman—"

Eli shoved the man in the back. "Don't speak to my mother in that manner. Be a gentleman and answer her question."

"Go to hell."

Gertrude jabbed her finger at him. "Watch your language, young man. We're church people and there's no need for you to think cursing helps your cause in any way."

Lillian Purdy said, "I'll find the Olsens if I have to open every door in this hotel. They have to be here somewhere."

"I'll help you," Mrs. Baldwin said.

"I'll help, too." Marjorie Cramer spoke up.

Three other women joined them and they all followed Lillian out of the room.

Grace moved to the window and yelled. "Lance, hold your fire. Everything is fine in here now. Come on in and take these outlaws to jail."

A stunned looking Lance followed by Jed, Virgil and Bryce came through the door. The men who had left the church to join them milled around on the boardwalk. All the men who had come with the women, with the exception of Eli Ellsworth, went outside to tell the others what had happened.

"What's going on in here, Grace?"

"We caught these awful men for you, honey."

"How in the world...?"

"Oh, big brother, let me tell you," an excited Nelda said. "Mrs. Ellsworth was our leader and we all came here to keep these awful outlaws from killing the people we love. You should have seen the lady, Lance. She was magnificent."

"Mrs. Ellsworth has always been magnificent," Jed butted in, then grinned at the older woman.

Mrs. Ellsworth beamed at him and there was a slight blush on her cheeks. She muttered, "Ah, shucks."

The reverend motioned toward the first man who had been captured. "This seems to be the leader of the gang, Sheriff."

Lance turned to look at the outlaw the reverend indicated. "It's Nate Tatum. He's one of the meanest outlaws around. The posters out on him say he's wanted in half the states in the West." He looked around at the group and asked again, "How in the world—?"

"It was Gertrude Ellsworth, honey," Grace said. "She was brilliant. She told us what to do and we just followed her lead."

Nelda took up the story. "Would you believe she captured the man you say is a hardened criminal with the handle of a broom?"

"You're kidding." Lance smiled at Gertrude. "I may just have to pin a badge on you, Mrs. Ellsworth. I could use another good deputy."

She beamed, but Eli said, "Don't encourage her, Lance. She thinks she can do anything with a broom."

Nate Tatum looked at Gertrude as if he wanted to murder her, but he didn't say anything.

Gertrude ignored him and grinned. She seemed to bask in the attention. "I've found that some of the vilest men are afraid of a broom. I captured several of the enemy soldiers in Savannah with one during the war."

The women who had searched for the Olsens came into the room followed by Effie, Mr. and Mrs. Olsen and Teddy. Luella Baldwin said, "He'd locked them all in one room and tied and gagged them, so they couldn't holler. He planned to take everything he wanted in here and skip town before church was over, then someone fired a shot and their plans changed."

Lillian Purdy added, "You know, after my experience last year, how much I hate men who try to rob honest working people."

"Why's that, Miss Purdy?" Jed asked.

"Because that awful friend of Kemp Newton's tried to rob me last year. Lance stopped him, but it made me realize what a horrendous crime robbery is."

Lance looked at Olsen. "Are your family and Effie all right, Frank?"

"We're fine, Lance, thanks to these brave women."

"Then I'll get these criminals in a cell and come back and talk to all of you." He smiled at Mrs. Ellsworth. "I'm sure there's a reward for their capture."

"Oh, Lance. I don't need any reward."

"You may not think so, but you've earned it."

Effie moved forward. "In the meantime, if those rascals didn't let the fire go out in the stove, I'll serve all you women a cup of tea and I'll get coffee for the men. I bet you need it after all you've done."

The women muttered among themselves about what a good idea Effie had. They ambled into the dining room and said they'd put the utensils back in the kitchen after drinking their tea.

"That won't be necessary, ladies," Henrietta Olsen said. "Teddy can gather them while I help Effie. I might even be able to find a couple of pies we can share with you while we wait for the sheriff to return."

"I can help," Grace offered.

"No, Grace," Miss Purdy said. "You have a seat with Nelda and your other friends. I'm going to help Henrietta."

"Thank you, Miss Purdy." Grace took a chair at the table her friends had chosen.

The reverend leaned over his mother's shoulder when she was seated at the table with Grace, Amelia and Nelda. "I'll go back to the church and explain what has happened. I'm sure Sophie Olsen will want to come to see that her family is all right. Margo and I will be back as soon as we can."

Gertrude patted his hand. "I'll be fine, but thank you, son."

"I believe you will be, Mother. You're more capable of taking care of yourself than I realized. I'm going to try to keep from nagging you about it." He kissed her cheek, smiled at her table companions and went out the door.

"It was sweet of him to admit he's been a little overprotective of you, Mrs. Ellsworth," Amelia said.

She chuckled. "He won't remember. He'll start nagging again tomorrow and you can bet on it. He thinks I'm a weak old lady and I need somebody to protect me. Truth is, I have to protect him from himself. He works too hard."

"Don't feel bad about that," Amelia leaned toward her and said. "Jed feels the same way about me. He'll probably give me a good talking to when we get home and explain all the danger I was in. Of course, he'll never mention that he could've been killed himself."

"Well, dear, Jed just wants to take care of you and I'm sure anything he says will come from his heart. He's just that kind of man."

Grace laughed. "Nelda, Mrs. Ellsworth thinks Jed Wainwright is the perfect man."

"That's right," Amelia said. "In her eyes, he does nothing wrong."

"Well, he is a wonderful man." Gertrude shook her finger at Amelia. "I've told you before and I mean it, if I was thirty or forty years younger, I would fight you for that man."

"And she wouldn't have to fight too hard," Amelia said. "Jed thinks she's about perfect, too."

The four of them burst into laughter and began talking about the adventure they'd shared on a sunny Sunday morning in Settlers Ridge.

~ * ~

Nelda and Wilma were sitting in their upstairs apartment over Brown's Mercantile having a cup of tea, eating cookies and discussing their day.

"I wish I had gone to church with you this morning, but you know I'd promised I'd stay with Mrs. Brown while Stanley took care of some business," Wilma said with her mouth full. "I would have loved to have seen Mrs. Ellsworth leading her brigade."

"She was marvelous. It was the most fun I've ever had at church. Even more exciting than the time one of the Lance's friends put a frog down Mrs. Baldwin's back."

"I remember that. At first your mother thought it was Lance and almost thrashed him for it. Then his friend finally confessed and saved Lance's behind."

"That's right. But today was different. This commotion actually did some good as well as being enjoyable."

"I would have loved to have seen your brother's face when he walked in and saw you had subdued all the outlaws."

Nelda giggled. "He and all the other men couldn't believe we'd captured them, but I think when they learned the preacher's mother was our leader, they were stunned."

"I'm sure they were."

"I think Mrs. Ellsworth was having the time of her life. I also think she made some of the women of Settlers Ridge realize they had power to do other things besides keep house, cook meals and have babies."

Wilma nodded. "Good for her, but I bet some of the men aren't going to like it."

"That's true. It wouldn't surprise me if it caused some arguments in some of the homes tonight. Especially the men who didn't go out to help Lance and Jed and that guy named Virgil."

"I'd like to be a fly on the wall in some of those homes tonight."

"Wouldn't you, though?" Nelda looked at Wilma with a puzzled look on her face. "Who is that fellow, Virgil, anyway? I don't think I've ever met him."

"You probably haven't. He came to town last year to find his brother." Wilma laughed. "I'll tell you the whole story sometime."

"Now you have my curiosity up. Go on and tell me now. We still have cookies."

Wilma giggled. "It's a long story, but let me see if I can give you a somewhat short version. It started when Shawn Parnell, his gambling pa, Nelson Parnell, and his uncle Rocky came to town and took over Sam McCormick's ranch. Shawn was kind of wild and Nelson was beating him every chance he got. Rocky tried to protect Shawn and was good to him, but Nelson had a terrible temper. Then Virgil showed up to save Shawn from Nelson. He's Shawn's older half-brother. When Nelson murdered McCormick, Rocky sent Shawn to tell Lance. When Lance went to arrest Nelson, the man tried to kill Lance, but the shot caught Shawn in the side. Lance killed Nelson. It turned out, Nelson wasn't Shawn's father. His real father had been killed and was Nelson's twin brother. Nelson had kidnapped Shawn, and his mother had been looking for him for years. On her deathbed, Virgil promised his mother he'd find Shawn, and he did. Now Shawn and his Uncle Rocky and Virgil live on what used to be the McCormick spread."

"That is convoluted, but I'll eventually get it straight in my mind. I'm just glad things turned out well for young Shawn. His brother, Virgil, is rather handsome."

Wilma laughed. "I think so too, but I hear Juliette Cramer is interested in him since she didn't get your brother."

Nelda frowned. "She and Lance were never close, were they?"

Wilma shook her head. "No, but when Juliette came back from boarding school, she decided she wanted Lance. It took a while for him to convince her that he wasn't interested, because she was sure he couldn't resist her."

"I'm glad he did. I don't think there's another woman in the world that could make him as happy as Grace has."

"You're right about that." Wilma sighed.

"What's the matter?"

"You know how close the four of us have always been. Amelia is happily married to her bounty hunger, Grace has the sheriff and you have your major and I'm still an old maid. I wonder if there'll ever be somebody for me."

"Of course, there will be, Wilma, but you're wrong about one thing."

"What's that?"

Nelda became serious. "I know you think my homecoming was only for the winter, but that's not true. I'm here for good."

"What are you saying?"

"I know you won't say anything until I'm ready to let it out. At this point nobody knows except Lance and Grace. I've left Spencer. I plan to see Mr. Cramer this week and start divorce proceedings."

Wilma stared at her.

"Aren't you going to say anything?"

"I don't know what to say, Nelda. I'm stunned."

"I figured since we were going to be working together you had a right to know."

"I appreciate you trusting me, my friend, but I thought you were happy in your marriage."

"I was until I found out my husband has a mistress and has had her for years."

"Oh, Nelda, that's hard for me to believe."

"It's the truth, Wilma."

"I'm so sorry."

"Thank you. Of course, you know it isn't the way I wanted my life or my marriage to go, but it has and now I've returned to Settlers Ridge to start my life over again." She gave Wilma a smile. "And I don't want to start in a down mood. Do we have any more cookies? I've eaten all of mine."

"Nelda, you had half a dozen cookies."

Nelda looked down at the plate and laughed "I never eat that much."

Wilma nodded. "I've eaten as many as you have, if not more."

Nelda sat the plate aside. "I don't think I should eat anymore tonight."

"Neither should I." Wilma sat her plate beside Nelda's.

"I know you've shown me everything I'm going to have to do in the store in the morning, Wilma, but I'm still nervous. I think that and all the excitement I've had today is why I ate so much."

"There's nothing to be afraid of. You know I'll be there if you have any questions. By the end of the week you'll be able to run the place by yourself."

"Do you think Stanley will come in tomorrow and check on how I'm doing?"

"I doubt it. He's busy helping his mother with her last-minute packing. When I was there, she said they wanted to get out of town as soon as they could. He said all that was left to do was to go to Mr. Cramer and have everything drawn up so there will be no question that you and I have a legal right to run everything here at the mercantile."

Nelda was glad they were ending their night on an up mood. She just hoped she wouldn't have a stomachache during the night from eating so many cookies.

Five

On Monday, Lance looked at his pocket watch and saw he still had a couple of hours before Grace brought dinner for the prisoners. He knew as soon as he got them fed, he'd accompany her back to the hotel to have dinner. Though Henrietta was getting better, Grace was still helping out for the midday meal. He didn't mind, but he was going to be glad when he could go to the house for his food instead of the hotel. It wasn't that they didn't have privacy in Grace's old room, but they had much more privacy in their own home. He knew better than to attempt to make love to her in her old bedroom, but at their house it was a different matter.

He shook his head and tried to get his mind off his beautiful wife by looking at the wanted posters lying on his desk. He was figuring up how much money the capture of the Nate Tatum gang was going to add up to. He was pleased that since there were so many involved in the capture that Mrs. Ellsworth had decided to donate it to the church, so they could finish paying off the building fund debt.

The door opened, and he glanced up. He was surprised when Spencer Barrington walked in. "Howdy, Spencer."

"Lance." Spencer removed his hat and nodded. "I guess you know why I'm here."

"I have a pretty good idea." He pushed the posters aside and asked, "Coffee's still hot. Want a cup?"

"Yeah. I've been riding pretty hard."

Lance nodded to the chair in front of his desk and stood to pour them both a cup of the strong brew. Handing a cup to Spencer, he said, "Is it true?"

"What?"

"The mistress in Denver."

"So that's what she told you?"

Lance nodded. "I ask again, is it true?"

"It's not what Nelda thinks it is. There is a woman in Denver, but it has nothing to do with me having a mistress."

Lance sat. "I don't know what you mean by that, but you know I'm going to protect her any way I can. My sister is hurt, and I don't want her to suffer any more than she has already."

"I understand, and I'm glad she came to you. I almost went crazy trying to find her. I should have come here first."

"Where else would she go but to her family?"

"The general thought she might have gone to Denver."

"She did. She came here afterward."

Spencer closed his eyes and cursed silently. Aloud, he said, "I hoped she wouldn't go there."

"Well, she did. She said she saw you there with a woman." Lance looked at his brother-in-law and thought he'd never seen a more defeated looking man. "If the woman isn't your mistress, then you should tell Nelda who she is."

"I can't, Lance."

"Why not?"

Spencer drank his coffee and sat the empty cup on the desk. "All I can say is I can't lose Nelda. She's the only woman I've ever loved and the only one I ever will love. I'd never betray her. I swear the woman in Denver has never been and is not now my mistress."

Lance rubbed his chin. "I don't know what to say, and I wouldn't dare presume to tell Nelda what to do. You two are going to have to work this out yourselves."

"I understand that. I just want to let you know that I love your sister and I never meant to hurt her in any way." When Lance said nothing, he went on. "I know I have to talk to her, but I'm afraid of what she'll say to me."

Lance felt sure the man was suffering, but he couldn't help thinking he brought it on himself. "I can't answer that for you either."

"I know you can't." Spencer stood. "Would you tell me where she is?"

Lance couldn't help feeling sorry for him. He knew he wouldn't betray Nelda's confidence, but he felt he had to help Spencer as much as he could. After all, the man could be telling the truth about loving Nelda. "I told her if you got in touch, I wouldn't tell you where she is, but I strongly suggest you go to Brown's Mercantile and ask there."

Lance nodded and started out the door. He stepped back when he met Grace coming in with a basket in her hand. He nodded and smiled, but didn't stop to talk.

"Come in, honey." Lance walked over and took the basket from her.

"What's Spencer doing here?"

He sat the food basket on his desk. "Looking for Nelda."

"Did you tell him where she is?"

"Kind of."

Grace frowned. "What do you mean, kind of? She asked both of us not to tell him if he showed up."

"I just told him that I wasn't going to say where she was, but maybe they could tell him at Brown's Mercantile."

Grace chuckled. "Lance, you're awful."

He winked at her and pulled her into his arms. "Seems like old times. You bringing food for the prisoners. I hope you brought enough for us like you used to."

"You know Effie wouldn't let me leave the hotel without enough food for her favorite sheriff."

He kissed her, then backed away. "Let's get those outlaws fed so we can have a few minutes to ourselves."

She began taking the food from the basket. "Sounds good to me."

~ * ~

Wilma looked up from the counter when Spencer walked in. She was shocked, but she managed to say, "Hello, Major. How can I help you?"

"I'm looking for Nelda, Wilma. Do you know where she is?"

"She's not here."

"Would you tell me where she is?"

Wilma wasn't sure what to say. She didn't want to tell him that his wife was upstairs stirring the stew they'd put on the stove that morning. Neither did she want to lie. How was she going to get out of this?

Finally, she said, "She left for a while."

Spencer raised an eyebrow. "Will she be back soon?"

"I'm not sure when she'll be back because she didn't say."

"But she is coming back, right?"

"I suppose so."

"Then I'll look around a bit and wait." Spencer moved to the rack of boots and looked them over.

Wilma wasn't sure what to do. She only hoped if Nelda didn't want to see her husband she'd stay upstairs until he gave up and left. She busied herself with dusting the tins on the shelf behind her and wished other customers would come in. But it was noon. Few people shopped at the dinner hour. They were too busy eating or getting ready to eat at their own homes or at the hotel dining room or the small restaurant that had opened down the street.

Then, she heard Nelda coming down the stairs and knew she had to do something. She decided to let her friend know her husband was here if she'd slow down and listen. "Oh, Spencer," she called loud enough for Nelda to hear.

"Yes."

"Nelda told me that you and your troops were out on maneuvers so much this time of year that she seldom saw you."

"Is that why she told you she came back to Settlers Ridge?"

"Yes. She said it would be nicer to be here with her friends and family than spend the winter with the women at the fort. I guess she thought she'd be too lonely there."

"I see. We are out a lot this time of year because it seems there are a lot of raids on the surrounding settlers. But I didn't plan to be gone as much as she thought I would."

"I see." Wilma heard Nelda creep back upstairs and relaxed. "Then she might change her mind about staying here."

"That's what I'm counting on, Wilma."

Almost thirty minutes passed, and they said nothing else to each other. Finally, he walked up to the counter and said, "Let me have five of those cigars."

"Certainly." She took them and started to wrap them in brown paper.

"I'll just put them in my pocket."

"Sure."

He paid her. "I think I'll go to the hotel and get something to eat. I'll come back by later and see if Nelda has returned."

"Maybe she'll be here then."

The bell rang again as he went out the door.

Wilma hurried toward the steps and met Nelda coming down.

Nelda grabbed her. "Thank you, Wilma. I would've stumbled right into him if you hadn't called out his name."

"It was all I could think of to do. I don't think he caught on."

"He didn't, or he would've grilled you like he does one of his men when he thinks they're lying to him." Nelda swallowed. "But what am I going to do if and when he comes back and wants to see me?"

"You can stay here at the counter and if we see him coming down the street you can go into the stockroom. From there you can hear what is said, or you can slip out the back door. I'll stall him as best as I can."

"I appreciate your help, Wilma. I don't think I can handle facing him any time soon."

Wilma patted her friend's arm. "There's one thing you must think about."

"What's that?"

"I got the feeling that Spencer isn't going to give up easily, which means you're going to have to face him sooner or later."

"I know, but I'm not ready yet."

"When will you be ready, Nelda?"

"After I get my divorce papers from Mr. Cramer."

"When are you going to see the lawyer?"

Nelda looked around the shop. "We haven't been busy today. The Browns might fire me, but I'm going to slip out and go to his office right now. I want to see how fast he can get the papers ready for me."

"What do I tell Spencer if he comes back before you do?"

She thought a minute. "Tell him I went to see somebody. If he wants to know who, tell him you don't know, but it could be Amelia."

"Do you think he'll believe me?"

"He should. He knows how close Amelia and I are."

"Then, go see Cramer before Spencer comes back."

"Thanks, Wilma."

Wilma walked her to the door and watched as Nelda looked up and down the boardwalk, then ran down the street to Hal Cramer's office.

Wilma wished her friend didn't have to sneak around like that, but if this was the way she wanted to handle it, there was nothing she could do, but help her.

~ * ~

Grace walked up to the table in the hotel dining room. "Would you like more coffee, Spencer?"

He looked up at her and nodded. "I saw you at Lance's office, didn't I?"

"That was almost two hours ago, and yes. I had taken food for the prisoners."

"I see. I know you didn't serve me when I came in here."

"It was either Mrs. Olsen or her daughter."

He nodded. "Grace, have you seen Nelda?"

"Yes, I have."

"Did she tell you why she left the fort in such a hurry?"

"Not right out, but I'm sure she told Lance."

"So, you don't know what she's thinking?"

"No, I really don't."

He waited a minute then asked, "If she's staying with you and Lance, wouldn't you hear when she told him?"

Grace bit her lip, but said nothing.

He narrowed his eyes. "She's not staying with you, is she?"

"She stayed with us when she first came back." Grace's voice shook when she added, "Now I'd better get back to the kitchen and—"

"Just a minute, Grace. If she isn't staying with you, where is she?"

"I don't think that's for me to say."

His voice became angry. "Why is everyone in this town trying to keep me away from my wife?"

"We're not trying to keep you from her, Spencer. We're only trying to protect her from more hurt. I guess everyone is like me. They know how very sad and hurt she is, and it bothers all of us to see her that way."

"The last thing I wanted to do was hurt her, Grace. I love Nelda."

"Maybe you do, but that's something I think you need to convince Nelda of, not me."

"I would try to convince her if I could find her."

Grace looked startled. "You didn't see her at Brown's Mercantile?"

"Wilma said she'd stepped out but was coming back. I waited for what seemed like an hour or more, but she didn't return. I thought I'd go back there after I eat."

"I think you should. Maybe she'll be there then."

He looked at Grace and frowned. "Will you tell me something, Grace?"

"I'll try."

"Why is everyone so sure Nelda will be at Brown's Mercantile sometime today?"

Grace swallowed. "Didn't Lance tell you?"

"No. He only said to go there. I went, and she wasn't there."

Biting her lip, Grace looked at him, but said nothing.

Spencer narrowed his eyes. It dawned on him that nobody wanted to tell him what his wife was doing at the mercantile. Why was everyone telling him to go to Brown's? It couldn't be because she worked there, could it? Nelda didn't have to work. He'd taken care of her since their marriage and he intended to continue taking care of her. But what other reason could it be? He couldn't think of one. There was only one way to find out and, knowing Grace, he was sure she wouldn't lie to him.

"Is my wife working at Brown's Mercantile, Grace?"

Grace hesitated, but when he kept staring at her, she finally said, "Yes."

He took a deep breath. "If she's not staying with you and Lance, is she staying at the hotel?"

Grace looked perturbed. "Spencer, please don't put me on the spot any more than you have already. You know that Nelda is my sister-in-law as well as a dear friend. I feel I'm being disloyal to her if I answer any more of your questions."

"Don't you think if you walked out on Lance without any explanation, he'd follow you? Wouldn't he try to get any information about where you are and what you're up to from anyone he could?"

"Maybe, but..." A couple walked into the dining room and Grace said, "Excuse me. I need to wait on those folks."

Spencer watched her hurry away and shook his head. He never dreamed the people in this town were so bent on keeping Nelda's whereabouts hidden. He wondered if he went to his small hometown back in Virginia to hide out if his old friends and relatives would be as closed mouthed about him. He chuckled to himself. *No way. They'd give me up in a minute. I would just be a guy who left the farm to seek my fortune elsewhere and no longer one of them.*

Shaking his head, he put his fork down and glanced out the window. His eyes grew wide when he saw Nelda coming from one of the offices down the street and hurrying toward the mercantile.

Trying not to draw attention to himself, he stood, threw more money on the table than he owed, picked up his hat and without a word to anyone, rushed out the door. He had to get to his wife before somebody tried to stop him again.

Six

As Nelda stepped inside the mercantile Wilma said, "I'm surprised to see you back so soon."

Nelda sighed. "I didn't get to see Mr. Cramer."

"What happened?"

"Somebody was with him and the man working there said I could see him after they left if his next appointment hadn't shown up. Then the man who had an appointment arrived and he told me I'd have to wait to see him until after this second man left. I figured it'd take too long, so I told him I'd come back later." She moved behind the counter and put on the white apron she'd left there. "I assume Spencer hasn't been back in?"

"No, he hasn't. Now why don't...Oh, my goodness, here he comes. Hurry upstairs."

Nelda ran to the stockroom and halfway up the stairs, then paused to listen. She wanted to hear what Spencer said when he came in.

The door opened, and he asked, "Where's Nelda, Wilma?"

"She hasn't come back."

"There's no need to lie for her now. I saw her come in here. Is she in the stockroom?"

"Stop, Spencer. You can't go back there."

"Don't try to stop me, Wilma. I'm going to talk to my wife."

"What if she doesn't want to talk to you?"

"Doesn't matter. I want to talk to her."

Nelda scurried up the steps and into the apartment above the store. She heard Spencer's boots in the stockroom.

"Please, Spencer. Come out of there. Nelda doesn't want to talk to you. Why don't you respect her wishes and leave her alone?"

He didn't answer until there was a tinkle of the bell over the front door. "Better go wait on your customer, Wilma. I'll come out when I find my wife."

"But—"

Nelda knew Wilma had given up because there was no more talking between the two. She then heard the back door of the storeroom shake. She knew Spencer was checking to see if it was locked. *Oh, why did we forget to unlock it this morning? Now he'll know I didn't go outside.*

The next thing she heard was the clomp of his boots as he climbed the stairs to their apartment. She felt paralyzed. What could she do now? She took a deep breath and bit her lip. She knew she had tried, but it was no use to attempt to escape him any longer. She'd just have to face him and get it over with. She jerked open the door at the top of the stairs and glared at him.

He smiled at her.

Bucking up her courage and using as unemotionally charged voice as she could, she asked, "What do you want, Spencer?"

He didn't answer until he got to the top of the steps and reached for her. She backed away and he dropped his hands to his side. "I want to talk to you, Nelda."

His voice was low and soft, and she had to look away. Why, after all he'd done, did his voice make her feel weak inside? She should hate him. Instead she wanted to reach out and grab him around the neck and pretend he'd done nothing to warrant her leaving him. She managed to fight off those feelings. "Then talk fast. I have to get back to work."

He came into the sitting room and closed the door behind him. "I don't want anyone to hear what I've got to say."

She tossed back her head and a lock of her sandy brown hair fell out of the twist. "Of course, you don't. If I were trying to sweet talk somebody with lies, I'd want privacy, too."

"You really are upset with me, aren't you, darling?"

"Don't you think I have a right to be?"

"I believe you think you have the right but if you knew the whole story, you'd think differently."

"I know the story and I don't believe you."

"To be honest, I didn't think you'd believe me."

"Then why are you here?"

"I'm here because I love you, Nelda. I loved you the first time I came through Settlers Ridge and laid eyes on you. I loved you when I was finally able to convince you to marry me. I love you now and I'll always love you. That will never change."

Oh, how she wanted to believe him. Though they'd been married almost two years, his presence still thrilled her. She loved this man so much. She knew if she would open her arms to him, he'd love her with his body, if not his heart and mind. But his actions belied his pretty speech. He didn't love her, no matter what his mouth said. He'd proven that the day she saw him standing on the porch of that house in Denver with that pretty blonde Antoinette pressed against him with her arms around his neck.

No. No matter what he said, he didn't love her. He might like to have her around for the times he couldn't get to Denver to his true love, but he'd never love her the way Nelda did him. She had to end it because she'd never able to trust him again.

She turned her face toward him. "Those are pretty words, Spencer. How many times have you said them to someone else?"

He frowned. "I've never said those words to anyone except you, Nelda. Furthermore, I never will."

"I don't believe that for a minute." She folded her arms across her chest and scowled at him.

"You think you know what's going on, but you don't, sweetheart. I swear you don't."

"Will you please stop addressing me with those terms of endearment? Save them for—"

"Please, Nelda, I..." He started toward her with his hands held out as he spoke.

"Don't you dare touch me, you...you..." She burst into tears and couldn't go on. Her heart was breaking, and she didn't know what she'd do if he actually put his arms around her. The other time he'd talked like this he'd promised her he'd never keep that woman as a mistress and she'd believed him. That time she went willingly into his arms and she thought things were going to work out between them. But it had been a mistake to believe his pretty words. She knew he'd lied then, and she was positive he was lying now. He would never give that beautiful woman up and he was not going to win his wife over with his fancy words. Not this time. She'd learned her lesson the hard way.

"Honey, I wish I could tell you—"

"You can tell me all the lies you want to, Major Spencer Barrington, but I'm not going to listen to you or believe your lies any longer. I've made up my mind what I'm going to do and there's nothing you can do to stop me."

She could tell he was getting frustrated when he said, "I'll use all the power at my disposal to keep you from doing something you'll regret, Nelda Barrington."

"I won't regret anything, but you might. When you find your girlfriend isn't what you think she is, you may wish you hadn't been so careless with the love I gave you."

His voice became defiant. "You don't know what you're saying, Nelda. I don't want you to throw away what we have. We love each other and we always will."

Her tears began to subside and with each word she spoke her voice rose. "You threw what we had away when you decided it was more important to go to Denver than to come home to your wife like the other troops did. Even Private Carson came back and everybody at the fort knew he and his wife fight like wildcats. But not you. You don't care that all the women at the fort are laughing at and talking about me behind my back. You don't care that you've broken my heart. You don't care a thing about me and I'm not putting up with it any longer. I'm divorcing you and if I'd been able to see Mr. Cramer today, I'd have had the papers here for you to sign." By the time she finished, she was screaming.

"We'll discuss this when you can be more reasonable," he said in a quiet voice and headed for the door. Then he turned and gazed at her. "Just remember one thing, Nelda. You can draw up all the divorce papers you want, but I'll never sign them. When I said our marriage vows, I meant them, especially the *until death do us part* line. I thought you did, too."

Nelda glared at the closed door and heard him going down the stairs. Shaking, but trying not to think about what had transpired, she got up and went to her bedroom. She poured some water from the pitcher into the bowl, dampened a cloth and washed her face. She straightened her hair and then went out the door and down the steps.

Wilma looked up. "Are you all right?"

"I'm fine."

"I know you don't want to talk about it, but there was a lot of screaming going on upstairs."

"I'm sorry. I didn't mean to make so much noise, but I kind of lost my temper."

Wilma nodded. "I'm just glad there were no customers in here at the time."

Nelda blushed, but didn't get a chance to answer because the bell over the door jangled and a couple of cowboys came in.

~ * ~

Lance came out the jail office door as Spencer headed toward it. "Did you need to see me, Spencer?"

"Won't take but a minute. That is, if you can spare the time."

"Sure. I was only going to the telegraph office to see if the circuit judge had responded. I have some prisoners and would like to get them tried as soon as I can. But I can take care of that any time today. Come on in."

"I heard about the way the women captured those outlaws when I was eating dinner at the hotel. I didn't mean to eavesdrop, but it seemed everybody was talking about it. You can't help but admire those ladies."

"The fact that they were led by a woman in her late seventies made the whole situation almost unbelievable. We sure have some spunky women in Settlers Ridge."

"Maybe some are just a little too spunky," Spencer muttered as he followed Lance through the jailhouse door.

Lance took his chair behind the desk and motioned for Spencer to sit facing him. "Now, what can I help you with?"

"I know you're loyal to your sister and you should be, but I need to know what Nelda has told you about me and about what she plans to do."

Lance looked at his brother-in-law and couldn't help thinking he was looking at an unhappy man. Maybe even a defeated man. "I don't think it's my place to say much of anything. You need to talk to Nelda."

"I've just come from a confrontation with her."

Lance lifted an eyebrow. He wondered what his sister had told Spencer. He didn't want to break a confidence, but he also wanted to see if he could help the man. He sure looked like he needed it and he realized he might even be helping Nelda in the long run. He knew his little sister fairly well, and no matter how she tried to put up a brave front, he could tell she was still in love with her husband. He would stake his life on that fact. He shook his head. "I'd know more what to tell you if you'd tell me what you and Nelda talked about."

"I have no choice but to trust you, Lance." He breathed deeply, but didn't pause long before he said, "She accused me of having a mistress in Denver and told me she planned to divorce me because of it."

Lance nodded. "She told me those things, too."

"I know this is going to be hard for you to believe, but she's dead wrong. There is no mistress in Denver."

Lance stared at him. Was he telling the truth? If so, who was the woman? There was nothing he could do but ask. "If she isn't your mistress, then who is the woman she saw you with when she went to Denver?"

"That's the thing, Lance. I can't tell you or Nelda or anyone. It's not that I wouldn't like to. I'd do anything to keep Nelda from leaving me. I just can't do it."

"If you'd do anything to keep your wife, then forget about why you can't tell her who the woman is and just do it."

"That is the one thing I can't do." When Lance gave him a puzzled look, Spencer went on. "If she knew what was really going on, it would put her life in danger, and that's something I'll never do."

Lance looked even more puzzled. "How could telling the truth put Nelda's life in danger?"

"If the people who are trying to ferret out this complicated matter I'm involved in had the least inking that

Nelda knew what was going on, they wouldn't hesitate to kill her."

Stunned, Lance could only stare at him for a minute. Finally, he said, "Are you sure it would put her in danger?"

"I'm positive, Lance, and to be honest, I may have put you somewhat in jeopardy just by coming here."

"I don't understand."

"I know you don't, and I wish could explain it all to you."

"But you can't?"

Spencer sighed. "I'm getting close to the solution, and hope to get to get it over with soon. I just want to keep Nelda from divorcing me until it's settled."

"And when it's settled, you can explain it all to her?"

"That's right."

"Then, I'll promise you this, if it'll help, Grace and I will do all we can to keep her from drawing up divorce papers for a while."

"I appreciate that, Lance, but please don't say anything to Grace. I don't want her in harm's way and I'm sure you don't want that either."

"Absolutely not."

"There's one other thing you need to know. I told Nelda she could draw up all the divorce papers she wants, but I'd never sign them. I meant that. I intend to go to my grave married to that woman."

Lance couldn't help smiling. "You've convinced me, Spencer. I believe you do love my sister."

"Thank God. I was afraid...well, never mind. I'm glad at least one person in this town believes me."

"I'll do what I can to calm Nelda down. But you and I both know I may not have much luck. When she sets her head to something, it's almost impossible to change her mind."

"I appreciate anything you can do. This should be over before too long. Then I'll be able to explain everything to both of you. I just want to keep her married to me until that time comes. I can't lose Nelda."

"As I said, I'll see if I can talk her into waiting to get those divorce papers drawn up. I want my sister to be happy and I know she's been happy with you until this came up."

"I appreciate it. I'll try to talk to her one more time before I go back to the fort, but I have a feeling it won't do much good. Not if she stays in the mood she's in now."

"Maybe it would be best if you let her stay in Settlers Ridge for a while. At least we'll know there isn't much chance of anyone coming for her here."

"I thought of that. As long as they think she's sure I have a mistress, they'll not bother her." He shook his head. "It will be awfully lonesome without her, though."

Lance nodded. "I'd be lonesome without Grace, so I sure can understand that."

"I do need your word that you won't tell Nelda that she could be in danger. I probably shouldn't have told you that much, but I'm a desperate man."

"Don't worry. What was said here today is between you and me and nobody else."

Spencer stood and held out his hand. "Thank you."

Lance took his hand. "You're welcome and you know if I can help out with your mission, whatever it is, don't hesitate to call on me. I'd like to see it over and you two back together again."

"I appreciate your offer, and I'll certainly keep it in mind."

"Good. As for your marriage, together maybe we can get things worked out faster than you think. I don't want to have to break in another brother-in-law. "

Spencer laughed. "I don't want to you to have to do that either."

~ * ~

"Oh, Nelda, these biscuits are wonderful. I could never make them as light and fluffy as these. I'm so glad you came up here and baked them to go with the stew." Wilma grinned and took another bite.

"Thank you. Spencer always liked...oh, Lord. I didn't mean to say that."

"Don't worry about it. You've spent almost two years with the man and he's a part of your life. There's no way you can stop mentioning his name every now and then."

"I know." She sighed. "Guess what he told me today."

"What."

"He said he'd never sign divorce papers so there was no need of me getting them filled out. He sounded as if he meant it."

"Maybe he'll change his mind."

"I doubt it. I've never known Spencer to change his mind when it was set on something."

"Does that upset you even more, Nelda?"

"I don't know. Maybe I should still talk to Mr. Cramer and see if there's a way I can get the divorce without Spencer signing anything."

"That might not be a bad idea, but you should think about that before you make up your mind."

"Why?"

"Well, you know how it's going to affect you when the word is out that you're divorcing your husband. What if

Juliette gets hold of the information? You know how she is. She would make it into something even bigger than it really is."

"You're probably right. I promise I'll think about it seriously before I do anything." Nelda took another bite of stew. "Now that's enough about my problems. How do you think I did in the store today?"

Wilma giggled. "I think you did great. Especially when those two cowboys came in and kept flirting with us."

"I guess I did scare them, didn't I?" She laughed, too.

"When you said you thought you'd better go get the sheriff, it sure quieted them down. I don't know if they thought you were the sheriff's girlfriend or what."

"That's why I didn't say anything else."

"They sure bought their tobacco and hurried away." Wilma leaned back. "I want to eat another biscuit, but I know I shouldn't. I'm about to pop out of this dress now."

The back door rattled.

The two women looked startled and Wilma said, "Go to your room and I'll see who it is."

When she got to the door she called, "Who's there?"

"It's me, Wilma. Just checking to make sure your door is locked."

Wilma turned the key. "Come in, Lance." She called, "It's Lance, Nelda. Come on out. It's safe."

Nelda walked into the kitchen. "What do you mean scaring us like that, big brother?"

"Get used to it, little sister. I always check all the doors on the businesses to make sure they're locked up for the night. I don't miss any. I go to the front door, the stockroom door and this one."

When Nelda started to protest, Wilma said, "He's telling the truth, Nelda. He always checks on me. I'm not usually up here, but I have been a couple of times. I guess I should've told you to expect it."

"Well, I'm glad he didn't do it just because I'm living here now."

"I'll do all I can to protect you while you're here, Nelda, but don't expect special treatment." He winked at Wilma. "I have a whole town to take care of."

Wilma laughed. "Spoken like a brother."

Nelda shook her head. "Would you like some stew, Lance?"

"No, thank you. I'll be meeting Grace shortly for supper. I think she said Effie was cooking a turkey somebody shot and brought in. Effie would have my hide if I didn't show up hungry."

"Then I won't try to tempt you with our stew. I know you've always loved turkey."

"Your brother might like turkey, Nelda, but he likes eating his supper with Grace much more. Sometimes it makes you wonder if they were destined to be together."

"I can answer that. We must have been." He laughed and looked at Nelda. "When you started dragging that silly little friend of yours home to aggravate me when you were young, I never dreamed I'd end up married to her. It had to be in God's master plan because it sure wasn't in mine."

"Oh, Lance. Grace fell in love with you when she was a little girl. She didn't think we knew, but we did, didn't we, Nelda?"

"We sure did. We just didn't let her know we'd figured it out. She had it rough enough with her bad foot and her terrible father. We didn't want to give anybody anything else to tease her about. Amelia knew, too. She's the one who told us we shouldn't say anything. And you know us, we always listened to Amelia."

"That doesn't surprise me. Amelia was always the instigator of the troubles the four of you caused in this town." He chuckled. "According to her husband, she can still stir up trouble. I think her little speech at church yesterday proved that."

"Did it ever."

"I'm still upset that I missed all the fun," Wilma said.

Nelda looked at Wilma. "I wish you'd been there, too. It was fun, and I know I sure want to get to know that Mrs. Ellsworth better. She's a super lady. I hope I can be that spry when I'm her age."

"I'm sure she'd like to get to know you, Nelda. She'll be coming into the mercantile soon. She seldom misses coming in during the week. When she does, just talk to her and I know she'll warm right up to you."

"Wilma's right. You'll like her. We all do." Lance put his hat on. "Now that I see you ladies are in here snug and safe, I'm going to meet my wife. Be sure to lock the door again when I leave."

"I'll see you to the door and lock it myself." Nelda hooked her arm in his.

"Thanks." He leaned down and kissed her cheek. "See you later."

Nelda closed and locked the door. When she turned back to Wilma she smiled and said, "He waited to make sure I locked it."

"That doesn't surprise me. He's very conscientious about his job."

"I'm glad you told me. I was afraid he'd hover over me, but maybe he won't."

"Maybe not. Now, let's have some of that cherry cobbler I made last night. I want something sweet."

"Sounds like we have the same taste, Wilma, my friend. I'll get the bowls."

Seven

A little man with a handlebar mustache, wearing a derby hat and a suit that only an Easterner would wear in Wyoming, got off the stage and brushed the dust off his coat. He looked around the small town and thought he'd never seen a place as unsophisticated as this town called Settlers Ridge. How in the world was he supposed to survive in a place like this? Even if he found that his trip here wasn't necessary, he couldn't leave until he got the word from his superior. He only hoped that word wouldn't take long in coming. He wanted to get back to civilization. And he considered civilization in this country only existed in the cities in the East. More specifically, Boston, New York and possibly Philadelphia.

Picking up the carpetbag the driver had tossed off the top of the stagecoach, he took a deep breath and headed for the hotel. Or what this town considered the whitewashed wooden two-story structure to be. He calculated that there could possibly be a dozen or so rooms in the place. He just hoped they had decent beds. So far, he hadn't found a comfortable one in any of the so-called hotels he'd had to stay in during his trip west.

"Good evening, sir," Frank Olsen said as the little man entered. "How can I help you?"

"I want to rent your room number six and I hope it's your best room, if you have such a thing as a best one."

If Frank felt insulted, he didn't show it. "For how long would you like the room?"

"A week to begin with, I suppose. Or maybe I should say, I hope that's as long as I'll be in this town."

"That's five dollars for the week."

The man took out a small leather bag and extracted five dollars. Handing it to Frank, he asked, "I suppose the dining room is the only place to eat in town."

Frank took the money. "There's a new restaurant down the street and of course, there's always the saloon. They serve meals, too."

"Those places do not sound too appetizing. I suppose the dining room here will have to do. It is open now, isn't it?"

"Yes, it is."

"Of course, I'll go to my room and wash up first. The trip here was horribly dusty and dirty."

"You'll be in room six, as you requested. I'll have some warm water sent right up."

The man nodded and took the pen Frank held out to him. He wrote his name on the hotel register.

Frank whirled the ledger back around and read aloud, "Marcel Guillaume Augustus La Gall. That's quite a name."

La Gall ignored him, bent and picked up his bag. Without saying anything else, he snatched the key Frank held out, turned and went up the steps.

When he stepped into the room, his heart sank. There was no bathroom. Only a chamber pot under a chair behind a screen. The floor had a rug that had seen better days, but it was clean. In fact, the entire room was spotless. "Well, I suppose that's something to be thankful for. Many of the rooms I've had to lay my head down in have been just shy of filthy. But my goodness, how crude this is! How do these people stand living in such a manner?"

Shaking his head, he set his bag on the only chair and began to unpack. His other suit was wrinkled, but he shook it and put in in the wardrobe. He opened the drawer of the small chest and placed his undergarments inside. A knock sounded on his door.

He frowned, but moved to it and said, "Yes? Who is it?"

"It's your warm water, sir."

At least the man downstairs was good as his word. He was going to have a nice wash-up, then go eat. He opened the door.

A young woman handed him a pitcher of water.

He took the water, nodded to her and closed the door without speaking. He put the water on the dresser, then turned back to his bag. When it appeared empty, he removed the false bottom and took out the velvet covered case. Sitting it on the bed, he carefully opened it and looked inside. He couldn't believe it. After all the shaking and terrible baggage handling, there was nothing out of place.

Each razor-sharp knife remained in its own slot in the case. All six of them were fine. They gleamed against the red velvet lining.

He grinned for the first time since arriving in Settlers Ridge. It always gave him a lift to look at his beautiful knife collection, a collection he considered the most important thing he owned. They had become the babies that witch in Paris wouldn't give him.

His grin widened as he remembered the day he came home with the collection. A collection that he'd scraped and saved to buy. The witch threw the case to the floor and all his beautiful knives fell out on the worn wooden floor. She yelled at him and he remembered distinctly what she said. *"You stupid idiot. We need bread and you come home with these horrible things. Where is your brain, you fool?"*

That was the day he realized what his knives could accomplish for him. It was so easy to gather them that day, select the one to do the job and turn to face her. She was still screeching at him in her high-pitched voice when he moved toward her. He looked at the knives in his hand and it was if a light shone down on one of them. He knew that was the one he had to use. He laid the others aside, gripped the beautiful dagger and smiled at her as he rammed it into her heart. He would never forget the look of shock and disbelief on her face as she slipped to the floor with the lifeblood draining out of her. He felt exhilarated when it occurred to him that she'd never yell and screech at him or any other person on earth again. It gave him a feeling of power he'd never experienced. He took his time cleaning the blade and putting it back in the velvet case with its siblings. Yes, that was the day the six of them became his perfect children. Children that would never let him down. He packed his valise with care, knowing no matter where he went, he'd never be separated from his beautiful collection again.

And he wasn't. By the time the superior recruited him, he'd used his special collection on three other people. Since he'd become known as 'The Blade' with those in power, he'd used the knives six more times. Every time he viewed the beautiful blades, he could remember which one had done the exciting deed for him. It was as if they communicated their delight in helping him.

Now that he'd come to this awful town at the request of his superior, he hoped the rumor they told him about was true, that the woman they were seeking had come here. If so, he already knew who would be the eleventh person to have the pleasure of feeling one of these perfect knives slip into her soft body at the opportune moment. He only had to wait until he found the woman and the knives would tell him which one would have the honor of slicing into her skin. Of course, if it was hard to find and identify her, he could always select someone who needed to leave this earth. Someone nobody would care had died and would not be missed at all.

~ * ~

In room seven, next door to the one he knew La Gall would request, Con Minton had stood at the window and watched the man get off the stage and he felt he had to prepare for whatever would happen on this assignment. He knew with his sharp hearing, he'd know when the man entered or left room six, which for some reason was the number La Gall always requested to stay in.

Con moved to the small table beside the bed and pushed the oil lamp to the side. He sat on the edge of the bed and laid his two pearl handled guns and the ornate Indian knife on the table. It would take a while, but he had to be ready to do his job now that the man had arrived.

He finished cleaning his guns, then turned to sharpen his long blade knife with the Indian carvings on the handle. The knife had been given to him by a young Indian brave who was in the process of trying to kill a half-grown grizzly bear with it when Con happened upon them. Con had shot the bear, not with the intention of saving the Indian, but wanting to save his own life before the bear decided to attack him. The Indian didn't realize the reason for his rescue, and vowed his eternal gratitude to the long skinny cowboy. He tried to give his savior a string of beads, a hunting bow, even an amulet used to ward off evil spirits, but Con didn't want any of those things. He'd seen the knife the boy had used and decided he wanted it.

The brave tried to explain that the knife had been a gift from his grandfather, the chief, and he would have bad luck if he parted with it. Con didn't like that answer, but took the amulet and tried to play dumb. He offered to help the Indian tend his wounds. The boy laid the knife aside and succumbed to Con's treatments. When the wounds were mostly taken care of, Con had stood, picked up a rock behind the Indian, and dealt the young brave a blow in the head. Stunned, the half-conscious boy watched Con take the beads, the amulet and the knife.

The young brave yelled at the man, telling him his people would make him pay for his actions. He then placed what he called a tribal curse on the cowboy.

Furious, Con lunged at the youngster and, using the knife, he ripped the young Indian's stomach open. He started to leave him for the vultures, but it dawned on him the tribe would know a knife cut from an opening made by a bear's claw. Con dragged both the Indian's body and that of the bear to the bank above the river, and rolled them over the ledge. He figured when they found him, if they ever did, they'd think he and the bear had fallen during their fight. He also thought if they looked for the knife, they'd think it was lost in the water as they fell. At least, he hoped they'd figure things this way. Just in case, he planned to steer clear of any Indians he came across in the future. In fact, he had grown paranoid about the curse as time passed.

Nobody knew the real story of how Con Minton came into possession of the beautiful Indian knife because he always said an Indian had given it to him for saving his life. He'd told the false story so many times he'd almost made himself believe it. Almost, but not entirely.

Since then, he'd used the knife several times when it wasn't wise to fire his guns, and it had become an important and most useful instrument. He'd never let himself think of it as an ill-gotten murder weapon, because to him it was only one of the many tools he used to do his job. He figured every time he'd used it, or his guns or even a heavy object, it was the correct weapon to rid the world of someone who had to die for the cause. Well, at least most of them had been for the cause. The other victims had made him mad enough to kill them in anger, and most of those were women who refused his attention. Of course, that didn't happen often because Con Minton considered himself a man who had a way with the ladies.

Finished sharpening his knife, he slipped it into his boot and grabbed his hat. Thinking about the women he'd had to show who was boss, he began feeling warm inside. He liked women who were a little afraid of him and he knew nothing would fill that oncoming need except a trip to the saloon. He was sure a town like this would have a few beauties who would show him a good time once he mastered them.

He hurried downstairs and glanced at the desk in the lobby. Nobody was there. "Good," he muttered. "I don't like the clerk knowing when I go out and when I come in. I like keeping my business to myself." He scooted out the door and didn't look back. "I especially don't want La Gall to see me and figure out I was sent here to keep an eye on him."

~ * ~

Nelda looked up as a handsome cowboy came into the mercantile. "Can I help you, sir?"

He chuckled. "Lordy, ma'am, you don't have to say sir to me."

"Then I won't. What do you need?" She almost said sir again, but stopped herself. She supposed she'd been around the fort too long and it came naturally to call most of the men sir.

"I'm Ward Kyler, the foreman at the Circle Two ranches. Cookie at Wainwright's section was up to his elbows in dressing a mule deer one of the hands brought in this morning and I volunteered to come get the supplies for him." He took a list out of his shirt pocket and handed it to her. "Is Stanley or Miss Wilma around?"

"Stanley isn't here, but Wilma will be back shortly. She went to the bank." Nelda looked at the extensive list. "You do need a lot of things, don't you?"

"It's a big ranch, ma'am."

"If I can't call you sir, then I'd appreciate if you don't call me ma'am. My name's Nelda."

He tipped his hat. "I'll do that, Miss Nelda."

The door opened and Wilma walked in. "Hello, Ward."

He removed his hat and grinned at her. "Miss Wilma. How are you today?"

"I'm just fine. I see you've met my new partner."

"Yes, miss."

"I hope she's been able to help you. I know you usually want those special cigars."

"I'll get some before I go, but I actually came for the ranch supplies. As I told Miss Nelda, Cookie is dressing a deer and I volunteered to come. I didn't want to finish up the deer for him."

"I understand, and it was nice of you. I'm sure Cookie appreciates it." She moved behind the counter and placed the money she'd gotten at the bank in the box on the shelf underneath. "Did you bring a list?"

"Here it is, Wilma." Nelda handed it to her.

"My goodness. Cookie has run out of a lot of things." She glanced at him. "Well come on, Ward. Cookie usually helps me gather up all his supplies, so I suppose you're going to have to help this time."

"It'll be my pleasure, Miss Wilma."

Nelda watched as they began to look through the shelves and barrels and tables for the items on the list. She couldn't help noticing that the man was especially attentive to Wilma. It occurred to her that the head foreman wasn't usually relegated to picking up supplies and he said he'd volunteered. She couldn't help smiling when she realized Wilma was probably the reason the handsome cowboy was doing that errand. That was a good sign. Wilma was going to need somebody to pay attention to her when Stanley left town. Ward Kyler could be the answer. Besides, he was much better looking and much manlier than Stanley Brown.

The bell over the door rang and a small man dressed as a dandy came through the door. He tilted his nose into the air as if he smelled something offensive and Nelda wondered why someone like him was in Settlers Ridge, and the mercantile in particular. He was certainly out of place in the store as well as in the town. But he came into the store; therefore, she knew she must wait on him.

"Good morning, sir. May I help you with something?"

"I doubt there's anything in here that I could want, young lady. But I will look around a bit to make sure."

"You're welcome to look all you want. Feel free to make yourself at home, sir."

He didn't answer, and began to look at the items on the nearest table.

Again, the door opened. Nelda sighed with relief when Gertrude Ellsworth came in. "Good morning, Mrs. Ellsworth. It's good to see you. How can I help you today?"

"Well, good morning, Mrs. Barrington. How are you doing?"

"Please call me Nelda and I'm just fine, ma'am, and you?"

"I will call you Nelda, and to answer your question, I feel the best I've felt in years."

"That's wonderful."

She leaned over the counter and laughed. "My son has had a stern talking to me every night since Sunday. Of course, I didn't pay him a lick of mind. I'd do the same thing I did Sunday again tomorrow if I had the chance. It was the most fun I've had since I left Savannah. Maybe even longer than that."

"I admit I enjoyed it myself, too. Sometimes I think men underestimate the will and the strength of a woman."

"You're right about that, young lady."

Nelda laughed. "Now, what can I get for you, Mrs. Ellsworth?"

"Margo is making some baby blankets for the coming winter. September's about gone, and it's getting a little cooler, but it won't be cold for a few weeks yet. I suppose she wants to get a head start."

"You're probably right. It's better than waiting until the last minute."

"I suppose so." Gertrude chuckled. "What she needs today is a spool of white thread, two sharp needles, and another batch of outing. Do you have anything with a pretty design?"

"I think most of the outing is white. Maybe she could embroider some flowers or put some trim around the edges of it."

"That's a good idea. How about giving me some colorful embroidery thread? Pinks, blues, yellows, and greens should do it. Also throw in a couple of needles and some colorful binding."

Nelda gathered the items and added them up. She was wrapping them in the brown paper they used for packaging when the bell sounded again. Glancing up, she gasped.

"Is something the matter, dear?"

She glanced away. "Not at all, Mrs. Ellsworth. I'm fine."

Striding to the counter, Spencer said, "Good morning, Nelda."

Not wanting to make a scene, she nodded.

He looked around. "So, this is what you've been up to?"

"Yes. I work here now, and I like it."

Gertrude interrupted. "I don't think I've met this handsome military man. I'm Gertrude Ellsworth, the preacher's mother, and you are?"

"How do you do, ma'am. I'm Major Spencer Barrington."

"Well mercy me. You must be Nelda's husband."

"Yes, ma'am, I am."

"Then I'll say it was a pleasure to meet you and go along and let you have a talk with your wife."

"It was my pleasure meeting you, Mrs. Ellsworth."

"Thank you very much, kind sir." She turned to Nelda. "Now young lady, you take care of this handsome major. He looks like a good one to me, so you don't want to let him get away. Good day."

"Good day, ma'am." Nelda's voice shook a little, but she didn't think Mrs. Ellsworth noticed.

When the door closed behind the elderly woman, Nelda hissed, "What are you doing here?"

"I came to see if you were in a more reasonable mood today."

"It doesn't matter what kind of mood I'm in. I have nothing to say to you."

Wilma called from the stockroom and interrupted. "Nelda, Ward and I are going out back to the shed to check on a couple of tools he wants. If you need me, call."

"I will."

When they were gone, Spencer said, "Now we're alone, could we have a talk."

"We're not alone. There's a man...." She looked around, but the dandy wasn't there. "He must have left, but it doesn't matter. I have nothing to say to you."

"Nelda, please. I love you."

"I don't believe you, Spencer."

"But it's true, darling. I've never loved any woman except you. You've got to believe me when I say that."

Nelda felt her anger building. "If you love me so much, why did you take a mistress?"

"Nelda, I—"

"Don't deny it. I know the truth, so you might as well not try any of your fancy talk on me today. I told you I was going to divorce you and I meant it."

"And I told you I'd never sign divorce papers and I meant that."

"Then we're at an impasse, aren't we, Spencer?"

"Nelda, please be reasonable. We can work this out."

"There's nothing to work out. My mind is made up."

"Please, come back to the fort with me and we'll try to set this right."

She shook her head. "I'm not going anywhere with you. There's no room in a marriage for three people. I'm staying right here in Settlers Ridge and making a new life for myself. A life without you."

"Nelda, a love like ours doesn't come along often. Please don't throw it away."

"What love, Spencer? You threw what we had away when you decided you couldn't give up your mistress." She put her hands on her hips. "Now get out of here and go back to her or to the fort or anywhere you want to go. I just want you out of my sight. In fact, I never want to see you again."

"But, Nelda—"

"I think the lady asked you to leave, mister."

Nelda turned around and saw Ward Kyler staring at Spencer. She hadn't heard him and Wilma come back in. "I can handle this, Ward."

"Are you sure?"

"Yes."

"Then I'll just stand by and make sure the man doesn't bother you anymore."

"This is between my wife and me, mister," Spencer spat at him and looked back at Nelda. "So, you you're saying you won't go back to the fort with me so we can work this out?"

"No, Spencer. I'm not going anywhere with you. Your actions have killed what was between us and that leaves nothing to work out. Now accept the fact that our marriage is over. The only thing I want now is for you to get out of my life and leave me alone."

"I won't give you up, Nelda."

She put her hands on her hips and glared at him. "You might as well give me up, since you have no other option."

He looked defeated, but stared at her for a minute. Then without saying anything else, he turned and walked out the door.

~ * ~

Crouched behind the bolts of cloth on a table in the back, Marcel Guillaume Augustus La Gall couldn't help smiling to himself. When he'd stepped into this rough looking, primitive store, he never dreamed he'd find the object of his pursuit. The meeting was more informative than he ever dreamed it would be. The major was certainly no surprise, but learning that the clerk was his wife certainly was. But what did she mean when she said she was going to divorce him? That didn't make any sense if the two of them were working as a team. He knew the major was working with a woman. Yet, this one did sound convincing. Maybe it wouldn't be a bad idea to swallow his pride and get to know this lady a little better. It could make his job more complicated and much more interesting if it turned out the woman she accused her husband of having turned out to be his partner. If so, where was the other woman? Was this one putting on an act? Could she be the one he was searching for?

He straightened and grabbed a small pouch off the shelf behind him. He marched up to the counter.

Nelda gasped. "I thought you'd left."

"No. I was only looking around. I didn't think I'd find anything I needed, but I was wrong. This is just the right thing to hold some of my objects." He laid the pouch down on the counter as he studied her delicate features.

Nelda lifted an eyebrow, but said nothing. He disregarded the look as she rang up the purchase. "That'll be sixty cents, please."

He counted out the money and decided this was the time he should show her he could be a gentleman. "Thank you very much, mademoiselle. You've been very helpful."

"I'm glad I could help you. Please come back and shop with us again."

He knew she was watching him leave with his purchase, but he didn't turn around or acknowledge the man and woman who were also in the store. He was planning his next move because he knew he had to learn as much as he could about the lady called Nelda.

Eight

As the door closed behind him, Wilma asked, "Who was that, Nelda?"

"I have no idea. He came in while you were busy with Ward, but he acted as if he was too good to shop in here. When Spencer came in, I lost sight of him and thought he'd left."

"I admit he looked out of place here. Fact is, it was hard to keep a straight face looking at those duds he had on. Besides that, he talked funny." Ward smiled at the women.

Wilma punched his arm playfully. "I admit I thought the same thing, but he did buy something, so I guess it was a good thing we didn't laugh at him to his face."

Nelda nodded, then burst out laughing. "Yes, I did make a sale, but unless he has a daughter, what in the world is he going to put in a little girl's reticule?"

Wilma laughed out loud, and it wasn't long until Ward joined in the laughter.

"Well, it sure looks like a party is going on in here." Lance came in and paused as he looked at them.

"Lance, come in." Wilma greeted him. "How can we help you?"

"It's close to dinner time and I thought I might take my sister out to eat, if it's all right."

"I think that's a good idea. She probably needs to get out of here for a while."

"I'm fine, Wilma. I planned to go upstairs and eat some of that leftover stew we had for supper last night."

"No, Nelda. I'm still helping Ward, but we're almost through. Why don't you go eat with Lance? I'll take care of the store until you get back, then I'll go eat."

"Miss Wilma has been such a good help to me, I'd be glad to take her to the hotel for dinner when we're through, just to say thank you," Ward said.

Nelda knew it would be a good thing for Wilma to be with Ward. "All right, I'll go eat with my brother, then Wilma can go." She took off her apron and hung it behind the counter.

"Great. Let's go, little sister. I'm hungry." Lance put his hand on the small of her back when she moved toward the door. "See you folks later."

On the plank sidewalk, Nelda said, "What is the meaning of coming to take me out to dinner, Lance? You need to be taking Grace, not me."

"Want me to be honest or make something up like I did when I didn't want to tell you the truth when we were kids?"

"I think we're past lying to each other, big brother. Now, answer my question."

He reached for her arm and looped it in his. "Effie's not feeling up to par and they needed Grace to cook, so Henrietta brought the dinner food for the prisoners. Mrs. Olsen's still not comfortable doing the cooking alone. Grace didn't feel she had any choice except to go help them out. She did send word for me to come to the hotel to eat. I was sure she wouldn't have time to eat with me, and I didn't want to eat by myself, so I came to drag you along with me."

"I guess that's honest enough, and to tell you the truth, I don't mind being your second choice, though I know you'd rather have had Grace than me."

"Don't worry. She and I will make it up for it when we're alone at home tonight."

Nelda stopped and looked up at him. "Lance, I can't believe you said that to me."

He blushed. "Sorry, Nelda. I guess I was just thinking out loud."

She patted his arm. "Don't worry about it. It does my heart good to see my brother so happy. Of course, I'm glad my good friend Grace is happy, too."

"I think she's happy with me. I certainly try to make her feel that way."

"There's not a doubt in my mind. You know she's loved you forever."

"She has told me she felt that way. I'm glad I didn't know. At the time, I might have hurt her feelings, but now it makes me proud she liked me."

They reached the hotel and Lance escorted her inside. He nodded at Sophie as they entered and guided her to his usual table near the back. After they were seated, Sophie came to the table. "Want me to tell Grace you're here?"

"I'm sure she's busy, but Nelda and I'll have whatever they've cooked up for the special today."

"It's beef, potatoes, and green beans."

"That sounds good to me. How about you, Nelda?"

"Yes. It will be fine."

"Do you want coffee, too, Mrs. Barrington? I know the sheriff does."

"Yes, please."

"I'll bring it right out. I'll also tell Grace you're here." Sophie walked away.

"She's grown into a lovely young woman. She was just a little girl when I left."

"She sure is. According to Frank, the young men are beginning to hang around. I'm not sure he likes it very much."

"How old is she?"

"Sixteen or seventeen, I guess."

Nelda lifted her eyebrow. "I was only seventeen and a half when I met...never mind."

"You really loved him, didn't you?"

"I thought I did. But I guess I was too young to know any better. He was older and so dashing in his uniform that my head was turned." She looked at him. "Why didn't you knock some sense in me?"

"I didn't think it was my place. Besides, I was sure he loved you, too, Nelda."

"Now you know better."

Sophie brought their coffee. "Grace said she'd come speak to you shortly."

"Thanks, Sophie." Lance smiled at her. When she moved away, he turned back to Nelda. "I believe Spencer loved you then and I believe he loves you now."

"If he loves me, why did he take a mistress? No man who loves his wife would ever do such a thing. I'm going to divorce him and find somebody who loves me and nobody else."

"Nelda, do you trust me?"

"Of course, I do, Lance. You're my brother. Why wouldn't I trust you?"

"Then will you take some advice from me?"

She gave him a sheepish grin. "If I like it, I will."

"You might not like it, but I hope you'll listen. Spencer came to see me before he left town. He convinced me he still loves you."

"So you believed his lies?"

"Maybe it's because I'm in love myself that makes me recognize another man who feels that way about his woman. I just want you to be sure you know what you're doing when you divorce the man. I don't want you to make a mistake."

"I don't think it's a mistake. He didn't tell you he'd give up his mistress, did he?"

"We didn't talk about her. I just know he wants you back."

"Well, he can want from now on, but that want will never be fulfilled."

"Just do me one favor."

"What's that?"

"Put off having Cramer draw up those divorce papers."

"Why?"

"For one thing, you know Spencer's not going to sign them. Getting them filled out now is a waste of time. For another, I don't want everybody in town talking about you because you've left your husband. Chances are, a little time is not going to change things, but it will give people more time to get used to you being back home alone."

She took a big breath. "If it's that important to you, I'll put it off a while, but I intend to divorce him sooner or later, no matter what anybody says."

Grace appeared with their food. "I hope this is to your liking. I'm not the cook Effie is, but I did my best."

"It looks wonderful, darling."

"He's right. It does look good, Grace. Can you join us?"

"Only for a moment. Things have slowed down a little, but I have some other things cooking."

"Will Effie be able to cook supper?"

"Probably not."

"So, I guess it'll be evening before I see you again."

"I'm afraid so."

Sophie walked up and whispered, "Grace, that man over there is giving me a hard time. He doesn't like this, and he doesn't like that. I'm about ready to yell at him and throw the soup he wanted in his face."

They all looked toward the little man at the table in the middle of the room. It was the Easterner.

Nelda smothered her laugh with her napkin. She then leaned over and whispered, "He came into the mercantile earlier. I almost fell over when he bought a little girl's reticule, then told me it was just what he needed."

Lance whispered back, "He looks like the type to carry one."

Grace punched him in the shoulder, but she had a big grin on her face when she shook her head. "You eat your dinner." She turned to Sophie. "Go to the kitchen, honey. You can help your mama and I'll take care of the worrisome customer."

Sophie scurried away, and Grace said, "Good to see you, Nelda. Maye we'll have more time to chat before you have to leave."

Lance grabbed her hand. "I'll see you later."

"I'll hold you to that."

"Is it possible for a man to get any service around here?" the Easterner yelled.

Nine

Marcel knew he shouldn't have called out like that as soon as the words left his mouth. But it was instinct. He'd been warned that things were done differently in the West and he'd have to adapt. He'd been ignored in other establishments after crossing the Mississippi river and had shown his displeasure to the workers. It didn't take long for his superiors to warn him to control his temper, but that hadn't been easy. He was used to things going his way most of the time. He'd do better, he promised himself. He'd even apologize to the waitress when she came back to serve him. After all, she was a mere child.

But it wasn't the child who walked up to his table this time. It was the woman who'd been talking to the sheriff and the major's so-called wife. He wondered why she limped.

"I understand you're unhappy with the service, sir. How can I help you?"

He started to say she could show him a little more attention. He was, after all, an important person. He thought better of it, though, and said, "I don't mean to be so much trouble, but my coffee is so strong I can hardly drink it and it is getting cold anyway."

"I'm sorry, but most of our customers like it strong. Would you like me to get you some cream for it or some water to weaken it?"

"Water would just make it cooler."

"I'll bring some of the hot water we use for the tea."

He couldn't believe his ears. "You actually have tea in this establishment?"

"Yes, sir, we do. A lot of our lady customers enjoy a cup of tea when they come in."

"That sounds wonderful. It will be so much better than this awful coffee. Please bring me a cup of tea with cream. That will be a pleasant change from this awful...I mean from the strong coffee you people are used to."

Grace lifted an eyebrow. "I'll bring it right out. Is there anything else I can get you?"

"Just the tea for now." He glanced around and saw the sheriff staring at him. He wondered why. Maybe the lawman had some idea who he was. No, that couldn't be. He'd made no move to let anyone in on his identity, with the exception of giving them his name. Of course, that name was beginning to be known, but mostly in the circles his superior traveled in. Not in towns such as this godforsaken place.

Grace returned with the steaming teapot and a cup. "Let me know if this is to your liking, sir."

"It will do. Tell me something if you can. Why is that lawman looking so intently at me? He seems to be unusually interested in what I'm doing."

"That's simple to explain, sir. That lawman is Sheriff Lance Gentry and the lady with him is his sister. He is my husband and he's protective of me. When he heard you yell out in an angry voice, he wanted to make sure you didn't berate me when I came over here to wait on you."

"What would he do if I yelled again?"

"Probably put you in jail."

His eyes got big. "You can't be serious."

"Oh, yes. I'm very serious. Men in the West are very protective of their women. They've been known to kill a man for making an inappropriate remark to their wife."

"Oh dear, aren't there laws against such things around here?"

"If so, the courts don't uphold them. No man has ever hanged for killing someone who mistreated his wife. Of course, my husband is a sheriff, so his motives would never be questioned if he shot someone who offended me."

Marcel could hardly believe what he was hearing, but he decided he'd better heed it. He'd be more careful how he talked to the women in this town. Especially those of the lawman's family. "Since you've enlightened me, I'll be more careful of what I say from now on."

"That might be a very good idea." Grace left him, and he watched as she moved back to the table where the sheriff sat.

She didn't repeat their conversation, but he heard her say, "It was good to see you two, but I need to get back to the kitchen."

"Did that man insult you, Grace?"

"No, honey. He's from the East and he doesn't understand our ways. I think I explained to him in a way he understands. He won't be upsetting Sophie anymore, either."

"I have to get back to work, too, Grace. Let's get together soon."

"We will, just as soon as everyone here is better and I can be away for a day. Amelia wants the four of us girlfriends to get together at the ranch soon. I suppose that will have to be on a Sunday when the mercantile is closed."

"That sounds good to me. The four of us haven't had a chance to do that since I returned. Of course, we'll have to dump Lance and Jed for the day."

Lance shook his head. "Don't worry about us. I'd enjoy a trip to the Circle Two and Jed and I can always find something to do out on the range."

"Who invited you, brother?"

"Nobody, but you don't think I'd let the three of you head out there without me, do you?"

Grace laughed. "I just told that gentleman over there that you were protective of me."

"That I am. It took me a long time to realize I wanted you and now that I have you, nobody's going to take you away."

So, she was telling the truth. Men do protect their wives in this wild country. I'm glad I found out before I made a wrong move. I'm assuming the third woman they're talking about is the other woman working in that awful store. Now I wonder who this fourth woman is. Maybe she's the one I'm looking for.

He sat back and sipped his tea. Though he wouldn't say anything to anyone, the tea was good. He planned to order it every time he ate in this establishment. He sure couldn't stomach that awful stuff they called coffee. Finishing, he placed some money on the table and left the dining room.

Back in his room, he took the velvet case from the false bottom of his valise. Placing it carefully on the bed, he opened the box. Taking the one with the longest and sharpest blade, he caressed it to his face, being careful not to nick his skin. "Hello, my lovely. I know you will be pleased to know I picked up an idea as to who our next prize will be while I was having lunch. We will have to take extra care this time, though. It seems the men around here will protect their women at all cost. But when we decide to strike, it won't matter. He will be too late to save her. Of course, we must wait until the other deed is done."

He placed the knife back in the velvet slot and took out another one and held it next to his chest. "Now, you are the honored one this time. I've chosen you to perform the required kill. You'll be happy to know I think I may have picked up a clue today. I'm not sure who this fourth woman is, but it seems she doesn't live in town. That makes me think she may be hiding, since she probably knows things she shouldn't know. Her name is Amelia and she lives at a place called the Circle Two. Have you ever heard such a ridiculous address? Circle Two. What can it mean?"

He put the knife back with the others and smiled. "I guess my job tomorrow is to inquire about this place called the Circle Two. It shouldn't take me long to find out where it is."

Looking at the other knives and touching each one, he said, "Don't worry, my pretty babies. I won't leave you out of all the fun. Surely, I can come up with something that will let you experience the joy of slicing into someone in this town before we find our real target. I'll be thinking on it. Just be patient.

He closed the red velvet box and returned it to the valise and moved to the window. He looked up and down the street and wondered what he could do to entertain himself for the rest of the day. A building at the end of the street caught his eye. In the bright sunlight, he could read *Wildcat Saloon* painted over the door. He hadn't been in the saloon since he arrived. Since he was in a town where nobody knew him or what his real purpose was, would he dare venture into this place just to see what it was like? Then the thought hit him. He might just find someone there who would ease his longing to use one of his babies.

"Why not?" he said aloud and opened his valise again. After making his selection, he headed out the door.

Ten

Major Spencer Barrington turned his horse in at the stable and walked across the dark compound to his quarters. He wasn't looking forward to going into the house. It would be dark and lonely without Nelda being there to greet him with her soft arms and her gentle kisses. He shook his head. Would he never hold that wonderful woman in his arms again? Lord, how could he cope without the feel of her small body lying next to him on their big four poster bed at night? He didn't want to think about it, though he knew there was the slight possibility she would never forgive him. She could be awfully stubborn when she wanted to be.

Of course, she'd understand if he told her the real reason he went to Denver, but he couldn't do it. He couldn't put her life in peril. He loved her too much for that. Even if it meant losing her temporarily, he couldn't take the chance on her getting killed. There was no way he could to live with himself if anything happened to the woman he loved.

There had to be some way he could protect her and still win her back. There just had to be. His life without Nelda would be worthless. There was no way he could keep his mind on his job and do what had to be done about Antoinette and help protect all those in danger. Not without the love and comfort of his wife. Nelda was what kept him stable. She was what gave him the strength to go on. She was his life.

"Hey there, Major Barrington. Good to see you back."

"Thank you, Sergeant Grimes."

"We weren't expecting you back so soon. I hope things were all right in Denver."

Spencer raised an eyebrow. "I went to Wyoming, Sergeant. Not Denver."

"Sure, sir. I understand." He was grinning.

Spencer narrowed his eyes and asked in a sharp voice, "Are you doubting the word of a superior officer?"

The man sobered. "No, sir. If you say you went to Wyoming, you went to Wyoming."

Spencer knew the man was lying, but he decided to let it go. "Then don't question me again, Sergeant, and get back to your duties."

"Yes, sir." The sergeant saluted and turned away.

Spencer figured there would be a discussion in the barracks tonight of how the major had given him a hard time because he mentioned Denver. What did it matter? There was no way to stop the men if they wanted to gossip about the officers.

He took a deep breath. Of course it mattered. Not only could this lead to Antoinette's discovery, but more important to him, this was the kind of talk Nelda had to put up with when he was away. He'd never thought about it, but it must have hurt his wife deeply. There was nothing he wanted more than to take that hurt away. But how? How was he going to correct all the damage that had already been done to the woman who was the most important person in his life?

There was an envelope left on the front door of his house. He grabbed it and went inside. Moving across the parlor, he reached the small table by the window where he knew an oil lamp sat. Lifting the globe, he took a match from his pocket and lit it. When he replaced the globe, a warm glow filled the room, but it didn't dispel the gloom he felt in the empty house.

Looking at the envelope he realized it was a telegram. He slid his finger under the seal, pulled it out and read: *Important. Come as soon as you can. CH*

What could have happened? The last thing I want to do now is go to Denver, but what choice do I have?

He decided he'd get a couple of hours' sleep before he pulled out for Denver. If two hours would make a difference, he was probably already too late for the emergency in the first place and he really needed to get some sleep. At least as much as he could without Nelda.

~ * ~

Lance was headed into his office the next day when he saw the Wildcat's barkeep, Ned Foster, coming in his direction. He paused and waited.

"If you're not too busy, can I talk to you a minute, Sheriff?"

"I'm not busy. The trial for the prisoners was this morning and I've just got them in the prison wagon headed for Cheyanne. Come on in, Ned."

"Thanks." He followed Lance inside.

Lance hung his hat on the peg and motioned to the chair in front of his desk. "Have a seat and tell me what's going on."

He sat and leaned toward Lance. "One of my whores was killed sometime last night or this morning."

Lance's eyes grew wide. "And you're just now telling me?"

"I just found out about it."

"What happened?"

"Hessie wasn't feeling good yesterday so I told her she didn't have to work last night. Our cook, Bertha, kept an eye on her and sent some soup up to her room at supper. She ate it, but didn't get any better so, Bertha ask me if we should send for the doc. I told her to go ahead. He came and told us Hessie might have something wrong with her stomach and she needed to rest. He told us not to give her anything else to eat for twenty-four hours. That's why she wasn't bothered any more last night or this morning. I told her if she needed something to let one of the girls know. Otherwise, we'd let her rest. But when she didn't get up or call out by the middle of the afternoon and we were getting ready to open the cribs for business, I told Meggie to go up and check on her."

"So, that's when you discovered she had been killed?"

"Yeah. Meggie started screaming. I went up to see what was going on, but she wouldn't stop screaming at the top of her lungs. It took me and my cook both a long time to calm her down, partly because the screams upset Bertha almost as much as they had Meggie. Anyway, she must have opened Hessie's door, then shut it without going in. I opened the door and glanced into the room. I knew immediately she'd looked inside and shut it again. I didn't blame her because it looked like the poor woman's throat was cut. Her head was hanging off the bed, almost severed from her body. There was blood everywhere. I didn't go inside. Instead, I got the girls downstairs and then sent Liza for Doc Wagner and I came to get you."

"I'll leave a note to let Bryce know where I'm going so, he'll go over there as soon as he gets here." Lance scrawled some words on a piece of paper, put a cup on it, then stood. "All right, let's go to the saloon. I'll see if I can piece together what happened to the woman."

When they entered the Wildcat three women came running toward Lance. "You've got to do something, Sheriff. I don't feel safe now," Liza said.

"None of us do," Meggie added through tears. "I can't believe this happened to poor Hessie and right here under this roof."

"I'd always felt safe sleeping here in the saloon," said another woman, who he thought went by the name of Pearl.

Lance put up his hand. "Ladies let me assure you, I'm going to do everything I can to capture whoever killed your friend. We don't want things like this happening in Settlers Ridge. Let me get upstairs and see if I can figure out what happened."

They were reluctant, but backed away and he started toward the steps.

Ned stopped him. "Lance, if it's all right with you, I'm going to stay down here and get things ready to open up for the night. There are some men outside already waiting to come in."

"Go ahead, Ned, but it'd be better if you didn't talk too much about this killing until we get to the bottom of it."

"I'll do my best, but I doubt I can get the girls to stay quiet."

Lance nodded. "Do the best you can."

He went on up the stairs and knew when he'd reached the right room because he heard the doctor muttering. "Senseless waste. Can't believe something like this would happen in Settlers Ridge."

He stepped inside. "Hello, Sheldon."

The doctor turned. "Come in if you've got the stomach for it, Lance."

"Bad, huh?"

"It's awful. Whoever did this wasn't some irate customer or somebody who decided to rob the woman. He knew exactly what he was doing."

Lance glanced at the body, but couldn't look long. He was afraid he'd lose his dinner. "How can you tell?"

"Whoever did this tortured the victim for a long time before he killed her."

"Why?"

"If I could answer that, I'd be written up in all the medical journals for the next two years."

"What did the bastard do to her?"

Sheldon looked up at Lance and shook his head. "I don't know all he did, but I do know he gagged her, so she couldn't scream for help. See the marks in the corners of her mouth. He tied the gag so tight it cut into her skin. I don't know in what order he did the things he did to her with a knife, but I would guess he started at the top. He cut around her ears, her eyes, her nose then moved to her breast and her private area. Then he moved to her legs, and arms, then her feet and ankles. I would guess she felt every cut because the wounds are deep enough to hurt, but not deep enough to kill. When he was finished, he slit her throat and of course, that killed her."

"He must be awfully evil to do such a thing."

"I'd say you're right there. I've been reading about this type of behavior in some of the medical journals I've gotten from back east. People with this mental problem aren't just mean, they're so malicious they kill for the thrill of it and they have no remorse. Some say they're born without a conscience. Now that I've seen Hessie in this shape, I'm beginning to understand what those journals are talking about."

About to gag again, Lance looked away from the body. "I wonder why they chose Hessie. She's not young anymore and she sure isn't very pretty. She was a middle-aged woman when I was a kid. I thought most men went for the younger girls when they came in here."

"True, but as you say, Hessie's been here a long time. She's at least in her late fifties, maybe early sixties. From what I've heard and read, killers like this don't care about a person's age. It doesn't matter if they're young or old. The kill is the thing that thrills them."

"I'm glad to say I don't know anybody in town who fits that description, Doc."

"Neither do I, and that makes me think it's probably a stranger. Maybe an outlaw or some wicked person just passing through."

The strange easterner in the dining room yesterday crossed Lance's mind. But could that little man commit a murder such as this? He didn't look to have the strength to overpower a woman. Especially one as wise and experienced in handling rough cowboys as Hessie, even if the woman had been sick. Surely it wasn't him, but he'd have to be checked out. Nobody seemed to know why he was in Settlers Ridge in the first place. It was time the man explained himself.

~ * ~

Grace came into the mercantile with a basket on her arm. "Hello, my friends."

"Hello, Grace." Wilma smiled at her.

Nelda waved from behind the counter where she was adding up an order for Juanita Garcia. "Four dollars and seventeen cents."

"Put it on Circle Two's bill, please," Juanita said in a soft voice.

Nelda looked confused.

"Nelda, you haven't met Juanita. She's the lady who keeps house for Curt Allison on the part of the Circle Two that used to be the Lawson ranch before my folks moved to Texas."

Nelda nodded. "Hello, Juanita. I'm delighted to meet you."

"I'm glad to meet you, too. I understand you're the sheriff's sister."

"Yes, that's right. I just recently came back to Settlers Ridge."

"Thank you for your help today." Juanita gathered her package and left the store, smiling at Grace on the way out.

"What are you doing here, Grace?" Wilma laughed. "Not that we're not always glad to see you, but why aren't you at the hotel?"

"Would you believe everybody is better today? Henrietta said she was ready to get back to her baking and Effie was as spry as always. I decided since they didn't need me, I'd come and pick up a few things, go home and cook a nice supper for my husband."

"I bet he'll be glad."

"I think so. He likes to eat at the hotel with me, but I think he enjoys being at home more."

"I know he does, because he told me so." Nelda put the book away where she'd recorded Juanita's order and joined the conversation.

"That's nice to hear. I like it better, too."

Nelda changed the subject. "Grace, has Lance said anything about the woman from the saloon who was killed last night?"

"He came by and told me to be careful going outside. He said they have no idea who committed the murder and he didn't want any of the women in town to take any chances. Other than the fact he thought it was someone who had come to town and not one of our regular citizens, he didn't have much to say about it. I think it upset him because she was so brutally killed. He said he'd never seen anything so horrible." She handed Nelda the short list she had taken from her drawstring purse.

"We've heard all kinds of things about it in here today. I thought you might know the real story." Nelda glanced over the list. "I'll start gathering this for you."

"Thank you, and I told you all I know about the murder. I'd certainly share with you if I knew anything more, but Lance doesn't like to tell me the gory details when there's a murder."

"That's because my brother wants to protect you."

Wilma said, "I'd met the woman who was killed a few times. She came in here once in a while. She didn't talk much, but she was always polite. Stanley waited on her most of the time, but I remember getting her a pack of needles and some thread once. She said something about having to repair the other women's dresses."

Lance came into the store and walked directly to Grace. "I thought I saw you come in here. What are you doing out on the street alone?" His voice sounded irritated.

Grace gave him a hard look. "I just needed a few things to fix for supper. I didn't realize I was breaking any law."

Lance's voice softened, and he slid his arm around her shoulder. "I'm sorry, honey. It just scares me when I think something might happen to you when I'm not around."

"Oh, Lance, it took me too many years to get you. I'm not about to let anything take me away from you now."

"Ah, isn't that sweet, Wilma?" Nelda grinned at them.

"It sure is. Makes you realize maybe there is such a thing as real love in the world."

Grace blushed. "Let me assure there is more love in this old world than you ever dreamed would be."

Lance frowned at them. "I can't help loving this woman, so you two quit teasing us."

"Then let me get the groceries she wanted, then you can walk her home, brother. I know that's what you're going to do, aren't you?"

"Absolutely. Got to see she gets there safe. Might just stay there and guard her for a little while." He winked at Grace.

Grace blushed again. "Now you're embarrassing me. Let's get the things I need and go."

After they left, Nelda shook her head and laughed. "I remember so well how he couldn't stand to be in the same room with Grace and me when we were teenagers. It looks like now he can't stand to be away from her for more than a few hours at a time."

Wilma sighed. "It would be wonderful to be loved like that."

"It'll happen for you someday, my friend. I feel in my heart that it will."

"What about you, Nelda? I thought the major loved you like that, and I know you loved him just as much."

"That's the sad part, Wilma. I did love him like that and I thought he loved me the same way, too. But I was wrong. He should have been a stage actor because he sure can pour out the sweet words. Too bad he didn't mean a thing he said."

"I'm sorry, my friend."

"Thanks, but I'll manage to survive without him."

They didn't talk anymore because the brass bell over the door jangled and the mayor's wife walked in.

~ * ~

Ned was checking the liquor stock when Meggie came into the saloon. "You're down earlier than usual."

"I was ready, so I decided I'd come have a drink before it gets busy. That is, if you don't mind."

"Don't mind at all, Meggie. Want some of the good stuff?"

"That'd be nice, Ned."

He reached behind the box under the bar and pulled out a bottle. Taking a clean glass, he filled it half way. Then repeated the act for himself. He put the bottle back, picked up the filled glasses and nodded to a table. "Want to sit over there and tell me what's on your mind?"

She nodded and followed him.

He put one of the glasses in front of her. "Something must be worrying you, Meggie? You don't usually come downstairs until you have to."

Taking a sip of the drink, she shuddered and halfway grinned at him. "Couldn't get Hessie off my mind. I wanted to ask if you'd heard anything about her killing?"

"Not yet."

She sighed. "I have a feeling you probably won't."

"What do you mean?"

"You know how it works, Ned. When a woman like Hessie gets killed there's some talk and a show of interest from the law for a few days, but when it comes right down to looking for the killer, they give up awfully quick."

"I think you're wrong this time, honey. Lance Gentry's a dedicated lawman. He won't let it go until he does everything he can to find the murderer."

"I don't know him very well. He never came around here to visit the women very often and he quit coming all together more than a year ago."

"That's because he fell in love, Meggie. A deep, passionate, everlasting love. That man loves his wife dearly, so don't expect to ever see him around here for anything except a drink now and again."

"I remember when he married that woman who worked at the hotel. I heard she's a nice woman. I know she's a lucky one."

"Yes, she is, but he's pretty lucky himself. You're right when you say she's a special lady."

"That's my point, Ned. If somebody like his wife was killed, he'd leave nothing unturned until he found the culprit, then jailed or even killed him."

"Lance will do the same for Hessie. Just watch and see."

"I hope you're right, but I can't help doubting it."

There was knock on the saloon door.

She frowned. "We don't open for another half hour today. Can't those cowboys read the sign?"

Ned laughed and stood. "Unfortunately, many of the ones we get around here can't read a word."

He opened the door. "Hello, Sheriff. Meggie and me were just talking about you. Come in. Want a drink? If not liquor, I have some coffee if you'd rather have it."

"I'm fine. I just came by before you opened because I wanted to ask you a few questions, if you don't mind."

"Don't mind at all."

Meggie stood. "I'll go back upstairs and give you some privacy."

Lance nodded at her. "Please stay, Meggie. You might be able to help me out, too."

"If you want me to stay, I will." She sat again.

"Sure, you don't want that drink while we talk, Lance?" Ned asked.

"Since you mentioned coffee, I'll take a cup."

Meggie jumped up. "I'll get it, Ned." She went to the bar and took the hot pot he kept there.

Ned motioned for Lance to have a seat at the table he and Meggie were sharing. "What did you need to ask me, Sheriff?"

"One of the main things is to ask you if you'd seen any strangers in here lately."

"Can't recall any. Of course, we've been pretty busy. Last night was no exception. Everybody seems to want to come in and ask about the killing."

Meggie sat the cup in front of Lance. "Did you forget about that funny little man who was here, Ned?"

He frowned, then it seemed he remembered. "Oh, yeah. How could I have forgotten him? He sure was a funny looking little duck."

"Was it the funny looking little easterner that's been in town for a few days? The one everyone is curious about."

"That was him, Sheriff." Meggie picked up her glass. "He was awfully quiet and timid, though. He only drank a little wine and complained that it tasted worse than horse pee."

Lance chuckled. "I saw him in the hotel dining room the other day. I can't imagine him knowing what horse pee tastes like."

Meggie laughed. "That's what he said."

"He insisted Grace serve him tea at the hotel, too. Didn't hear him say what he thought it tasted like."

"He did look like a tea man, but we don't serve tea in this establishment." Ned grew serious. "Was there anything else you needed to ask, Lance?"

"I know it seems unlikely, but did the dandy say or do anything out of the way to any of the women?"

"Meggie would know more about that than I would."

They both looked at her and she said, "I don't remember anything except the complaint about the wine. I think Pearl asked him if he wanted a sarsaparilla. We laughed when the fool didn't even know what that was."

"Did any of you mention that Hessie was sick or wasn't working?"

"Not to him." She wrinkled her brow as if in thought. In a minute, she said, "I think Spud Winkler did ask where she was. Like Rolo Pullman, he's been a customer of hers for years, so I told him she was sick and couldn't work."

"What did he do?"

"Just said that he guessed he'd have to save the button he'd sewed on his shirt for her."

They all laughed and Ned said, "I guess Hessie's button collecting is widely known. She showed them to me a while back and let me tell you she had three one-gallon jugs full, and another one almost full. She said she planned to get half a dozen full before she quit the business. The old gal almost made it."

"I never knew much about her myself, but I hear she was quite a woman." Lance shook his head. "Are you sure nobody overheard you tell him she was sick, Meggie?"

"I don't know. There's a lot of noise in here, but I guess they could have heard if they'd been listening."

"I see. I guess that's about all I need to ask for now. If either of you remembers something you think I would want to know, please come tell me. Every little thing helps in a case like this."

Meggie frowned. "There was one other man I'd never seen in here. He came in after the funny easterner left. He looked something like a gunman. He kept pawing Pearl, but she'd promised to go upstairs with somebody else as soon as she finished serving drinks."

"What did he do?"

"I'm not sure. Maybe Liza would know. I think he talked to her, too."

"Can you describe him a little more, Meggie?"

She told him what she could remember and ended with, "He did have a wicked looking knife. Somebody asked him about it, so he was showing it around and telling everyone some Indian had given it to him. I don't know why."

"Do you know if he was staying in town or if he was just riding through?"

"I have no idea, Sheriff. As Ned said, we were awfully busy last night."

"Again, thank you both for the information. In the meantime, do you mind if I come back if I think of something else I need to ask?"

"Come any time, Lance."

Lance drank his coffee. "Meggie, I don't want you or any of the women to put yourselves in danger, but I'd appreciate it if you'd keep your eyes and ears open when you're working. I need all the help I can get to catch the bastard that did this to Hessie. We don't want him to get away with doing something so brutal to a woman in our town."

Meggie gave him a smile. "You're really going to try to find the killer, aren't you, Sheriff Gentry?"

Lance stood. "Yes, I am. I don't want somebody getting with away such a heinous crime."

Meggie smiled. "I'll do anything I can to help you, Sheriff."

"We all will," Ned said as he walked Lance to the door. "Hessie was a whore, but she was part of our family here and we cared for her."

"Don't worry. It may take a while, but we'll eventually catch him."

Ned closed the door and turned back to Meggie. "Now, what do you think?"

She downed the rest of her whiskey. "You're right, Ned. Lance Gentry is not only a good sheriff, he's a good man. I believe you now. I think he'll do all he can to catch the man who killed our Hessie."

"I'm glad you found that out. Now, why don't you go talk to the girls and have them keep their eyes and ears open while they're working the saloon. But I want you to take Lance's advice and be careful. I don't want any of you hurt."

"I know you don't, Ned and you can bet we'll be careful, but we'll sure keep our ears open. We all liked Hessie." She started for the stairs. "We'll be down in ten minutes to open up."

Ned smiled at her and headed back behind the bar. He trusted the sheriff and he trusted his girls. He was satisfied that things were going to work out and the murderer would soon be behind bars or possibly hanging by his neck from the gallows.

Eleven

It was a balmy day on Saturday, as the town gathered in the church yard for a dinner on the grounds to say goodbye to Mrs. Brown and Stanley. Families for miles around were represented by one or two members, if not by all of their relatives. Andy came in from the Circle Two where he worked, and joined his mother and brother at the table set up especially for them. He promised in front of the crowd to visit them in Chicago, but he said he was happy living on the ranch and working as a cowboy for Jed Wainwright and Curt Allison. He also made it clear, he had no intention of ever moving away from Settlers Ridge.

The church ladies, who had arranged the gathering, were pleased with the turnout and the mountains of food the people brought for the event. Touched, Mrs. Brown cried, and Stanley made a shaky speech about how much he'd enjoyed growing up in Settlers Ridge and how he was going to miss the people. He also assured them he was leaving the mercantile in the capable hands of Wilma Lawson and Nelda Barrington, and that business at the store would go on much as it had in the past.

After the eating and the speeches, the men who were accomplished on the fiddle, harmonica, guitar and banjo, gathered and impromptu dances began taking place. When Reverend Eli looked as if he wasn't sure that was the right thing to do in front of the church, his mother got his hand and pulled him up to dance with her. That was all it took to turn the event into a big party.

Nelda danced with her brother a couple of times. Wilma even danced with Stanley. And the strange little easterner sat at a table and watched the proceedings. Everyone was stunned when he asked Sophie Olsen to dance. She did dance with him once, but they both looked uncomfortable and they didn't repeat the process.

After dancing with his wife, Jed Wainwright took Gertrude Ellsworth for a slow waltz. Everyone stood back and watched the couple and applauded when they finished. Mrs. Ellsworth curtsied like a princess and Jed bowed. He then kissed her cheek.

Mrs. Ellsworth turned a little pink and called out, "Amelia, I mean what I've told you before. I'd fight you for this man if I were forty years younger."

Amelia smiled and blew her a kiss. Everyone else laughed and applauded.

Nelda also laughed at the exchange, then her eyes roved over the crowd to where her brother sat with his wife. They were holding hands and slipping glances at each other. That gesture seemed to tell everyone around them that at this moment they were so much in love that nothing in the world mattered except being together here or anywhere else in this old world.

Nelda knew all the people were having a good time and they were relating to each other as friends and neighbors should. She realized this was what she'd missed most about her hometown. Nothing like this ever happened at the fort. If Spencer hadn't been a military man maybe they could've settled down here and taken part in everything that went on in the town. If life had turned out that way, maybe he wouldn't have taken a mistress and their marriage would still be a good and happy one.

She glanced back to Amelia. She was sitting on a bench with her son on her lap and after seeing Mrs. Ellsworth to her chair Jed walked over and joined his wife. He sat down, slipped his arm around her shoulder, pulled her closer to him and kissed her cheek. Baby Aaron reached up and patted his father's arm. Then it was as if the three of them were lost in a world of their own. A world where they only needed each other.

The perfect family. That's what I wanted. I didn't want to spend the rest of my life being forced to go to teas and entertain other officers' wives every Saturday afternoon. I didn't want to have to sit at home and wonder if my husband was being killed by some renegade Indian or an evil outlaw. I didn't want to learn that my husband had a mistress and would never love me the way Jed loves Amelia or Lance loves Grace. I now know, I'll never have what either of my friends has. I'm trying hard not to begrudge them their happiness just because it's too late for me. Someway, somehow, I'll go on. I will find a measure of happiness sometime. It may take a while, but I'll do it. I promise myself that.

Her thoughts were interrupted when the easterner walked up and bowed. "May I have a dance?"

Nelda was too stunned to refuse. She stood and took his hand. He led her to the area where several couples were dancing. He took her in his arms and she found out immediately that he was a wonderful dancer. He said nothing, so she decided to break the silence, "I've seen you in the mercantile, but we haven't been introduced. I'm Nelda Gentry."

"Oh, somebody told me your last name was Barrington."

"Well, technically it is, but my husband and I are not together right now and I'm thinking of taking back my maiden name. Since you're a stranger I thought I'd try it out on you." She frowned at him. "You didn't tell me your name."

"It's Marcel Guillaume Augustus La Gall."

"Wow, that's a mouth full. What is it, Greek or something?"

"It's French. We speak French in the country I came from."

"I thought you were from somewhere back east, and now I learn you're all the way from France."

"I'm not from France, but a small country where French is spoken." He took a deep breath. "I have been in New York for some time. I consider that my home now."

"I thought so. How do you like the West, Marcel Gillian Augustus Gall?"

"It's Marcel Guillaume Augustus La Gall."

"People around here will never be able to handle all of that. How can we shorten it?"

"Maybe Mr. La Gall would suffice."

She shook her head. "No. People around Settlers Ridge aren't so formal. How about Marcel? I think everyone can handle that."

"Then since you say you no longer wish to be married, you should be Mademoiselle Nelda."

"Let's shorten that to Nelda."

"Are you sure?"

"I'm sure, Marcel. Now tell me something. What is a man like you doing in a town like Settlers Ridge?"

"Do you realize I've been here for over a week and you're the first person to ask me that question?"

"I'd believe it. People here are interested, but they won't be nosy."

"Then I'll tell you. I'm here on a scouting mission."

"Scouting what?"

The song ended, and he escorted her back to her seat. "I'm here on the behalf of a conglomerate that is interested in possibly starting a newspaper in Settlers Ridge."

"Oh, that would be wonderful. I've often said we needed a newspaper." It had been her secret dream that Spencer would give up the military and start a paper or some other business in Settlers Ridge, especially since he came from such a background. He would've been wonderful at it. But there was something about being a cavalry officer that kept him tied to the military. Nelda swallowed and added, "If there's any way I can help you, let me know."

"I'll do that, Nelda, and I thank you for the dance." He bowed. "Now, if you'll excuse me, I think I'll head for the hotel. This was an interesting gathering, but I'm beginning to become fatigued. I'm not as young as I used to be."

"You're welcome for the dance and I do excuse you, but you might miss something exciting if you don't stick around."

He didn't reply, and she watched him walk away and head for the middle of town where the hotel was located.

Lance and Grace came up. "May we join you?"

"Of course, you can. Glad to have you."

"Saw you dancing with the man everybody is curious about. Just had to come over to see what you managed to find out from him, little sister."

"How do you know I found out anything?"

He tweaked her nose. "Because I know how nosy you are."

"I guess you're right about that." She laughed. "Well, let me see. He has a long name, Marcel, something or other, La Gall. I told him I'd just call him Marcel. He's from a country that speaks French."

"You did find out a bit."

"I'm not through. He was sent here by some big company that is thinking of setting up a newspaper in Settlers Ridge. He said he was trying to see if it was feasible and if it would be profitable to locate here."

"At least I'm glad to know he's not here for some sinister reason."

Grace laughed. "Lance is always suspicious of somebody he doesn't know. I have to admit, the way Mr. Marcel acted in the dining room when I was working, I thought he was an unpleasant man, if not downright suspicious."

"I felt the same way when he came into the mercantile."

Grace said, "I'm not sure the man likes our town at all. He'll probably tell whoever wants to start a paper that it's not a place where they should invest their money."

"I hope not. As I said, I'd like to see a paper here."

"Maybe you could start one, Nelda."

"Oh, Grace, I don't think I have the expertise for that."

"Well, girls," Lance said. "Looks like people are beginning to leave. I'm about ready to go myself. How about you two?"

"I'm ready, too, honey. I'm a little tired and I think I'd like to go home and put my feet up for a while."

Lance looked scared. "Are you feeling all right?"

"Don't worry. I'm fine. As I said, I'm just a little tired."

"Go on home and don't worry about me, Lance," Nelda said. "I need to go say good-by to Mrs. Brown and Stanley. Then I'll round up Wilma. Since Grace is tired, you should see to her first. I'll be fine."

"I don't want to leave you alone, little sister. Wilma might get tied up, but if she doesn't, we'll escort the both of you back to the store."

"Even if I have to walk home alone, I'll be all right, Lance. Besides, your wife is tired."

Lance looked as if he were torn.

Grace shook her head and spoke before he could. "Lance is right. We want to walk you back. Now, both of you stop worrying about me. I'm fine."

"Grace is right, honey. Since we've already said good-by to the Browns, we'll wait right here for you."

Nelda saw it was useless to argue with them. "Then, if you insist. I'll be back in a minute."

Nelda was gone only a short time. "Well, you're going to only have the pleasure of my company. I asked Wilma to come along, but she is spending some time with that man named Virgil. He said he'd see she got home safely."

Grace looked over to where Wilma and Virgil were standing at a table and drinking punch. "They might make an interesting mix. Virgil Danforth is a nice man and I would like to see him find someone to make him happy. And of course, you know I want to see Wilma happy. Stanley was such a disappointment to her."

"Maybe she shouldn't have depended too much on him liking her back," Lance said.

Grace and Nelda both looked at him. Grace said, "I don't see anything wrong with hoping that someday the man you've been pining for will return your love. It worked for me."

Lance laughed and put his arm around her. "I guess that was a dumb remark about Wilma's feelings and I shouldn't have said it."

"A little dumb, I admit," Nelda said. "But in this case, you were right. Wilma just had those feelings about the wrong guy." She didn't add– *like me*?

"Okay, now that we've settled Wilma's love life, let's head out. As my wife said she wanted to do, I want to get home and put my feet up and relax."

"Do you need to get your bowls or something, Grace?"

"No, Nelda. I helped Henrietta fix the food and we brought it all in bowls from the hotel and on the trays that belonged to the dining room. Frank said he'd take them back."

Lance locked Grace's arm with his on one side and put Nelda's in the other. "Now I'm going to escort the two most beautiful women at this gathering to their doors."

They both laughed.

~ * ~

Marcel stood in the shadows and watched as Lance walked away with the two women. He thought of wiring the superior and telling him there must have been a mistake. After talking with Nelda Barrington, he was almost sure nobody in this town knew a thing about what was going on. Almost.

There was still the slightest of possibilities that she and her women friends were only cagey. They could all know about the plan and had made a pact that they wouldn't whisper a hint to another living being. That's how it worked with some people in this country. Keeping a secret was important to them.

He knew he had only two choices. He could continue to investigate around this town or he could rid the situation of the possible threat. What would the superior want?

Disgusted, he knew the answer.

The one in charge would want him to make sure before he used any of his babies on them. He remembered the statement as if he were hearing it being said at this moment. "We don't want extra bodies piling up unless they're necessary, Mr. La Gall. I know it's hard for you to restrain yourself, but as long as you are connected to our cause, you must. You know the price you'll pay if you don't heed my warning."

He did know. He'd be taken back to his country and he would never see his priceless knives again or have the thrill of feeling them in his hands as they did their perfect work. He'd spend the rest of his life in a dank dark place with no chance of being able to do another deed for the party. He would render himself useless to those who depended on him. He couldn't let that happen.

But it would be so much fun if the chosen one were as beautiful as were Nelda, Wilma, Grace and Amelia or maybe that one called Juliette. He sighed. *That Juliette seems almost as much out of place as I do in this town. Therefore, I don't suspect her as being a part of the group who wants to stop us. She just doesn't have it in her. Yet, she is beautiful. One of my babies would love to carve into that lovely creamy skin of hers. I will consider that if I have the chance.*

He was pleased that he knew all their names and was fortunate enough to see the four suspects at the gathering. They were the perfect choices. He could only hope that they were all involved. No matter what the sheriff or any other man did, they couldn't save these women if he found out they were the ones who could destroy the plan.

Patting the pocket where he'd placed the special knife, he whispered, "We'll have to wait, my pretty, but don't despair. The time will come when you get your reward."

He turned and slipped down the street and into the hotel. Nobody would ever know he'd been out here watching for his prey.

~ * ~

Con Minton was standing at his hotel window observing La Gall lurking in the shadows. He looked up the street to see who or what the man was watching. Then he saw the sheriff walking down the street with the two women, one on each arm.

"Lucky man," he muttered. "I don't see why I can't find a beautiful woman to be my friend. I'd take either of those. Why should that lawman have two?"

As soon as he saw La Gall slip into the hotel, he waited until he heard his footsteps in the hall, then the door close.

He knew he was safe because the man probably wouldn't leave the hotel again tonight. Con strapped on his guns, picked up his hat and headed for the door. "I'm going to the saloon and see if I can get lucky. Maybe that little redheaded Pearl won't be busy with someone else tonight. I'll get there early and make sure nobody else gets her before I do."

As soon as he heard La Gall's room door close, he went out his door with a smile on his face.

~ * ~

Spencer and his horse were both tired and ready for a rest when they pulled into the fort. Oh, how he wished Nelda were here to welcome him and hold him in her soft arms as he rested his tired body against her welcoming one. But she wasn't here. She was in Wyoming living above the mercantile and hating him because she thought he had a mistress. How did his perfect life with his loving wife come to this?

He knew the answer as soon as the thought crossed his mind. He had brought it on himself. He never should have married Nelda in the first place. She was too young and beautiful to be in the middle of this conspiracy. But he'd loved her so much. No other woman had thrilled him the way this little woman from the small town in Wyoming had. Not only had she captured his heart with her gentle smile and her beautiful hazel eyes, but she'd also captured his soul. He knew that as long as he lived, there would never be another woman for him. Nelda was the only one he would ever love.

Now he knew he had to get to Settlers Ridge to protect his woman. He didn't care if she wanted him there or not. He also didn't care if they tried to court martial him over it.

The only thing that mattered to him was keeping Nelda safe, and from what he learned in Denver, she was not at all safe.

He turned his horse over at the fort corral and walked in long strides to General DeLay's office. He hoped the general was alone, but it didn't matter. Now that he'd made up his mind as to what he was going to do, he'd give the general the courtesy of talking with him.

Spencer stood behind the private as he knocked on the general's office door. "Major Barrington's here to see you, sir."

Gilbert didn't have a chance to say anything because Spencer stepped through the door. "I need to see you immediately, sir."

DeLay nodded and held out some papers. "Take those dispatches to the post office, Private. You, come on in, Major."

When the outside door closed, Spencer blurted, "I need to leave the military service today, sir."

"Please, sit down, Spencer and tell me what you're talking about."

Spencer dropped into the chair in front of the desk. "I'm sorry to rush you, General DeLay, but I'm in an awful hurry."

"Your actions tell me that, Major. Try to relax and tell me what this is all about."

"I have to get back to Settlers Ridge, Wyoming, as fast as I can. Every minute counts."

"What's going on in Settlers Ridge, Wyoming, that's so important?"

"Lives are in danger, sir."

The general lifted an eyebrow. "Go on."

"Sir, you know I was sent here by Washington for a special mission. A mission I can't discuss with even you."

"Of course. That's why I've given you so much leeway on going to Denver and elsewhere. Now, I think it's time you explained to me what's going on."

"I wish I could, General, but if I did, not only would I put your life in danger, but it would endanger your wife and anyone else close to you."

Gilbert frowned. "You're sure about this?"

"I'm positive, sir."

The superior officer took a deep breath. "How long will you have to be gone?"

"To be honest, I have no idea. All I can say is that I have to go."

"Then I guess I have no choice." He started scratching in his desk for some papers. "I'll make this leave open ended. When you get back, we'll fill in the date. Will that work?"

Spencer hated to say what he knew he had to tell his superior officer. "Sir, this may be the last time I'm in this fort. If that turns out to be the case, I want you to know it has been a pleasure to serve under you."

Gilbert gave him a confused look. "What are you saying, Spencer?"

"Nothing except what I said. If Washington thinks my service time is over here, they'll get in touch with you and I'll let you know where to send our personal items."

Surprised the general stared at him. "Are you telling me this is good bye?"

Spencer sighed. "Possibly, but as of this moment, I can't be sure."

"Then if you refuse to enlighten me further, I guess we'll have to leave it at that." He stood and held out his hand. "It's been my pleasure to serve with you, too, Major Barrington. Let's just hope we can forget this conversation ever took place and you will be returning to your post in the near future."

Spencer nodded and shook the general's hand. "That's a possibility, too, sir."

Less than an hour later, Spencer saluted the sergeant at the gate as he rode out on a fresh horse. He rode north for thirty minutes then pulled his steed under the shade of a grove of trees. Dismounting, he hurriedly removed denims, a white linen shirt, a black vest, a blue silk kerchief and debated about taking the jacket from his saddle bags. Deciding it wasn't cool enough for it, he shoved it back. He took off his uniform, folded it and stuffed it in the saddlebags with the jacket. He donned the clothes he'd taken out, strapped a holster around his waist and climbed back on his horse. He knew he'd have to stop somewhere along the way and pick up a Stetson or some appropriate hat. Then, no matter where he went, he'd not be looked at as an army officer. He'd simply be another cowboy traveling about the countryside or one settling down for a time in the town of Settlers Ridge, Wyoming, where he hoped to finish his assignment and reclaim his wife.

Twelve

On Monday afternoon Nelda turned from the ladder where she stood stocking the shelf behind the counter and glanced at the door where the bell had rung. She smiled. "Did you get the Browns off?"

Wilma laughed. "Finally. Mrs. Brown had a million suggestions of what we should do to keep the business running successfully."

Nelda shook her head. "As if she hadn't already given us a hundred detailed instructions several times over."

"I thought the stage driver was going to have to gag her and stuff her into the stagecoach so he could get on the way. Finally, he said he was going to leave without her if she didn't get aboard. She'd probably be talking yet if he hadn't told her that." Wilma moved to the counter and reached for one of the aprons hanging there. "Now, what can I do to help?"

"There are several bolts of dress goods I found in the stockroom under some other supplies. They were pretty prints and I thought they would sell. I planned to put them out on the table when I finished here."

"Sounds like a good idea. I'll go get them."

"Thanks, Wilma. I'll be through with this in a minute, then I'll help you."

As Wilma disappeared into the stockroom to get the cloth, the bell over the door jangled again.

"Hello, Nelda," Juliette Cramer said as she waltzed in.

Nelda climbed down and tried to smile. It was hard because Grace had told her how Juliette had tried to get Lance to be interested in her even after he and Grace had announced their engagement and were married. "Good morning, Juliette. How can I help you?"

"Mother wants some yellow ribbon."

"How much does she want?"

"Three yards should be enough."

Nelda started toward the area where the material and sewing notions were located.

Following, Juliette asked, "How's Lance doing, Nelda?"

Nelda raised an eyebrow. "He's doing fine. Why do you ask?"

Juliette shrugged. "I was only wondering. I don't see much of him since he got married."

"When he isn't working, he likes to spend his time with his wife." She reached for the roll of yellow ribbon and began to measure it. She couldn't help adding. "I don't think I've ever seen a couple as much in love as he and Grace.

Sometimes I wonder if they think they're the only two people in the world."

Juliette shook her head. "It sure surprised me when they got married."

"I don't see why. All you have to do is be around them a few minutes and you'll know they were meant for each other." Nelda cut the ribbon. "I gave you a few inches extra just in case your mother needs a little more."

Without thanking her for the extra, Juliette said, "So, you like Grace?"

"Of course. I think the world of her. We've been friends since childhood."

"But don't you think she and Lance are mismatched?"

Nelda tried not to sound irritated when she answered. "Absolutely not. They're perfect for each other. Why would you think otherwise?"

"It's just that Lance is so vital and healthy, and Grace is crippled."

"Grace is not crippled. She has a little limp. Nobody, except you, even notices it. Lance certainly doesn't. He loves her with all his heart."

Wilma came in with several bolts of cloth in her arms. She dropped them on the table beside the women. They made a heavy thud. "Sorry about the noise, but they're heavy."

"I would have helped you bring them in."

"I know you would, Nelda, but I decided to bring as much as I could carry so we wouldn't have to make so many trips." She took a deep breath. "Hello, Juliette."

Juliette nodded.

The bell rang again and a tall cowboy walked in. For a few seconds Nelda didn't recognize him, then it dawned on her it was Spencer. It was the first time she'd seen him in public without his uniform. Her heart began to beat fast and it angered her inside that she couldn't help the shiver that went down her spine. Before she could stop herself, she noticed how he filled out the tight denims and how the rolled-up sleeves of his white shirt showed his powerful arms. Arms that had once lovingly held her. She also couldn't help noticing the way Juliette Cramer looked at him. It was all Nelda could do not to let the woman see how her attention to Spencer irritated her. She bit her lip and said, "Come to the counter and I'll wrap the ribbon for you, Juliette."

Juliette ignored her and turned toward Spencer. "I don't think we've met. You must be new in Settlers Ridge since I've been out of town in school in St. Louis."

Nelda jumped into the conversation. Her voice was harsh and too loud. "What do you want, Spencer?"

Juliette glared at her. "What's the matter with you, Nelda? Isn't it important to be polite to customers when they come in?"

Wilma took the ribbon from Nelda, then moved beside Juliette and took hold of her elbow. "Come with me. I'll wrap this for you."

"But..."

Wilma had a firm grip on Juliette's arm. "I'm sure your mother is in a hurry for her ribbon and I'll have you out in a matter of minutes."

When they were out of earshot, Nelda whispered, "What are you doing here and why in the world are you dressed like that?"

"Why are you whispering?"

Still whispering, she said, "Hush. I don't want Juliette to hear."

"Why not?" He whispered back."

"Please, Spencer, don't say anything else until she leaves."

He lifted an eyebrow and smiled at her. "As you wish."

Juliette's voice carried across the room. "Why are they whispering?"

"I don't think they want us to hear what they're saying."

"Why not?"

"Maybe because what they're talking about is none of our business."

"Don't be silly, Wilma. He's a stranger. Why would they have secrets?"

Wilma shook her head and handed the small package to Juliette. "Here you go. I'll put it on your father's account. Thank you for coming in."

"Are you throwing me out?"

"Of course not, but you have what you came for. There is no need to stay here any longer, is there?"

Juliette grabbed the package. "I knew Grace and Amelia would always snub me, but I thought better of you, Wilma."

"I'm sorry, Juliette. I didn't realize you felt snubbed. Is there something else I can help you with?"

Juliette gave her a snide smile. "Not today." She whirled around and stalked out.

As soon as the door closed Nelda took a deep breath and said, "I thought I made it clear I had nothing more to say to you, Spencer Barrington."

"I know you did, but I knew that someway and somehow, I had to talk some sense into you. We can't leave things this way."

"I have plenty of sense, thank you. I know exactly what I want and what I intend to do to get it."

"Of course, you think you do, but I think differently. Did you really expect me to give up, leave here and let you get your divorce?"

"I don't see why not. Then you'll be free to spend all your time in Denver with *her*."

"I'm not going to spend my time in Denver with her or anyone else."

"If you don't like Denver, maybe you can move your mistress to another town. After the divorce, I don't care what you do."

"I'm not letting you get a divorce, Nelda. You might as well get that through your head. If you try, you'll be sorry."

"We'll see about that. I'm going to ask Mr. Cramer if I can't get one without you having to sign anything."

"I've already checked. The only way you can divorce me without my signature is if I walk out on you. And you may as well get it through your head, I have no intention of disappearing from your life."

Nelda's temper flared. "Why do you want to hang on to a marriage that's dead, Spencer Barrington?"

"Regardless of what you think, our marriage isn't dead and I intend to win you back. I love you and I aim to grow old with you, Nelda."

"There's no hope for us ever being together again, much less, growing old together."

He gave her the smile that always went straight to her heart. "There's always hope, my love. All we have to do is talk it out."

"No, Spencer. There will be no talking things out. We've already said enough, and you need to accept the fact that our marriage is finished."

"I'll never accept that, Nelda. You're my wife. I love you with all my heart and though you're mad at me right now, I know you love me, too. I want us to get past this and for you to come back to me where you belong. I'm not going to rest until you do."

Nelda took a deep breath and shook her head. "I've said all I intend to say and I'm not going to argue with you any more today. I'm tired of arguing. Please leave now, Spencer."

He hesitated for a minute, then sighed. "All right, I'll go this time, but I'll be back. In the meantime, I'll be at the hotel if you find it in your heart to come talk with me." He started out.

"Wait."

He turned. "Yes?"

"What do you mean, you'll be at the hotel? Don't you have to go back to the fort?"

"I'm not going back to the fort until you decide you'll go with me."

She fought back the threatening angry tears, tossed back her head and gave him a sneer. "Then, if they don't court martial you for deserting your post at the fort, I guess you'll be living at the hotel for the rest of your life."

"No, I won't, Nelda. You'll see. I'll win you back, and we'll be living together again sooner than you think."

She glared at him. "You couldn't be more wrong."

"You'll see, my love. You'll see." He winked at her, turned and went out the door.

Nelda stared at his back as the door closed. She shook her head and returned to the counter where Wilma was busying herself folding a box of fancy ribbons. "Did you hear what he said to me?"

"I sure did."

She looked a little worried. "Do you think he means it?"

"It sounded to me like he meant every word."

"But I know I can never trust him again."

"Well, in the meantime, come here. You need to see this."

"What?" Nelda turned toward the window where Wilma pointed outside to the sidewalk.

Nelda gasped as she looked at the couple on the street. Juliette had sidled up to Spencer. In a matter of minutes, she locked her arm in his and they walked down the street.

In spite of everything Nelda couldn't control the jealously that flashed through her. "Oh, my Lord! What do you think they're saying to each other?"

Wilma shook her head and shrugged. "Knowing Juliette, if what he says is to her liking it'll be all over town by evening."

"I know. That's what I'm afraid of."

"Well, there's nothing you can do about it now." She patted Nelda's arm. "Come on. Let's go get the rest of the material out of the stockroom before another customer comes in."

~ * ~

Spencer sat at a corner table in the saloon with a glass of beer before him. He didn't particularly like the brew, but he knew the barkeep wouldn't want him sitting there watching the patrons without something to drink. Never having been a friend of hard liquor, except for an after dinner bourbon or a splash of whiskey in his coffee now and then, he settled for a beer. He figured the stronger drinks there in the Wildcat wouldn't go down as well.

Actually, he would have rather spent his evening having a nice dinner with Nelda, then taking her to his hotel room and holding her in his arms all night. Just the way he'd done every time he'd been at home with her at the fort. But that was all before she got in this mood of hers. A mood he knew he was going to have a devil of a time combatting. Of course, he did know better than to invite her out to eat then. In the mood she was in, she would probably shoot him if she could get her hands on a gun. The woman had it in her head that she wanted to have nothing to do with him. Otherwise, she would have never threatened a divorce.

He frowned. There was no way he was going to let her get away with that. He loved her with all his heart, and he knew she loved him, though she didn't think so just now. He only wished he could explain everything to her, then she would understand why he'd been making those trips to Denver. But there was no way he could tell her. It would not only put the mission in jeopardy, but it could get her killed. Keeping her from getting hurt was more important to him than anything. Telling her what was really going on wasn't only something he was sworn not to do, it was something he was unwilling to do. He would never put her life in jeopardy. And since he'd got the word their prey was in the West, he had to make sure she was safe at all cost.

He looked around when somebody pulled out a chair at his table and said, "Mind if I join you?"

Giving the man a half smile, he muttered, "Not at all, Lance. Have a seat."

Lance sat. "What are you looking so gloom about, brother-in-law, or do I need to ask?"

"As you probably already know, it's your sister. Had another little talk with her and made no headway at all. That woman is exasperating."

"Don't I know it? She gave me fits when she was a kid. Always thinks she's right, no matter what anybody else thinks. My guess is she's doing the same thing with you."

"You're right about that, but this time she has good reason. I just wish I could explain everything to her and then she'd realize I don't have a mistress and never have had. In fact, since the day she and I said *I do*, I've never even thought about looking at another woman, much less being with one."

"Have you told her that?"

Spencer nodded. "Little good it did. She's convinced I'm lying to her and until everything comes out into the open, I don't think she'll ever believe me."

"Wish I could help you."

"Maybe you can later." He changed the subject. "In the meantime, what are you doing here in a saloon just after suppertime on a Monday night? Haven't had a fight with Grace, have you?"

"Not at all. Grace knows exactly where I am and why. It would be nice if all crimes were committed in the daytime, but that's not about to happen. My sweet wife accepts the fact that sometimes my job takes me away from home in the evening."

"Something happen here today that has taken you away this evening?"

"Not today. There was a murder here a few nights ago. I'm doing everything I can to figure out who did it. It's a puzzling case."

"What happened?"

"Somebody tortured and carved up one of the prostitutes who worked here."

Spencer raised an eyebrow. "Carved up?"

"Yeah. According to Doc Wagner, they started at the top of her head and cut different areas of her body in a way she'd feel the pain, but not die right away. The last cut was a slice across her throat. That one did kill her." Lance frowned. "You look as if you've heard about a murder like this before, Spencer."

"Did read about something like that happening in Chicago."

"Chicago?"

"Yeah. One of the officers at the fort knew about it because he knew the woman's cousin or something."

"I can't imagine a person coming from Chicago all the way to Settler Ridge to do such a deed."

"You're probably right, but when you mentioned it, it reminded me of the case."

Before Spencer could answer, a tall woman with brassy red hair and a painted face walked up. "Thank you for coming, Sheriff Gentry."

"I was happy to. You sent word that you had something to show me and you know I need all the help I can get."

She nodded and glanced at Spencer. "Maybe I'll tell you later."

"It's all right, Meggie. This is my brother-in-law. You can talk in front of him."

She still looked scared.

"Would it make you feel better if you left whatever you found with Ned and I picked it up a little later?"

"It might be better if I did that. Then nobody will know I said anything to you except to ask you if you want a drink."

"That's good, and if you think it will help keep you from being suspected of something, bring me a beer."

"I'll do that, Sheriff Gentry." She smiled at Lance, then glanced at Spencer. "You want another one, mister?"

"Sure, why not?"

She nodded and headed to the bar. Some communication must have taken place between her and Ned because the bartender said loud enough that everyone could hear, "Come on back behind the bar and get their beers yourself, Meggie. I've got something else to do."

Meggie disappeared behind the bar.

"What do you think she found that could help you, Lance?"

"I don't have any idea, but I'll go by the bar in a little while and pick it up. I don't intend to rush up there to get it. If the killer happens to be in here, I don't want to put her or anyone else in danger."

"You're a smart man, Lance. I guess that's why you're a such good lawman."

Meggie came back with the drinks and Spencer handed her some money. "Might as well let me pay for this round, Lance. Next time you can buy."

"Thanks." Lance took the beer and Spencer watched as his brother-in-law's eyes traveled around the room. He figured Lance was looking to see if anyone was taking any special notice of them.

There didn't seem to be anyone giving them any extra attention, and this puzzled him. Hearing the description of the murder, he knew that often the killer or killers stayed close enough to his crime to find out what the local authorities were doing in the investigation. Though this killing had been different from some of the others, Spencer had the feeling it was one of the men the conspiracy group was using to throw him off. Given the brutality of the woman's death, her killer could very well be the man they considered the most brutal of all.

But nobody stood out in the crowd tonight, unless one counted the burly mountain man who seemed to be extremely upset because the prostitute he liked wasn't there. That could be an act, but Spencer didn't think so. The man seemed to genuinely care about the woman. Of course, knowing how the men working for the conspiracy seemed to operate, that could be an act. He could be like the man caught in Colorado. That fellow had fitted in with the locals. In fact, he'd been well liked by some of them. It was too bad the fellow died before he could be questioned by the right people. It had solved a murder for the local sheriff, but it left Spencer and the others trying to break up the conspiracy with no more clues to follow.

After a while, Lance thanked Spencer for the beer, bade him good night and headed to the bar. Spencer watched as the barkeep handed Lance an item and the two men said a few words. The sheriff then nodded to a couple of people he knew, and left the saloon.

Spencer decided to have one more beer and watch the crowd. If nothing else happened to make him think the killer could be in the saloon, he'd leave, walk by the general store to make sure it was secure for the night, then he'd go to his hotel room. He smiled inside knowing how upset Nelda would be if she knew his room looked directly at the corner of the Brown's General Store where the apartment she shared with Wilma was located.

Thirteen

It was the middle of the morning when the brass bell over the mercantile door jangled, Wilma turned from her position behind the table where she was straightening the large selection of men's shirts that had come in. She looked at a skinny cowboy as he sauntered into the mercantile. He wore a pair of holsters on each hip with pearl handled-revolvers inside. For some reason, he made her feel uneasy.

Taking a deep breath, she said, "How can I help you, sir?"

He gave her a searing smile. "From the looks of you, honey, you could help me a lot."

Wilma gasped. "How dare you!"

"Sweetheart, I dare a lot of things." He chuckled. "Especially where pretty women are concerned."

She didn't answer, and he went on, "Anybody else here except you?"

Wilma wasn't about to tell him that, at the moment, she was alone. "Of course, there is."

"That's strange. I don't see nobody else."

"They're in the back."

He continued to give her the sleazy grin. "I don't think I believe you."

"I don't care whether you believe me or not. It's the truth."

He held out his tobacco pouch. "In that case, fill this with tobacco for me and I'll be satisfied this time. We can get to know each other better later."

"I don't think so." Wilma grabbed the pouch and hurried to the counter where the tobacco was kept. She filled it and held it out to him. "That'll be twenty-five cents."

He took out the coins and dropped them in her hand. "Here you go, sweetheart."

Wilma jerked her hand back and he laughed. Before he could say anything else, the bell over the door jangled again.

Never before in her life had she been so glad to see Juliette Cramer. "Hello, Juliette," she called. "How can I help you today?"

"Is Nelda here?"

"She should be back soon." Though Wilma knew Nelda would be out for another hour or so, she didn't want Juliette to leave her alone with this strange man. "Why don't you look around and wait for her?"

"I'll do that."

The stranger turned and looked at Juliette. "Wow. Is this town full of beautiful women?"

Juliette moved to the counter and smiled. "Thank you, sir."

"You're very welcome, Miss Juliette."

"I don't believe we've met. You know my name, now, what's yours?"

"My name's not important, but you can call me Con."

Wilma wished Juliette would cease talking to this man, but for some reason, she didn't interfere. She only wanted the man to say what he wanted to, then leave.

"Don't you have a last name, Con?"

He moved away from the counter where Wilma stood and headed toward Juliette. "I don't know your last name and you don't know mine, pretty Juliette. I think that's fair, don't you?"

"Well..."

He reached out and took hold of Juliette's arm. "Why don't you and me go down to that little café and have a drink or something? We can get to know each other better there."

Juliette's eyes blared at him. "Take your hands off me, you ruffian. I don't know you and you have no right to touch me."

"Mister, you have no right to accost a lady like that. Let her go," Wilma said.

"Oh, come now. She likes it. I can tell."

"I do not like it. Let go of my arm!"

"All right, sweetheart." He dropped her arm. "Maybe we'll meet again when your friend here isn't around to interrupt us."

"I never want to see such an uncouth person as you ever again."

"Don't be too sure of that, girly. We might have more in common than you think."

"There's no way I have anything in common with the likes of you."

They all looked around when the bell over the door rang. Two young boys stepped inside. Teddy Olsen and Joel Wagner were best friends and everyone in town knew they spent most every day together. Everyone liked them. Joel, the doctor's stepson and Teddy, whose parents owned the hotel, only caused anyone trouble by accident. Everyone knew that and excused them.

"Hello, boys," Wilma called.

"Hello, Miss Wilma. Me and Joel want to buy some chaps."

"You do?"

Joel grinned. "Yeah, we do."

"Chaps are kind of expensive. Do you have the money for them, fellows?"

"We don't know, but we thought we'd look and you can tell us if we have enough," Teddy said.

"How much money do you have?"

"The sheriff gave us fifty cents to dig Ms. Grace a new flower bed under the window. I don't think he wanted to dig it his-self. Is that enough money?" Joel asked.

Wilma bit her lip to keep from laughing. At the same time, she noticed the stranger's face take on a dark look at the mention of the sheriff. She couldn't help wondering why. To the boys, she said, "I'm afraid that won't be enough to buy two pair of chaps today, fellows. Maybe you can find some more jobs and save up the money."

The man turned to Juliette. "I've got to go this time, darling. I'll see you later, though."

"No, you will not!"

He chucked her chin, winked at Wilma and said, "See you later, too, babe."

Before she could answer, he walked out the door.

"Who was that, Miss Wilma?"

"I don't know, Joel. He came in to buy tobacco."

"I don't think he was very nice to you ladies," Teddy offered.

"You're right. He sure wasn't. In fact, he was horrible," Juliette said.

"He had a funny looking knife in his boot. It looked like the kind an Indian would carry. Maybe he's an Indian. A mean one, not a good one like Mr. Jed."

Wilma smiled. "Yes. Mr. Jed is a very good Indian."

Juliette smiled and nodded. "Most people think he's a good one, but he's still part Indian, so you never know."

Teddy butted in. "I don't know that man's name, but he's staying at the hotel. Him and that funny looking dandy came about the same time. They're both still staying there."

"It's the first time he's been in here. I bet you haven't ever seen him either, have you, Juliette?" Wilma looked at her.

"Not until today. He was an awful man and I never want to see him again. He really scared me."

"I think he looks like a gunman," Teddy said.

"How do you know what a gunman looks like, Teddy?" Juliette asked.

Teddy shrugged.

"If he's not an Indian, I bet he's an outlaw," Joel said.

"He might be," Teddy said. "I heard Mama tell Sophie not to wait on him if he came into dining room to eat. She told Sophie she'd do it."

Wilma looked at him. "Why was that, Teddy?"

"I don't know, but he's not come in there to eat, so neither of them has had to wait on him."

"Where does he eat?" Juliette asked.

Teddy shrugged. "The café or the saloon, I guess."

"Let's not talk anymore about that strange man. I'm just glad he's gone." Wilma smiled at the boys. "Now, since you don't have enough money for chaps, how about a stick of candy?"

"How much does that cost?" Joel asked.

"A penny each stick."

The two boys negotiated as if they had a great decision to make. Then left the store sucking on a peppermint stick they bought and broke in half.

Wilma laughed, and Juliette shook her head. "I can't believe they didn't buy two sticks of candy."

"I guess they're going to try to save enough money to buy the chaps they want."

"Forget them. I'm sure glad that man is gone. Are you sure he hasn't been in here before, Wilma?"

"I'm sure. It's the first time I've ever seen him. I don't think Nelda has seen him either. She would've mentioned it to me."

"I didn't like him at all. I thought he was awful and I think I should tell Lance what happened to me while he was here."

"For once, I agree with you, Juliette. When I get a chance, I plan to tell Lance about the way he acted. He might want to keep an eye on the man while he's in town."

Juliette slung back her hair. "I'm sure Lance would be more interested in the man if he knew the rogue had accosted me."

Wilma shook her head. "Lance would be interested no matter who the man accosted. But I dare say, he'd be livid if it had been Grace instead of you or me."

Juliette looked at Wilma as if she wanted to hit her. Instead, she walked out of the store without saying anything else or buying a thing.

Wilma couldn't help laughing as she wondered why Juliette had come into the store in the first place, but she didn't care. Since the man, who called himself Con, scared her, she was grateful Juliette had shown up when she did.

~ * ~

Spencer headed down the street and saw Juliette going into the sheriff's office. Though he intended to go to Brown's Mercantile and have another go at trying to get Nelda to be reasonable and discuss their situation, he wondered if he should go to Lance's office to see what the Cramer woman was up to. He had heard how the woman had tried to get Lance to take up with her instead of Grace last summer. He had a suspicion Juliette was still interested in trying to break up Lance and Grace's marriage. If so, he might be able to help his friend get rid of the woman. Though he and Nelda were estranged at the moment, he still considered Lance a friend. At least his brother-in-law seemed to be willing to help get his sister to listen to her husband.

Reaching the office, he pushed open the door and stepped inside.

Juliette was saying, "I knew you would want to know what a terrible experience I had at Brown's this morning, Lance."

"What happened, Juliette?" He nodded at Spencer and motioned for him to come in.

Juliette looked around and the expression on her face told Spencer she didn't appreciate the interruption. "I have business with the sheriff, Mr. Barrington. Maybe you could come back later to see him."

"I have business with him, too, Miss Cramer. I'll just have a seat over here and wait until you're through." He knew Juliette had been miffed at him ever since he hadn't warmed up to her when they met outside Brown's Mercantile the day he came by to talk to Nelda. Though she had waited for him outside that day, he'd merely walked away with her and talked of unimportant things. He wasn't about to tell her what he'd been fighting about with his wife.

The only reason he left with Juliette in the first place was to make Nelda jealous, if possible. He knew she was watching them out the window and he hoped it would bother her seeing him with another woman on his arm.

Lance turned back to the woman. "Juliette, please go on with your business. I need to talk with Spencer."

She gave him a seductive smile. "Well, Lance, I'm surprised you're not more interested in what happened to me than having a chat with your friend."

"For heaven's sake, Juliette. If you have something to tell me, please get on with it. I'm a busy man."

She dropped her head and her voice came out in a whisper. "A man accosted me today in Brown's Mercantile."

"What happened?"

"I just told you. He accosted me right there in the store."

Lance raised an eyebrow. "How did he accost you?"

"He grabbed my arm and wouldn't let me go. I thought he was going to kill me right there."

"Did you know the man?"

"No, Lance. I didn't know him." She batted her eyes at him. "But he was a terrible creature. I was afraid for my life and I knew you'd want to go arrest him immediately."

"It would be a little hard for me to arrest the man without knowing who he is or what he looks like."

She huffed. "He said his name was Con and he was a horrible looking monster. He's probably some kind of killer and I'm sure he wanted to kill me."

"Anything else?"

"I knew you wouldn't want him to hurt me, so I came here to tell you about him."

"I don't want anyone in town to get hurt, Juliette. Now, tell me, was he tall or short? Skinny or fat? Old or young? I have to have some kind of description."

"He wasn't very fat, and he was taller than me. You will arrest him for me, won't you, Lance?"

"If I can find him, and I find out he's done something wrong, then I'll question him."

"After all we've meant to each other, I'm surprised you're not in more of a hurry to find a man who wanted to kill me."

"For heaven's sake, Juliette, don't start that foolishness again. We've never meant anything to each other, and furthermore, we never will."

"How can you say that, Lance?"

He ignored her question. "I'll see if I can find the man, but until I do, go on about your business. If you see the man again, let me know."

"Don't you want me to tell you how he grabbed my arm and called me sweetheart, darling and other such personal names?"

"I've heard enough, Juliette. Now, go on and watch out. Like I said, if you see him again, let me know and I'll see what I can do to stop him."

She jumped up and snapped, "Some sheriff you are, Lance Gentry. You don't care about anything except that silly crippled wife of yours, do you?"

"Yes, I care about my wife. I love her with all my heart, Juliette."

Wheeling around, she gave Spencer a hard look and flounced out the door, her fancy skirt swinging as she went.

Spencer couldn't help it. He laughed out loud. "There's nothing as dangerous as a spurned woman, is there, Lance?"

"Don't I know it? Juliette Cramer is awfully dangerous. She's been a thorn in my side ever since she came back to Settlers Ridge last summer." Lance got up and poured two cups of coffee from the pot on his stove. He held one out to Spencer. "Now that she's gone, how can I help you?"

"The only way you can help me is to get that hard-headed sister of yours to realize we belong together, whether she thinks so or not."

"Sorry, friend. You're on your own there." Lance sipped his coffee. "I did convince her not to go running to Mr. Cramer about the divorce. Told her it would create too much gossip, and you weren't going to sign the papers anyway."

"Thanks for that. It gives me time to convince her to come home."

"Anything else I can do?"

"Not really. The only reason I came in was because I saw the Cramer woman sashaying in your door. I heard about your problems with her last year, and I thought I might run interference for you."

"I appreciate that. I'm sure she'd have given me more trouble if you hadn't been in here."

The door opened again and Wilma came in. "If you're busy, I can come back, Lance."

"Come on in, Wilma. We're just talking. What can I do for you?"

"I just wanted to let you know about a little trouble we had at the mercantile this morning."

Lance and Spencer glanced at each other. Lance said, "Juliette was here a little while ago telling me a man had tried to kill her in the store this morning. How about you tell me what really happened?"

Wilma smiled. "He didn't try to kill anybody, but he did grab Juliette's arm. He talked like he might try something more, but he didn't because Joel and Teddy came in."

"Where was Nelda?" Spencer sounded concerned. "Did he hurt her?"

"No. She wasn't there when he came in. She'd gone to Miss Purdy's Dress Shop to take her some material and supplies she'd ordered."

Spencer relaxed.

"Were you alone when he came in or was Juliette there?"

"I was alone, but let me tell you, it was the first time in my life I was glad to see Juliette Cramer come into the store." The men smiled, and she went on to describe the incident. She ended with, "I'm not sure what he would have done if the boys hadn't come in, but I know he didn't have killing Juliette in his mind."

"I didn't think so." He smiled. "What'd he look like, Wilma?"

"He was tall, clean shaven and had black hair. He carried two guns low on his hips and I didn't notice, but one of the boys said he had wicked looking knife in his boot." She grinned. "Joel said he might be a mean Indian, not a nice Indian like Jed Wainwright."

Lance laughed. "Jed will be glad to know the children think of him as a nice Indian."

Wilma nodded. "I thought that, too."

"Anything else?"

"Yes. He told Juliette to call him Con and Teddy said he was staying at the hotel."

Spencer lifted an eyebrow. "I wonder why I haven't seen anyone of that description there."

"Teddy said he hasn't eaten in the dining room."

"Maybe that's why we've missed each other."

"Wonder why he hasn't eaten there," Lance said.

"I don't know, but I think they're glad. I also think the hotel staff is leery of him."

"Did Teddy say how long he'd been at the hotel?"

"Yes. He said he arrived about around the same time the funny Mr. La Gall did."

Again, Spencer and Lance looked at each other. Then Lance said, "Wilma, you've been a big help. I'll go over to Olsen's right away and see what I can find out." Lance stood. "If you think of anything I need to know, don't hesitate to come and tell me."

"I will, Lance." She stood. "I better get back to the store. I don't like leaving Nelda there alone. The man might come back."

Spencer got up, too. "I'll walk you back, Wilma."

"That's not necessary, Spencer."

"I know, but there's no need to tempt fate." He opened the door. "I'll come back later and see what you found out, Lance. I'll also keep my eyes open at the hotel."

Lance nodded.

"Come on, Wilma. It makes me nervous thinking of Nelda being alone in the store."

Wilma gave him a strange look, but he grinned at her and she said nothing more.

~ * ~

Lance opened the door to the hotel lobby and stepped inside. He walked over to the registration desk where Frank Olsen was looking into an account book. "Hello, Frank."

"Hey, Lance. I bet you're here to have dinner with Grace."

"I probably will eat with her, but right now I want to talk to you."

"Sure. What can I help you with?"

"Do you happen to have a man staying here named Con something or other?"

"As a matter of fact, I think we do. Let me look up the name." He turned the registration book around and looked through the names. "He signed in as Con Minton."

"When did he register, Frank?"

"He's been here a week. As a matter of fact, he registered a day before the La Gall man did."

"Did they both come in on the stage?"

Frank shook his head. "Couldn't have. Minton registered the day before the stage came in. He must have ridden in on his horse or in some kind of wagon."

"Sounds like it."

"If I had to bet, Lance, I'd say he came on his own horse."

"Why's that?"

Frank glanced around. "The man has the look of a gunman or maybe a bounty hunter. I don't think he'd be driving a wagon."

"Has he given you any trouble, Frank?"

Frank shook his head. "At first, I thought he might, but we haven't seen much of him. He's not eating in the dining room and I don't think he's always in the hotel at night. I assume he's probably spending some time at the saloon, maybe even eating there."

"Is he here now?"

"I'm not sure. He could have come in while I was away from the desk."

"I think I'll check his room just in case. What number is it?"

"Number seven. It's on the front at the end of the hall."

"Thanks, Frank." Lance headed upstairs.

~ * ~

"What are you doing here?" Nelda almost shouted when Spencer walked in with Wilma.

"Do you have a problem with me seeing your friend safely back to work? There seems to be a mad man about."

Nelda swallowed, looked contrite, but didn't answer him.

"Spencer was with Lance when I went to tell him about the man who came in here. They both seemed to think he might be a danger in town. When Lance went to check him out at the hotel, Spencer insisted on walking me back here."

"I see," Nelda muttered. "Now that Wilma is safely back in the store, you may leave."

"I'll leave, but I just wanted to be sure you were safe, too, Nelda."

"As you can see, I am."

He turned to leave. "Just remember one thing. I'm here to protect the woman I love and there's nothing you can do to stop me from doing the job."

"Well, you might as well stop loving me, because I hate you."

"You may think so, sweetheart, but I know better." He smiled at her and opened the door. Before he could step outside, a shot rang out. He fell backward to the floor with blood running down the front of his shirt.

Fourteen

"No!" Nelda screamed and ran to her husband.

Wilma followed her and knelt beside Spencer. Nelda had put his head in her lap as she held him and blood poured out of the wound in his chest.

Feeling his neck, Wilma said, "He's alive, Nelda. I'll get the doctor."

Through tears and in a weak voice, Nelda muttered, "Hurry."

As Wilma ran out, she met Lance running toward the mercantile. "What happened?" He asked.

"Spencer's been shot. See if you can help Nelda. I'm going for the doctor."

Lance nodded and continued to run. When he reached the store, he hurried inside and saw his sister sitting in the floor cradling her husband's head. She looked up at him.

Tears ran down her face. "I killed him, Lance. It's my fault that Spencer is going to die."

"Don't talk foolish, Nelda. You didn't kill anyone." He squatted by his sister. "Let me see what I can do to help him until the doctor gets here." He turned to the bleeding man and began tearing off his shirt.

"Is he going to die? Oh, God, please don't let him die."

"It looks bad, Nelda, but Doc will be here in a minute. He'll be able to help him. In the meantime, I'll do what I can."

"Please try to save him. I didn't want him dead."

"I'll do my best. Go get me something to pack in this wound until Sheldon gets here."

Nelda continued to look into Spencer's face. "The last thing I said to him was that I hated him. Those are awful words to hear before you die, aren't they?"

Lance ignored her remark. "Give me that apron you're wearing."

"He can't die thinking I hate him, Lance. He just can't."

"Nelda, get hold of yourself and take that apron off." Lance's voice became stern. "That way I can at least try to stop the bleeding. When Doc Wagner gets here, he'll know what to do."

"He can't die now, Lance. He just can't. I don't want him to die thinking I hate him." She continued to cry and ignore her brother.

When she didn't remove her apron, Lance knew she wasn't completely aware of what was going on. *Must be in shock. I've heard of that happening to people in a crisis.*

With her in this condition, he knew there wasn't any use trying to get her to help him. He jumped up and ran to the table where he saw a bolt of soft white cloth. He tore off a length and returned to Spencer.

The blood was gushing out of the man's side. Lance rolled the cloth into a ball and shoved it against the bullet wound. *Hurry, Doc. It doesn't look we have much time. I don't want Spencer to die here in my sister's arms. She'll never get over it if he does.* He shook his head. *And she says she doesn't love him anymore. What a lie.*

It wasn't long until the doctor ran through the open door. Wilma was behind him. Without a word, he knelt beside Spencer. "Get your sister away from here, Lance, and let me do what I can to help him."

Lance stood and took hold of Nelda's shoulders. "Let's move over here, honey. The doctor needs room to work on Spencer."

"No. I can't leave him."

Wilma looked at the doctor. "Is there anything I can do, Sheldon?"

"You might be able to help me after I see what's going on."

Lance finally pulled a protesting Nelda away from Spencer and ushered her to a bench near a barrel of flour. "I know it's hard, but you have to stay calm, honey."

"I want to hold my husband's head. Let me go. He's going to die thinking I hate him if I'm not there with him when he takes his last breath."

"Spencer doesn't know you're there, Nelda. We have to stay out of Sheldon's way, and let him work on the man. We'll be in the doctor's way."

"No. I have to be with him when he dies."

"He's probably not going to die if we stay back and let Doc care for him. You want him to have that chance, don't you, sister?"

She nodded, but didn't say anything as her sobs continued.

Esther came through the door with another black bag. "I brought some things I thought you'd need if you have to remove a bullet, Sheldon."

"Thank you, honey. It sure looks like I'm going to have to." He glanced at Wilma. "Is there a table I could put him on to do the operation?"

"I'll make one." She ran to the table displaying children's clothes. In a few swipes, she pushed everything to the floor. "Bring him over here."

In a matter of minutes, they had Spencer lying on his back on the table. Sheldon and Esther began working on him right away. Wilma moved back.

The bell jangled over the door and Virgil Danforth walked in. He frowned. "I heard a shot. What in the world is going on in here?"

Wilma hurried over to him. "Spencer Barrington has been shot and the doctor is here. I'm sorry, I'm too upset to wait on you now, Virgil."

"I understand, Wilma. Is there anything I can do?"

"I guess you could keep people from coming in here for a little while."

"I can do that, but why don't you close the door and put up the closed sign? Several people were headed this way. I suppose they heard the shot same as me."

She shook her head. "I'm so upset, I don't know what I was thinking. Of course, that's what I should do. If not, it won't be long until half of Settlers Ridge is coming in to see what happened."

She moved to the door, closed it and hung the closed sign in the window.

When she returned to Virgil, he asked, "Who is Spencer Barrington, Wilma? I don't believe I know him."

"Nelda's husband."

"I see." Virgil nodded. "Can I do anything else?"

Lance's voice rang out before she could answer Virgil. "Wilma, if you'll come over here and take care of Nelda, I'm going to go see if I can get a lead on who did this to Spencer."

"Can I help you, Lance?"

"Yes, you can. Thanks, Virgil."

"Do you have any leads?"

Lance shook his head. "It doesn't make a lot of sense. Spencer has only been in town a couple of days. Certainly not long enough to make anyone angry enough to shoot him."

When Lance moved, Nelda started to get up. Wilma hurried to her and put her arm around her shoulder. "Sit still, Nelda. The doctor will tell us how Spencer is soon."

Lance and Virgil slipped out the door.

"I don't want Spencer to die thinking I hate him, Wilma."

Wilma patted her arm. "He won't, Nelda. The doc is going to pull him through."

"What if he doesn't save him?"

"He will. I'm sure of it."

Nelda didn't say anything, but she burst into tears again and clung to her friend.

~ * ~

As soon as the bullet left the gun and Spencer fell, the man smiled. "That was easy enough," he muttered and stashed the rifle behind some thick bushes at the side of the Miss Purdy's Dress Shop. He knew he'd look suspicious if he went down the street carrying it. Especially just after people heard a shot fired.

Stepping out of the shadow of the building, he glanced up and down the street. Everything looked normal, though some people were headed toward the area where they thought the gunshot had occurred. He saw two boys dash out of an alley chasing a ball, but he was sure they hadn't noticed him aim and shoot the man in the doorway of the store.

Ignoring them, he hurried to the back of the shop, then worked his way behind the two businesses and around to the front of the hotel. Moving swiftly and acting as casual as his excitement would let him, he went up the stairs to his room. Inside, he hurried to the window and looked out toward the people heading toward the mercantile. For the first time, he smiled, though it wasn't a fully satisfied smile. Not yet, anyway.

He watched the woman run out of the store, and in an instant or two, he saw the sheriff run into the business. It wasn't long until a doctor arrived. He knew this because he carried a medical bag. He was followed by the woman who worked in the store. Another woman soon followed them. She had something in her arms, but he couldn't tell for sure what it was. Then another man went into the store. He'd seen that man in town, but didn't know who he was

He continued to watch the scene and hoped they'd leave the door open. He wanted to watch the man on the floor and the people working on him. If they stayed in this position, he could watch it until the end. That way, he'd soon know if his shot had hit its mark, though, he was positive it had.

But it didn't happen that way. In only a moment the door was shut, and a closed sign appeared in the window.

"Damn." He muttered, and shook his head. "I would've had the pleasure of watching him die, if they hadn't closed the door. Now, I'll have to get the news with the rest of the town." Little doubt entered his mind that the man was dead. He just didn't want that slight bit of uncertainty since the doctor had come to work on the man.

It wasn't long until the sheriff came out the closed door. The last man who had gone in, came out with him. The lawman peered up and down the street and then both men began talking to the crowd that had gathered outside the store.

The man at the hotel window gave a smile to the empty room. "Won't do that lawman any good. He'll not find me, no matter where he looks. I know better than to let some backwater town sheriff catch a professional like me."

He knew there was nothing else interesting to see. He moved to a chair and poured himself a drink from the bottle sitting on the table beside the bed. It wasn't very good whiskey, but it was better than going to the saloon for a drink.

He lifted the glass into the air. "You didn't think I knew who you were since you'd dressed up as a cowboy, did you, Major? I wanted to kill you later, but you were getting too close to finding out who is in this little town," he muttered. "Next, you'd have helped the lawman figure out who killed that whore. Then, the whole mission could fall apart. Good thing I'm here and am one step ahead of you. If I had been able to find the woman you're protecting, our mission in this country would be over, and I wouldn't have to do the distasteful thing I was sent here to do." He drank the whiskey in one gulp.

~ * ~

Nelda felt almost numb as she sat on the bench with tears running down her cheeks. She clung to Wilma's hand as she watched Sheldon and Esther rip the rest of the bloody clothes from Spencer's mangled chest and drop them to the floor. She almost knew she was watching the man she loved die right before her eyes. The man she'd told she hated and never wanted to see again. She didn't mean it, but he would never know that. It had all been a terrible mistake. A mistake that could have been avoided if Spencer had either given up his mistress or had never come to town.

Why had he come to Settlers Ridge in the first place? Oh, she knew he said he'd come because he loved her and wanted her back, but she was sure that was a lie. She'd seen the woman in Denver. Seen her well. She'd been beautiful. Tall and willowy with long blonde hair. Though Nelda hadn't seen her eyes, she figured they were crystal blue. She knew Spencer liked blue eyes. She also knew she could never get the picture of those long arms and hands encircling Spencer's back out of her mind. Though she hadn't seen him kiss her, she knew he did by the way his head had bent over the woman.

How could he do it? How could he have thrown away what they had? Now, there was nothing he could do to change what had happened, or what she'd witnessed. Now, he'd never know that she'd been almost ready to relent and tell him she'd come back to him if he'd stay in Settlers Ridge and not go back to the army. Nobody would ever know she'd thought this.

"Oh, Wilma. I don't want him to die."

"I know you don't, Nelda. Neither do I, and if there's any way he can stop it, Sheldon won't let him die."

"I know he'll do his best." Nelda held her hand tighter. "Did Lance leave?"

"Yes, honey. I'm sure he wanted to see if he could catch the person who did this."

"I hope he catches him or her. I want them to be punished for what they've done." Nelda looked at Wilma and saw a frown on her friend's face. "What's the matter?"

"You said a woman or a man. A woman couldn't have done this, could she?"

"Of course, she could. Women are vicious." Nelda dropped her head. "Maybe his mistress heard he was in Settlers Ridge trying to get me to come back to him. She could have come here and shot him."

"Oh, Nelda. I don't think that would happen."

Nelda pulled her hand out of Wilma's and stood. "I've got to see what Doc's doing to him. Maybe I can help."

Doc must have had heard her. "If you want to help me, Nelda, clean off one of those small movable tables so I can put my instruments on it where Esther and I can reach them better."

"Come on, Nelda. I'll help you." Wilma took her arm and moved her to the nearest small display table. It happened to have stacks of books, pencils, and a collection of children's toys.

Nelda began raking the items to the floor and Wilma reached out and stopped her. "You know we'll have to put all this back. Let's try not to break or tear up anything."

"What difference does it make, Wilma?"

"It makes a lot, Nelda. Now, try to get hold of yourself and let's do this right."

In a short time, the table was clean and they pulled it close to Sheldon and Esther.

"Oh, Wilma," Nelda cried and threw herself into Wilma's arms when she looked at her husband's bleeding body. "I don't think I can stand it if Spencer dies. I just don't think I can go on living."

"He's not going to die, Nelda. Now, let's go sit down and wait for Doc to tell us what's going on. I'm sure he will as soon as he can."

Esther smiled at them. "She's right. He'll let you know as soon as we can, Nelda."

Nelda let Wilma lead her to the bench. When they sat, Nelda dropped her head to Wilma's lap and sobbed inconsolably as she mumbled, "I know I said I didn't love him, but I do. No matter what he's done, I can't get him out of my heart."

"I know, Nelda." She soothed her friend. "I think I've known all along."

~ * ~

In the alley, Teddy tossed the ball against the side of the building. He paused and looked at his friend. "Joel, when we were chasing the ball, did you see that man who upset Miss Wilma and Miss Juliette throw that rifle in the bushes next to Miss Purdy's store?"

"I sure did. Why you reckon he did that?"

"Maybe he's the one who shot at something a while ago."

"Do you think he meant to throw it away, Teddy?"

Teddy shook his head. "I don't guess so. Who would throw away a perfectly good rifle?"

Joel shrugged. "Papa says people do stupid things sometimes. He's always having to go doctor somebody who has done something crazy."

"Do you think we should go get the gun?"

"Let's wait and see if somebody goes to get it. A lot of people are gathering on the street in front of the mercantile. We don't want somebody to see us and think we're trying to steal it." Joel looked at his buddy.

"All right, but if nobody gets it, I think we should."

"What are we going to do with one gun? It wouldn't be right for you to have it and not me."

"I would share it with you Joel. You're my best friend and we could own it together."

"That might work."

"Or we could sell it and get enough money to buy the chaps we want."

"That's a good idea. I want those chaps."

"Me, too."

"I saw Mama and Papa go in the store a little while ago. Somebody must have been hurt. They could've got shot or something. Maybe that's the shot we heard."

"Maybe they did something stupid like your Papa said some folks do and they need a doctor."

"That might be why the man threw away the gun. He could've done something stupid and shot somebody he didn't mean to."

"He might have even killed somebody."

"Why do you say that?"

"It must be pretty bad because Mama doesn't usually go with Papa unless it's something bad or some woman is having a baby."

"Oh, I see."

They ambled to the plank sidewalk, paused and watched the store for a minute. They then saw Sheriff Lance talking to some of the people.

Teddy frowned. "I bet he's goanna get the gun."

"How could he? He didn't see the man throw it away. We did."

"I forgot." He looked at Joel. "Should we go get it now, or do you want to wait a while longer?"

Joel looked pensive. "We better wait. If somebody sees us get it, they might say it's theirs and take it away from us."

"I guess you're right. Why don't we get up closer to the crowd and see if we can find out who was shot?"

"Yeah, let's do that."

They headed toward the crowd, never giving a thought to the fact they had witnessed a possible murderer leaving the scene of his crime.

~ * ~

It was dark when Lance climbed the back steps to the apartment his sister shared with Wilma. He knocked on the door and Wilma opened it. "Hello, Lance."

"Hello. I went by Doc's to check on Spencer and was surprised when he told me Nelda insisted they leave him here for her to look after."

"That she did. She's in her bedroom with him now." She stood back. "Come in."

He stepped inside and removed his hat. "Can I see her?"

"Sure. I know you probably want to see her alone."

"I don't mind if you're here, Wilma. In fact, there's something I want to say to both of you, so please come with me."

"Of course, I want to hear what you have to say. Then, while you're here with Nelda, I'm going downstairs for a little while. I have something I need to do down there before we open in the morning."

"I won't keep you long."

"Then, follow me. Nelda's room is the one on the right as you go down the hall."

"Thank you, but I remember moving her in."

"Of course. I forgot."

When they reached the room, she pushed open the door and he saw Nelda sitting in a chair beside the sickbed. "Hello, little sister. I came to check on Spencer."

Nelda looked around. "Come in, Lance. He's sleeping now."

Wilma moved to the foot of the bed without saying anything.

Lance walked up beside his sister. "How's he doing?"

"He hasn't opened his eyes since Sheldon worked on him, but so far, he's holding his own."

"What did Sheldon tell you about his condition?"

"He was hopeful, but he said Spencer had to have constant care to pull through. I intend to give him that care." She glanced at him. "Did he tell you something different?"

"The only thing he told me was that Spencer should be in one of the beds in his office, so he could keep an eye on him."

Nelda shook her head. "I wouldn't know what was happening to him if I had let him go there. Here I'll know, and I want to be with him when and if he wakes."

"I'm sure Sheldon would let you visit him as much as you want to."

"No, Lance. The minute he wakes up I have to tell him that I didn't mean it when I said I hated him."

"He knows that already, Nelda."

"How could he know?"

"He told me he knew you still loved him, but you were too stubborn to admit it."

She didn't say anything for a minute. "How could he say that? The last thing I told him was that I hated him."

"I know. You've told me that before, but I don't think it matters. I'm sure Spencer really loves you, Nelda and from the way you're acting, no matter what you say, I think you still love him."

She looked up at her brother with tears in her eyes. "I'll always love him, Lance, but that doesn't mean I can stay married to him."

"Why not?"

"Because he has a mistress."

"Are you positive, Nelda?"

"Yes, Lance. I told you. I saw him in her arms."

"Maybe you misunderstood."

"No. I didn't. She was blonde and beautiful and according to the busy-bodies at the fort, her name is Antoinette." She looked at her brother and changed the subject. "Did you find the person who shot Spencer?"

Shaking his head, Lance said, "No, honey, I haven't found him yet, and there's something I want you ladies to do until I get the man behind bars."

"What's that, Lance?" Wilma asked.

"I don't want anyone to know Spencer is staying here with you until I tell you differently."

"Why not?" Nelda asked.

"Because they might try to get to him here. I don't think they'd be foolish enough to attempt it at the doctor's office, but they might think it'd be easier here. After all, with only two women..." His voice drifted off.

Nelda gave him a hard look. "I can't believe anyone would try to get to Spencer while he's here."

"It depends on how bad they want him dead."

"Why would anyone want him dead?"

"What should we do, Lance?" Wilma asked, before he could answer Nelda's question.

"I talked it over with Doc. We decided that it's best if nobody in town knows he's here. In fact, if you two will go along with it, we want the shooter to think Spencer is dead or at least dying."

"Why would you want us to do that?" Nelda glared at him.

"Because if the man thinks he got away with murdering Spencer, he might make a mistake and give himself away."

"So, you want us to pretend Spencer died or is going to from the gunshot wound?" Wilma looked at him.

"Yes. That's exactly what I want."

"If you think it's important, I'm willing to do it if Nelda is."

Nelda nodded. "I'll do anything to help you catch the man who wanted to kill Spencer."

"Good. Now as far as anyone else is concerned, I just came by tonight to comfort my sister. Not to check on Spencer's condition."

"I'm glad you came to check on me, big brother."

He smiled at her. "It's true that I wanted to check on you, honey. I also had another reason for wanting to see you."

"What other reason could you have?"

"I wanted to find out if you might know what could have brought this on."

Nelda shook her head. "You've probably already guessed I don't know a thing."

"How about you, Wilma? Do you have any idea?"

She shook her head. "I'm afraid not."

"I didn't think you would, but I had to ask."

Wilma smiled at them both. "Now, while you're here to visit with Nelda, I'm going downstairs to get ready for opening up in the morning. I'll probably be back before you leave."

"I'll see you later, Wilma."

After she left, there was a short silence. Nelda broke it. "Who could have shot him, Lance?"

"I don't know yet, but I intend to find out."

"Good. I know you won't give up. Though I still intend to divorce him, I don't want somebody getting away with shooting him."

Lance didn't say anything else about his sister and her husband's relationship. Instead, he said, "Nelda, I'm sorry to ask you this again, but are you sure you don't know anyone who would want to kill Spencer? Maybe somebody at the fort? A disgruntled soldier he had to discipline or someone he had a confrontation with?"

She frowned. "Unless his mistress decided to do it. I don't know anyone."

"You know that's ridiculous."

"Then, I'm sure. I don't know of a soul. As far as I know, everybody who knows Spencer, likes him. I just don't understand it at all."

"You understand why I had to ask, don't you?"

"I guess I do, Lance. I wish I did know somebody who could have done this, but I assure you, I don't."

He touched her shoulder. "Don't fret about it. It may take a while, but I'll find out who did this to your husband."

"Does Grace know Spencer was shot?"

"Yes. I told her as soon as I went home. She wanted to come with me to see you, but I told her I was going to Sheldon's first and I wanted her to wait until tomorrow to visit you. She agreed. She said for me to tell you she was praying for Spencer and to give you her love."

"Thank her for me, Lance."

"I will."

"She's made a wonderful wife for you, hasn't she?"

"Yes, Nelda. She has. I never dreamed I'm be as happy as I am married to her."

She gave him a sad smile. "When we were children and spent time trying to spy on you and your girlfriends, it never occurred to me that you'd end up with Grace. She was such a shy little thing, especially after that tree limb fell on her ankle and left her with a limp."

"It never occurred to me either." He smiled back at her. "But I have to admit now, that you bringing her home from school and making her a part of our lives, was the best thing that ever happened to me."

"You know I'm happy for you and her both, don't you?"

"I know you are, Nelda. I know you and Spencer will be happy again one day soon."

She didn't answer, and he leaned down and kissed the top of her head. "I better go now. I don't want to leave Grace alone too long."

"I understand."

"You know if you need anything, all you have to do is let me know and I'll see you get whatever it is."

"I know, Lance. I could always count on you because you've never let me down." She reached out and squeezed his hand. "All I really want is for you to find who did this horrible thing to Spencer. I want to see them severely punished."

"I will do my best. I promise you that."

She stood and hugged him then re-took her chair and turned her eyes back to her husband.

Lance smiled at her and slipped out of the room. He reminded Wilma, who was back in the kitchen when he entered, to make sure nobody knew Spencer was here, then said a quick good-by to her. He went out the door and waited until he heard her flip the lock. Going down the steps, he wondered where he could look next for some kind of clue that would help him find the rascal who shot his brother-in-law. He hoped to come up with something fast. If he didn't, the sister he loved, and her friend would be in danger just because Nelda insisted on taking care of the man the killer wanted.

He tried to recall all the conversations he and Spencer had had. He knew the man was into something secret, but he had no clue what. He was sure, though, this shooting had to do with whatever Spencer was trying to accomplish.

Fifteen

Meggie leaned on the bar and watched as the strange little man from the east rose from the table in the corner of the Wildcat Saloon, pushed away the drink he'd ordered because he said he had something to celebrate and went out the door. She almost smiled when he'd sat down and she realized he was only taking baby sips. Though by then everyone knew his name was Marcel La Gall, he was still a mystery to most people. At one time she couldn't help thinking that he might have been the one who had killed Hessie. But she decided he just wasn't the type. He was too...well, too something. It had to be somebody else.

Later, her eyes shifted to the long tall cowboy she'd mentioned to the sheriff. He swaggered through the batwing doors shortly after La Gall left. He seemed sure of himself and the guns he wore announced he was probably the type to commit murder. Doubtless for a price. But he would more than likely use a gun. Not a knife. Though, he did have that wicked one he'd showed off the first time he was in the saloon.

Tonight, he ordered a bottle, settled in a chair and eyed Pearl. Meggie wondered if she went over to his table, he'd say something that would let her know whether or not he was a killer.

Before she could make up her mind, Ward Kyler came through the swinging doors. She couldn't help smiling. She liked to think of Ward as one of her regular customers, though she hadn't been with him often. But since she'd first met him, she'd liked him. Well, maybe more than liked him. He had always been kind and he treated her well. Of all the men she'd entertained, she often had day dreams that one day Ward would decide to take her away from this life and move to a town where nobody would ever know she had been a saloon whore. But reality would set in and she'd know it wasn't going to happen. Ward worked for Jed Wainwright as one of the foremen at the big Circle Two Ranch. There was no way he'd ever give up such a prestigious job. Not only that, he was a respected man and he'd never marry a woman like her and introduce her to the rich and fancy Wainwrights. She might as well give up on that dream, but it was hard to do. She was only twenty-two. Much too young to give up all her dreams.

She jumped when the lean cowboy grabbed her arm and a gruff voice said, "Let's go upstairs, girlie. I have something to celebrate and I want you to help me."

Jerking her arm away, she snapped, "I'm busy."

"You don't look busy to me." Without her agreement, he began roughly pulling her toward the stairs.

For some reason, Meggie felt afraid of this man. She didn't like the look in his eyes, and the way he wore his guns low on his hips made her wonder if he wasn't some gunman, with little or no feelings. "I'm waiting for a customer who has already spoke for me," she said, hoping he'd turn her loose.

"Forget him. You're going to be entertaining Con Minton tonight."

She wondered if him giving his full name was because he thought it would mean something to her. He could be a gunman who thought his reputation preceded him. It crossed her mind again that this could be the man who had killed Hessie. He did have that awful knife.

That made her shiver inside and she tried another tactic. Maybe if she played up to him, he'd be reasonable. "I'd be happy to go upstairs with you any other time, but as I said, I can't go now. Could you come back later or maybe tomorrow night?"

"Don't hand me that crap. I'm in the mood for some loving and you're the one who I want it from."

"But my customer..."

He jerked her forward, making her stumble and almost fall. "I told you to forget him. Now, start moving toward those stairs or I'll drag you."

Meggie had a feeling if she went up those stairs with him, she might never come down again. She knew there was nothing she could do but try to get away from his grip any way possible. Her first impulse was to reach out with her free hand and slap him, and she did.

Slapping him had been a mistake. He balled up his fist and hit her on the chin.

"No saloon whore slaps me and gets away with it. I guess I'll have to carry you upstairs." He reached to pick her up, but before he could, a strong hand grabbed his shoulder and pulled him backward.

He went for his gun, but didn't get a chance to use it. The bartender, Ned Foster, rammed a shotgun in his side. "Nobody treats my girls that way. I think you'd better get out of here before you…"

"Oh, no?" The man slung around, missed the bartender and landed a right fist on Ward Kyler's jaw, sending him into the legs of the men standing at the bar.

In a matter of seconds, Ward grabbed the man and sent him to the floor with one punch. Again, the man went for his gun, but another cowboy kicked it away.

Scrambling to his feet, he yelled, "What the devil is wrong with this place? All I came in here for was a woman. Why is everybody defending that whore?" He pointed at Meggie, who had managed to get off the floor and slip behind the bar.

"We defend any woman who is being abused," Ned said.

"But she's just a whore."

"Call her that one more time and I'll…."

"Let it go, Ward," Ned said. "There's no way you can ever reason with a fool like him."

"Maybe not, but it'd make me feel better to knock his teeth out."

"Me too, but I don't want to end up in jail. And if I'm not mistaken, neither do you."

"I guess you're right." Ward turned and walked over to the bar. "Are you all right, Meggie?"

"I'll be fine."

"Your face is beginning to swell. Why don't you go …"

The cowboy had his swagger back. "If she goes anywhere it'll be upstairs with me. I'll show her how she should treat a man who is here to do business with her."

"Maybe somebody should teach you how we treat the women in Settlers Ridge." Ward looked at Ned. "Should we throw him out of here?"

"I'd be much obliged if you would."

"I'll help you," the cowboy who had visited Pearl earlier, said.

"Me, too," came from another one.

In a few seconds, ignoring his yells and cusses, three men dragged Con Minton to the door and tossed the struggling man to the street.

The batwing doors closed as they went inside. It didn't prevent them from hearing him yell, "I'll get every one of you bustards for this."

Ignoring the yelling, Ward took Meggie's hand and smiled at her. "I want you to go to your room and wash your face. Then lie down and rest a bit. You must be upset with what that bastard did to you."

She smiled back at him. "I'll be fine, Ward."

"Please, Meggie. You need to take care of yourself."

"Listen to him, Meggie," Ned said. "You need the rest."

She knew she probably shouldn't have said it, but before she could stop herself, she looked at Ward and said, "After what happened, I'm afraid to be by myself. I'll go upstairs if you'll go with me?"

"Of course, I'll go with you, Meggie." He offered her his arm and they walked up the stairs together.

Meggie felt her heart flutter, though she knew she shouldn't feel such a thing with a customer. But this was Ward, and it was hard to think of him as only a customer.

He meant so much more to her, though he didn't know it - and never would.

~ * ~

Wilma assured Nelda that she didn't mind opening the store alone the next morning. She'd worked in the store alone before, even when Stanley Brown was still in town. Often, he'd go to check on his mother and be gone as much as a half a day and as of yet, Wilma hadn't had any trouble waiting on all the customers that happened to come in.

Today, she'd already sold a box of handkerchiefs to Luella Baldwin, a sack of flour to Effie Vaughn for the hotel and had gathered the supplies the ranch cook had come to pick up for the Circle Two Ranch. She was about to go into the storeroom to bring out some of the merchandise she saw was getting low when the bell over the door jangled. She looked around and swallowed. It was the cowboy who had caused a scene when Juliette was in the store. She took a deep breath and moved behind the counter.

It wasn't the best of protection, but at least it would be a sort of barrier between her and the man. At least she hoped it would be.

He walked up to her. "Good morning, pretty lady."

She nodded, but said nothing.

"In case you forgot, I'm Con."

Wilma didn't acknowledge his remark. "How can I help you, today?"

He chuckled and gave her a wink and tossed his tobacco pouch on the counter. "I'm low on tobacco and papers to roll my cigarettes, sweetheart. I'm sure you must have some here."

"Of course, I do." She frowned at him and moved down the counter and pulled out the papers and a tin of tobacco to fill his pouch. She laid them on the counter in front of him. "Is there something else?"

"Might as well pick up some matches." He was still leering at her.

She got them for him. "Anything else?"

"Don't think so. How much do I owe you?"

She told him the total and he handed her the money. She took it and gave him the things he'd bought.

"Thanks." He smiled at her. "By the way, word is that somebody was shot in here yesterday. What happened?"

"Yes, there was a shooting."

"Is that all you can tell me?"

The bell rang again and she didn't have to answer him. Gertrude Ellsworth came in.

"Hello, Mrs. Ellsworth."

"Hello, Wilma. How are you today?"

"I'm fine. How can I help you, Mrs. Ellsworth?"

"I'm just going to look around a bit. Margo took the baby to the doctor for a checkup and I didn't want to sit in that crowded office. A person can get sick that way, you know."

Wilma smiled. "I guess you're right."

"I also want to know how that man who was shot here yesterday is doing."

Wilma looked away. Everyone who had come in the store today had wanted to know about the man who was shot. Wilma couldn't bring herself to say he was dead or dying, so she thought she'd come up with the perfect solution as an answer to their question. "I'm not sure. The doctor took him away."

"I see. I sure hope he's going to be all right. From all I've heard, he's a nice man."

"That's what I've heard." Wilma glanced back at the man called, Con. "Is there something else you need?"

"No, ma'am. I have all I came in here to get." He tipped his hat to Mrs. Ellsworth and headed out the door.

Gertrude frowned. "I don't think I know that man."

"I think he's new in town." Wilma smiled at her. "Are you sure there's nothing I can get for you?"

"Where's Nelda? Does she know how her husband is doing?"

"She's making dinner."

"I see." Gertrude leaned over and whispered, "Don't get upset, but that funny little Mr. La Gall is heading into the store. I saw him coming this way when I glanced out the window. I think I'll go before he comes in. I'm sorry to say, but there's something about him that I don't fully trust."

"I know how you feel, Mrs. Ellsworth." Wilma sighed. She figured Marcel La Gall would be someone else she'd have to lie about Spencer to.

~ * ~

Con Minton dashed into the alley when he saw Le Gall headed for the mercantile. Breathing hard, he grabbed his head. He knew better than to rush when he had such a hangover. A hangover that never should have happened. But he'd drank an almost full bottle of whiskey before going to the saloon last night, then another bottle when he'd got back to the hotel.

It was after his anger subsided that he realized what a fool he'd been. Now, he had to remedy any mistakes he'd made. The trouble was, he wasn't sure what those mistakes had been. He vaguely remembered being thrown out of the saloon, and declaring he'd get even with the men who had done it. Now, though he didn't want to admit it, he realized they had been right. He shouldn't have been so rough with the saloon whore. But at the time, he had been past reason.

He knew better today, and his only hope was that nobody would finger him and have that sheriff throw him in jail. If that happened, there would be a lot of things he'd have to square with the superior. In fact, if his actions derailed the mission, it would probably cost him his life.

~ * ~

It was almost time for Wilma to come up for dinner when Nelda headed into the bedroom where Spencer lay in her bed. She had a bowl of the chicken soup she'd made. She hadn't eaten much breakfast and she was hungry. She hoped Wilma wouldn't be upset because she ate a little before they sat down for the meal. As she cooked, she thought about what had happened to Spencer and she knew she still intended to tell him that she didn't hate him. Yet, she didn't want him to think she'd forgiven him for all he'd done to her and their marriage.

She couldn't help being a little shocked when she stepped through the door and saw Spencer lying there with his eyes open. "You're awake," she stammered, setting the bowl on the table beside the bed. "How do you feel?"

He didn't answer her question, but whispered, "Where am I?"

"You're in my room above the mercantile."

He frowned, then grimaced, but managed to gasp out in a raspy voice, "Why?"

"It doesn't matter, Spencer. Try to relax. I can tell you're in pain. We'll talk later."

"But ..."

"No buts. Do you think you could eat a little?"

When he only continued to look at her, she added, "Doc said to make sure you ate as soon as you woke up so you'll get your strength back. I'll feed you this soup then go get another bowl for myself."

"Wait. We must talk."

"Not yet." She moved beside him and placed extra pillows behind his back. She pulled the chair closer to the bed. Picking up the bowl, she took a spoonful and held it out to him. "Now, please eat this."

He shook his head.

"Don't be difficult, Spencer. It'll be good for you."

He took the bite and swallowed. "What happened to me, Nelda?"

She gave him another bite. "You were shot."

"Shot?"

"Yes, shot."

"Who shot me?"

"We don't know, but Lance is trying to find out. Here, have another spoonful of soup."

He opened his mouth, took the soup, swallowed, then tried to get up again. He fell back.

"I told you not to do that."

"But I can't stay here in bed. There's something I need to do." He tried again to get up.

"For heaven's sake, Spencer. Quit trying to get out of bed. You were badly hurt and the doctor said you're lucky to be alive. But you have to use your head or you won't be alive much longer."

"I feel like hell, but it can't be that bad."

"I assure you it is. Now, relax and eat more of this soup."

He seemed to relax and took a bite. Finally, in a calm voice, he said, "I need to talk to Lance."

She raised an eyebrow. "I'm sure he'll come back by tomorrow."

"What time is it?"

"It's almost noon."

"I need to see him today." He started moving in the bed as if he was trying to get up. He didn't make it and fell back against the pillows.

She shook her head at him. "I've told you not to try that again, your foolish man. You'll hurt yourself worse than you're hurt already."

He looked at her for a long minute. "You sound as if you might care what happens to me, Nelda."

"I don't like seeing anyone hurt." She looked away and sighed. "I know the last thing I told you was that I hated you, Spencer."

"Are you saying you don't hate me anymore?"

She swallowed. "I'm not sure how I feel about you but I hate what you've done to me and to our marriage. I do know I don't hate you enough to want to see you shot down in cold blood."

He gave her a smile. "At least that gives me hope."

She shook her head. "Don't start hoping, Spencer. The fact that I don't hate you doesn't change a thing. I'll never live with a cheating man. I still intend to divorce you."

Sixteen

Wilma moved to the door to pull the shade, put up the closed sign saying she'd be back by one-thirty, and then lock the door. She smiled as she watched Teddy and Joel come down the street. They were looking around as if they thought someone might be watching them and they were talking in whispers to each other. She knew that because they would hold their hands to their mouths and move their heads to talk into their pal's ear. Fascinated, Wilma continued to watch them.

In front of Miss Purdy's dress shop, which was across the street at an angle from the mercantile, they came to a complete stop. Again, they looked up and down the street, shared a few more whispers, then moved slowly to the side of her building and began looking in the bushes.

"In the name of heaven, what are those little rascals up to?" Wilma smiled and simultaneously, shook her head. Then her expression turned into a frown when she saw what they had retrieved from the bushes. "I've got to find out what's going on with them."

She opened the door and stepped outside. "Hi, fellows. What in the world are you two doing with that gun?"

They froze and stared at her for a few minutes. Finally, Teddy said, "We found it."

"You did?"

"Yes, ma'am."

She could tell by the way they fidgeted and keep glancing around there was more to the story than a found gun. "Well, how about that? Finding a gun is something special, isn't it?"

"It sure is." Joel nodded. "We're lucky we found it before anybody else did."

"I suppose you were at that." She knew she needed to find out about this found gun, but she didn't want to upset the boys or scare them. "I wonder who lost that gun."

They looked at each other, then Teddy shrugged. Joel did the same thing.

She softened her voice. "Do you think we should try to find the owner?"

Again, they glanced at each other, then Teddy said, "He don't want it."

"Why doesn't he want it?"

"Cause he threw it away," Joel explained.

Wilma was surprised at this explanation. "Did you see him throw it away?"

They both nodded and Joel said, "Yeah. He just looked around then threw the gun under the bushes, then ran around the back of Miss Purdy's shop. We knew he didn't want it or he would've taken it with him."

"Yeah," Teddy added. "We decided we'd come back and get it when nobody else was looking, so they wouldn't take it away from us."

Her heart began to pound. Could this be the man who shot Spencer? Not wanting to frighten them, she asked, "Did you see him shoot the gun?"

"No, ma'am. If he shot it, it was before we saw him."

"I see." Wilma nodded at Teddy. She knew she had to get the gun away from them, but she didn't want to tell them what had probably happened. "What did you plan to do with this gun?"

Joel grinned. "We thought we would share it or maybe sell it for enough money to buy us some chaps."

"I see." She knew she had to keep them from leaving with the rifle, so she added, "Why don't you fellows come in the store and let me look at that gun?"

Teddy frowned. "Why, Miss Wilma?"

"Well, just in case I think it's worth a couple pair of chaps. If I do, we might talk about a swap. That way you wouldn't have to sell the gun."

"That's a good idea, Teddy. Let's do it."

Teddy nodded. "All right."

She went inside the store and the boys followed. Closing the door, putting the 'closed' sign in the window and pulling down the shade, she turned to them. "I forgot to ask if you guys knew the man who threw the gun away"

"Sure," Teddy said. "It was the man who is staying at the hotel."

"The funny little easterner?"

"No, ma'am. The one that was mean to you and Mis Juliette that day we were here."

"Oh, my goodness. Not him."

Teddy frowned. "What's wrong, Miss Wilma?"

"Aren't you afraid of what he'd do if he knew you took his gun?"

Joel joined Teddy in frowning. "But he threw it away."

"Are you sure?"

"Yeah. We saw him do it. Didn't we, Teddy?"

"We sure did."

"Are you sure he threw it away?"

Teddy fidgeted. "What do you mean?"

"Maybe he was hiding the gun, not throwing it away." When they said nothing, she added, "What if he intends to come back and get it when nobody is watching him? He'll be furious when he finds it gone and I don't know what he might do."

Their eyes got big. "What do you think he'll do, Miss Wilma"?" Joel asked.

"I'm not sure. You were both here when he acted so rude in the store. You probably can figure out what he'd do as well as I can."

Teddy looked at his friend. "What do you think, Joel?"

"I don't know." He looked at Wilma. "Should we put the gun back?"

"I don't know about putting it back, but it may be dangerous to keep it."

"Do you think he saw us get the gun?"

"I can't be sure, Joel. You know Miss Purdy's shop can be seen from the hotel. Maybe he wasn't looking out the window."

"Think he'd shoot us, or use that awful big old Indian knife of his on us, Miss Wilma?"

She shook her head. "Maybe you fellows should let the sheriff know about the gun. I'm sure he could tell you what you should do."

"I think she's right, Teddy. Let's go tell Sheriff Lance."

"I agree with Joel, Miss Wilma. I think we'll go tell Sheriff Lance. Will you keep the gun in here for us? I'm sort of afraid to take it with us."

"Yes, boys, I'll keep it. Just tell the sheriff I have it here in the store in case he wants to see it." She turned and opened the door.

They rushed out without noticing she watched to make sure they got to the sheriff's office without incident.

~ * ~

Within fifteen minutes Lance knocked on the back door of the upstairs apartment over the store. Wilma opened the door. "Saw your closed for dinner sign in the window and figured you wanted me to come this way."

"I did." She stood aside. "Come in, Lance."

He stepped in and removed his hat. "I'm a little confused. Teddy and Joel told me you had a gun I needed to see."

She led the way into the parlor. "Have a seat."

"Thanks." He sat on the settee. "Now, tell me about this gun."

"Didn't the boys tell you how they found the gun?"

"No. They acted scared. Just said you had a gun you thought I should to see. Then they hurried out saying they needed to get home for dinner."

"I'm afraid I may have scared them."

"What do you mean?"

"Let me begin at the beginning, Lance."

Nelda walked into the room. "We heard company in here. Hello, brother."

"Hi, Nelda."

"I asked him to come. Why don't you join us?" Wilma nodded to a chair.

"Spencer thought it might be you, Lance. He wants to talk to you."

"Then why don't we go into the bedroom? You and Spencer need to hear what I have to tell Lance."

After Wilma told them what the boys had told her, she added, "Even if the guys said they didn't see him, I'm sure that's the man who shot you, Spencer."

Lance nodded. "Is that the same man who Juliette said accosted her?"

"It is."

"He's been hanging around the saloon. I wonder..." Lance's voice trailed off.

"You're going to arrest him, aren't you, Lance?" Nelda interrupted.

"I am." He started to stand.

Spencer said, "Lance, before you go, I need to talk with you a minute."

"Sure." He sat again. "What is it?"

Spencer turned to Nelda. "Honey, if you don't mind, I'd like to speak to Lance alone."

She frowned. "Why?"

"Please, Nelda."

Wilma put her arm on Nelda's. "Come on, my friend. Let's let the men talk. Besides, I'm hungry and we need to finish up dinner so I can get back to the store."

Nelda looked reluctant, but she stood and followed Wilma out of the room.

After the door was closed, Lance said, "Now that we're alone, what is it, Spencer?"

"Pull your chair closer. I'm going to talk low because I don't put it past Nelda to not listen. What I have to say is for your ears only."

Puzzled, Lance moved the chair nearer the bed and waited for Spencer to say what he wanted only him to hear.

"First of all, I hope I'm not putting you in jeopardy by taking you into my confidence, but since I have this bullet wound and can't get out of bed, I don't have any other choice. Things seem to be coming to a head and since I'm in no shape to handle them, you're the only person I trust to do it for me."

"You should know, I'll do what I can."

"In that case, let me tell you a story."

Seventeen

Con Minton had been watching for his chance to grab one of the kids ever since seeing them take his rifle from the bushes. It was ironic he had happened to look out of the window the minute the two had glanced around then went directly to where he'd stashed the gun.

He instantly knew they had to see him discard the gun or they couldn't have gone directly to its hiding place. Did they see him shoot the major? Cursing, he knew he had to make sure of what they knew and what they'd seen.

He also knew he had to play it carefully. He couldn't go directly and grab the two of them, especially after he saw them go into Brown's store. What were they telling the pretty little women who worked there? If it was that they'd watched him shoot Barrington – he knew he'd have to get rid of, not only them, but the pretty women, too.

Continuing to watch, he saw them come out. He cursed again as he watched them head to the sheriff's office. They weren't there long. Coming out they headed in different directions. One went down the boardwalk and the other went in the direction of the hotel. The sheriff didn't come out behind them.

"Maybe they only told him they found a stray gun," he muttered, then sighed. "Doesn't matter though. I'll have to grab the one coming here, the first chance I get. Can't take a chance of them remembering something about the shooting." He then began to plan his escape, though he didn't look forward to it. Not that he minded grabbing a kid. That didn't bother him at all. It was that damn stuff he'd have to use to do it.

Con Minton wasn't afraid of man nor beast, but he had strong fear of that strange liquid he kept in the tightly sealed metal bottle. He was almost as afraid of it as he was of Indians.

He shook his head, knowing he would have to use the evil concoction the association had supplied. He didn't like the stuff because he'd heard if you used too much, you'd kill your prey, too little and it didn't work. He figured if you didn't handle it right, you could injure yourself. He despised the mixture so much that he'd refused to use the name, though he was pretty sure it was called chloroform but it could be that new thing he'd heard about called ether. He hoped it wasn't that since he'd heard ether was as dangerous as nitro.

This would be the second time he'd be forced to use the stuff, but it couldn't be helped. He had to knock the kid out without killing him at first. Kids were loud and nobody could ever guess he had anything to do with the kid's disappearance. All he had to do now was be patient. His chance would come. The kid went all over the hotel. Therefore, he had to come down this hall sometime soon.

~ * ~

After going to the telegraph office and sending the strange message to Denver to somebody called CH, Lance headed back to the office. Though he was sure Spencer hadn't told him the entire story, he could hardly believe the tale his brother-in-law did tell him. A story he was sure he'd never have heard if Spencer hadn't been shot. No wonder the man had tried to keep his secret life from everyone, especially his wife. He was right. If certain people thought Nelda knew what was going on, her life would be in danger, and as Spencer had said, it probably was anyway. The people they were after didn't have to have proof someone was involved to kill them. And that was easy to pull off because one of the killers wasn't as interested in serving the cause as he was in the thrill of the kill.

Opening the door to the jailhouse, he saw the deputy looking over the wanted posters. Putting on a face he was sure wouldn't give a clue as to his conversation with Spencer, he said, "Anybody familiar in those pictures, Bryce?"

"Nobody I've run into yet. Didn't know where you were when I got here, so I decided to look through them while I waited for your return." He pushed the posters aside and eyed the rifle Lance carried. "So, now you're walking the street with an extra gun?"

"You're going to be surprised where I got this extra gun." Lance came in and laid it across his desk. He hung up his hat and took his chair. "A couple of kids saw a man throw it in the bushes beside Miss Purdy's dress shop."

"You're kidding."

"No, Bryce. I'm not kidding. They ended up taking it to Wilma at Brown's store. She realized it could be the rife used to shoot Spencer Barrington, and sent them to get me."

"Was it the gun he used to shoot the major?"

"Probably was. Now, all I have to do is prove it."

"How're you going to do that?"

Lance had no intention of telling Bryce the plan he and Spencer had devised. He simply said, "Not sure yet. But together, maybe we can think of something."

"I'll help any way I can."

"Thanks. I know you will." He leaned back in his chair. "I think the first thing we should do is question the boys again. Separately, this time."

"Sounds like a good idea."

"Why don't you head over to Doc's place and talk to Joel. I'll go to the hotel and see what I can find out from Teddy."

"Will do." Bryce got his hat and headed out the door. Lance followed him, thankful his deputy hadn't asked any more questions.

~ * ~

"When I grow up, I ain't never going to work in no old hotel," Teddy muttered as he carried the two full buckets of hot water to room eight. "People shouldn't come here to take a bath. They ought to do it before they come. I get tired of lugging this heavy water up to them."

He sat a bucket down and knocked on the room door.

A pretty woman with black hair opened it and smiled at him. "Thank you, young man. Just empty them in the tub where you put the others."

Teddy knew where to put the water, but he nodded and dumped it into the hip tub. He then asked the question his father always instructed him to ask. "Is this enough, ma'am?" He sure hoped she said it was. He wanted to hurry and head for Joel's house so they could make their plan for the rest of the day. He didn't have time to keep lugging those heavy buckets up the stairs. It was too bad Sophie was busy in the kitchen and couldn't help him. Pa used to make her help when she was younger, but now that she was almost grown up, she worked more in the kitchen than helping him carry water and stuff. It didn't seem fair.

"I think this will be just fine," the pretty woman said, and held her hand out to him. "This is for doing such a good job."

"Thank you, ma'am." He stepped into the hall, set one of the buckets down and looked at the coin she'd given him. His face lit up. Maybe it was a good thing Sophie didn't help him. He had the whole nickel to himself. He put it in his pocket and picked up the bucket with a smile on his lips. He couldn't wait to tell Joel how much closer they were to having enough money for the coveted chaps.

He was so engrossed in his good fortune he didn't notice a door down the hall behind him open. The next thing he was aware of was a man's hand going around him and covering his mouth and strong arms picking him up. He slung the bucket against the wall, and struggled enough to get his nose from under the foul-smelling cloth. He realized he shouldn't have done it when the man hit him hard in the nose, scattering blood in all directions. The last thing he remembered was hearing the coin drop from his pocket.

~ * ~

Spencer wasn't sure he'd done the right thing by telling Lance as much as he had about the mission the government has recruited him to do. But what choice did he have? There was nothing he could do as long as he didn't have the strength to get out of bed, much less be able to move on the information he had about the men staying in Olsen's hotel. They had to be taken care of.

At least he was glad Lance had had the foresight to tell the public the major was hanging on to life, but the doctor didn't think he'd be able to pull him through. The sheriff said he did it because he thought it would possibly cause the shooter to make a mistake. That was well and good, but Spencer knew it would keep the conspirators from putting more innocent people in danger and possibly killing them. Nelda included.

Sighing, he looked toward the door. Why hadn't she come back after Lance left? Was she still upset because he asked her and Wilma to leave the room while he talked to Lance? He was sorry if it did. But he couldn't let her know what was going on. Someday he could tell her, but not yet.

Then he remembered she did come back. She brought him coffee. He shook his head as he realized his thinking was beginning to slow down. How could that be? He remembered he'd refused the pain medicine when Nelda had wanted to give it to him after Lance left. He didn't like the way it muddled his mind and made him go to sleep. She told him she'd bring him a cup of coffee to help him relax.

A smile crossed his lips and he shook his head. He'd forgotten how sneaky Nelda could be. She'd probably put the medicine in his coffee. That woman would never stop amazing him. He still had the smile on his lips when he closed his eyes and went to sleep.

Eighteen

Frank Olsen took the coffee his wife, Henrietta handed him. "Thanks, dear. I needed this."

"I figured. You hardly had time to eat before the crowd descended on us."

"Well, I have them all in rooms and satisfied now."

The front door opened and he looked up, hoping it wasn't another customer. It wasn't. "Hello, there, Sheriff."

"Hello, Frank." Lance removed his hat and nodded to Henrietta.

She smiled back. "I just brought Frank a cup of coffee. Would you like one, Lance?"

"No, thanks, Henrietta. I just came by to see if I could talk with Teddy for a few minutes."

"Don't tell me our son has broken the law." Frank chuckled.

"Not at all. I just wanted to ask him a couple of questions about the gun he found."

Henrietta frowned. "Teddy found a gun?"

"Yes. Didn't he tell you?"

"No, he didn't."

"According to Wilma, he and Joel found it and took it to Brown's to see if they could trade it for a couple a pair of chaps."

"He's been talking about chaps for a while now," Henrietta said. "But I'll get that little imp for not telling his father or me about the gun."

"So, will I." Frank turned to his wife. "Tell him to come in here right now, honey."

"I'll do that." She turned and left the two men alone.

Frank shook his head. "I don't understand why Teddy didn't tell us about finding the gun. It's usually hard for him to keep quiet about something he'd think was this exciting."

"Maybe they were just too excited about the possibility of getting chaps."

"Could be." He nodded toward the settee in the lobby. "Why don't you make yourself comfortable while you wait, Lance?"

"I will in a minute. First, I need to ask you something." He looked around, then leaned closer to the counter. "What can you tell me about that man calling himself Con Minton who, I understand, is staying here?"

Frank wondered why the sheriff wanted to know about the stranger, but he figured he had his reason. "Can't tell you much. He pays by the week and I see him go in and out occasionally, but he sticks pretty much to himself. Doesn't even eat here. I assume he's taking his meals at the café or the saloon."

"So, he hasn't given you any trouble?"

"Not a bit."

"How about that dandy who everyone calls that funny little man?"

Frank shook his head. "At first, he gave the ladies in the dining room a fit, but as you must already know, your wife set him straight."

Lance chuckled. "Yeah. I happened to be in the dining room that day."

"Since then, he's been pretty easy to get along with."

Henrietta came back into the lobby with a concerned look on her face. "Frank, I can't find Teddy anywhere. Last time I saw him, he was taking water up to the lady in room eight. Sophie and Effie both said they hadn't seen him since then either."

"I didn't see him come back through here, but maybe he used the back stairs."

She still looked worried. "I hope he didn't use them to slip out. He knew we needed him to stay here and help out today."

"If he didn't use the back door, he'd have to come through here."

Lance interrupted. "Maybe you should check upstairs. For some reason, he might not have come down yet."

Henrietta headed for the lobby stairs. "I'll go."

Within a matter of minutes, a woman's scream echoed down the stairs.

"That's Henrietta!" Frank hit the stairs running.

Lance followed.

~ * ~

"Stop that blubbering, you brat!"

Teddy cowered in the corner of the old abandoned barn on the edge of town. Tears ran down his cheek and his voice faltered. "I... I... want to ... go home."

217

"You're not going anywhere."

Teddy began to cry harder.

"I said for you to shut up."

"I ... I can't."

The man stepped closer. His hand was raised and his voice grew harsher. "I asked you before and I'm going to ask you one more time. Where is my rifle?"

"I told ...you. I give it ...to Miss Wilma."

"Why?"

"We ...I thought ...well, we want some chaps."

"What did you see?"

"Huh?"

"How did you know where the gun was?"

"You threw it away."

"I didn't throw it away."

"But..."

"Listen, kid. I'm tired of you stalling. I guess I should go get your friend. Maybe he would be willing to answer my questions." Con laid his hand on his gun. "I wouldn't need you at all then, would I?"

"No! I'll answer anything. Don't shoot me!"

"All right. Tell me what you told the sheriff."

Teddy wiped his eyes on his sleeve. "You mean about the gun?"

Con looked disgusted as he raised his hand. This time he slapped Teddy. "What have we been talking about, you little idiot? Of course, I mean about the gun."

Teddy fell backward on a patch of scattered hay. His tears began again and he tried to crawl away, but Con grabbed his leg.

"If you don't want me to beat the life out of you, you better start talking."

Through his tears, Teddy's voice was shaky. "We told him we found the gun and Miss Wilma told us to go tell him we did. She kept the gun."

"Did you tell him you saw me shoot the gun?"

"No."

"Why not?"

"We didn't care if you shot it or not. We just wanted the gun."

"So, that's all you told the sheriff?"

"We told him to go see Miss Wilma. I don't know what she told him."

Con thought a minute. If the kid didn't finger him, he'd be taking a big chance on killing the boy. There would be a lot of questions if and when the body was found. On the other hand, he could tie him up and leave him here in this abandoned barn. Eventually, he'd either be found or he'd starve to death. Probably the latter, but either way his mission in Settler's Ridge would be complete and he'd be gone. Now, all he had to do was to decide which would be the best thing to help him accomplish his plan. And that would depend on whether or not the major lived.

~ * ~

Esther Wagner looked up from the account book she was working on as the doctor's office door opened. "Hello, Deputy. I hope you're not feeling poorly."

Bryce removed his hat. "I'm fine, Esther. Just came by to ask Joel a few questions about the gun he and Teddy Olsen found."

She frowned. "They found a gun?"

"According to the sheriff, they did."

"He hasn't said a word to me about it."

"I didn't mean to say something out of turn, but I figured he'd told you."

"He hasn't, but maybe he told Sheldon." She stood. "Let me latch the door. If anyone comes for help, they'll bang on the door. We'll go into the house and see what the young man has to say."

"I hope you don't mind me talking to him."

"Of course not. I want to know what's going on and I'm sure Sheldon will want to know, too. Now that he's finished up with the last patient, I bet my husband is headed for the kitchen and a cup of coffee."

Bryce chuckled. "Doesn't take you wives long to catch on to our little habits, does it?"

"Not at all." She smiled at him. "We just watch and listen and you men give yourselves and your habits away."

"Lettie's good at that."

As predicted, Sheldon was pouring himself a cup of coffee as they entered the kitchen. Looking around, he said, "Hello there, Bryce. I hope you're not here to arrest one of us."

"Don't think so, Sheldon. You haven't broken any laws lately, have you?"

"Not that I know of. How about a cup of coffee?"

"No, thanks."

"He's here to talk to Joel about a gun he and Teddy found." Esther put her hands on her hips. "Has he said anything to you about it?"

"I think he mentioned it when he came home, but Miss Simmons was here and I admit I only half listened to him. Told him we'd talk about it at supper."

"Where is he? I want to get to the bottom of this."

Bryce looked at Esther. "Would you mind if I talked to him alone first? I assure you he hasn't done anything wrong and he's not in any trouble. I just think he might talk more freely if he's not worried about what you think."

"But..."

Sheldon butted in. "What would it hurt if we listened in?"

"Nothing really. It's just that Lance and I are pretty sure the gun they found was the one used to shoot Spencer Barrington."

Esther gasped. "What are you saying?"

"The boys found the gun in the bushes next to Miss Purdy's Dress Shop." He continued to explain the situation and ended with, "Just to make sure they didn't see the shooting, I thought he'd be more forthcoming with me alone."

"He's right, Esther."

She frowned, but finally said, "If you think so, I'll call him in. I think he's out back in his tree swing."

"Don't bother, Esther. I'll go talk with him out there." Bryce smiled at her, nodded to Sheldon, then went out the back door.

~ * ~

As Frank and Lance came into the upstairs hall the woman from room eight was trying to comfort Henrietta.

Frank reached his wife first. "Why did you scream, honey? What's going on."

Henrietta reached for him. "Oh, Frank. Teddy is gone."

"What are you talking about?"

"He dropped the buckets after giving Miss Wilson her bath water."

Frank shook his head. "I don't understand."

Lance glanced at him and muttered. "See if you can calm Henrietta and I'll talk with Miss Wilson." He turned and introduced himself to the attractive woman.

"I don't know much to tell you, Sheriff. Young Teddy brought water for me and as I was putting the soap flakes in the tub, I heard a disturbance in the hall."

"What kind of disturbance?"

"At first, there was a clatter. I ignored it because I thought the boy had dropped the water bucket. Then it sounded like a scuffle. I decided it was time to investigate. It was then I discovered the dropped buckets and the blood on the floor. I also found the nickel I'd given him in the corner. Then Mrs. Olsen screamed when she came in the hall looking for her son."

"Show me the blood."

"Sure." She moved to the side and pointed down, then raised her arm. "Some is here on the floor and there are a few splatters on the wall."

"You didn't happen to see anyone out here, did you?"

"No, Sheriff. I didn't."

"Did Henrietta see the blood?"

"I'm afraid so. That's why she screamed."

"Thank you, Miss Wilson." He turned to the Olsens. As he did, he saw La Gall coming down the hall.

"What's going on?" the man asked.

"Did you grab my son?" Henrietta glared at him.

Lance spoke before anyone else could. "Frank, please take your wife downstairs. I'll come down when I finish up here."

Frank nodded, and led a protesting Henrietta away.

"Don't take offense at what she said, La Gall. Her son is missing and she's upset."

"I understand," Marcel muttered, though his eyes said he didn't understand at all. He turned to unlock his room.

"Before you go inside, let me ask a question. Did you happen to see anyone with the Olsen boy on your way into the hotel or on your way up the stairs?"

"I haven't seen that boy all day."

"Thank you, Mr. La Gall."

La Gall didn't answer as he went through his door and closed it behind him.

Lance shook his head, then thanked Miss Wilson for her help and told her he would get back in touch if he had more questions.

She agreed to help in any way she could, then tuned and went through her door.

Lance headed downstairs to organize a search for Teddy Olsen.

Nineteen

Con Minton pressed his body against the wall of the gun shop in the alley when he heard a man say, "Hey there, Shawn Parnell. Want to join the search for Teddy Olsen?"

"What happened to Teddy?"

"A man kidnapped him and there's a search party gathering to look for him."

"Who would kidnap the kid?"

"The sheriff is almost positive it was that man staying in the hotel who grabbed Teddy Olsen. Something about a found gun, but I didn't get the straight of it."

"I wonder what it could all be about, Andy."

"Who knows? I was in the dining room there when Frank Olsen came in and asked if anybody there was willing to join a foot posse to search for Teddy. Before we started out, Lance came in and told us the man who took the boy was dangerous and to keep our guns ready. He then told us to check door to door for the boy."

"Who was the kidnapper? Do you know?"

"Some drifter called Con Minton."

"Don't know him, but I'll be glad to help out. I just need to go tell Virgil. He's at Brown's Store."

"Go let him know what's going on and I'll check in the gun shop. I'll go to the medicine shop next. Meet me there after you let your brother know what's happening."

The voices faded and Con cursed under his breath. He realized he'd made a mistake by grabbing the brat, but he did think it was a good thing he'd heard the couple talking as he'd headed back to his room in the hotel. He had to rethink going back there.

He was sure they were searching or had already searched the hotel. Would they have looked in his room? That was a foolish question. Of course, they would have. Didn't the man say the sheriff suspected him? Even knew his name.

Not knowing what to do, he let his mind consider his options. Should he try to get back in the hotel and retrieve his saddlebags? They did have some sensitive information in them. On the other hand, he figured the sheriff had already gone through the bags, so there was no need to worry about what was in them.

After considering every situation he could think of, he had a feeling his best choice was to work his way to get his horse and slip out of town as quickly as he could. Deciding there was no way to warn La Gall, he headed toward the back of the building so he wouldn't be seen working his way to the livery stable. It didn't really matter anyway. La Gall didn't know he'd been sent there to watch him. The man would have to take his chances without help.

~ * ~

Wilma latched the front door of the mercantile, placed the closed sign in the window and pulled down the shade. Turning toward the stairs in the storeroom, she ran up to the apartment. "I'm going to check the back door to make sure it's locked, Nelda."

Nelda turned from the stove. "I'm sure it is. What's going on?"

"We've got to make sure." Wilma moved to the door and doublechecked. "You're right. It's locked."

"Told you. Now, it's your time to tell me what's happening."

Wilma dropped to a chair at the kitchen table. "Andy Brown came by looking for Con Minton, the stranger who has been making a nuisance of himself."

"Why in the world would he be looking for that man?"

"I'm not positive, but he said something about the man kidnapping Teddy Olsen."

"What?"

Wilma sighed. "I'm afraid it's my fault, Nelda."

"How could it be your fault?"

"After Teddy and Joel left the gun with me, I sent them to get the sheriff. What if that awful man was watching?"

"Calm down, Wilma. I'm sure you had nothing to do with this."

"Yes, but…"

A knock on the back door interrupted her.

"I'll check." Nelda moved to the door and peeped out. "It's Grace and Lance." She opened the door and they came inside.

Wilma blurted, "Have you found Teddy?"

"Not yet, but we will." He didn't give her a chance to say anything else. "I've brought Grace to stay with you until we do find him."

Grace moved to a chair at the table. "He didn't want me to be at home alone until this man they're after is caught."

Nelda patted her arm. "I'm glad you're here."

"Before I get back out there, I need to talk to Spencer if possible."

"Why, Lance?"

"I just need to see what he thinks."

She shrugged. "I gave him a dose of his medicine earlier, but you might be able to wake him. It was a light dose."

Lance nodded and headed to the bedroom. He heard Wilma ask, "What in the world is going on, Grace?"

He didn't hear his wife's answer but he knew she would explain that he needed to speak to Spencer in private for some reason he couldn't tell them at this time. He stepped into the bedroom and closed the door behind him. Moving to the bed he looked down at his sleeping brother-in-law. Touching his shoulder, he muttered, "Can you wake up, Spencer?"

It surprised Lance when Spencer immediately opened his eyes, though they didn't seem to focus well. "Try to clear your head. I need to ask you a couple of questions."

Spencer closed his eyes and nodded. In a minute, he opened them again. He did look more aware. "What's going on, Lance?"

Lance talked about unimportant things until he was sure Spencer was aware of what was happening. He then explained about Teddy being missing, and about searching

Con Minton's room. "I was shocked when I found some papers in his saddlebags. They gave me some idea of what you're into, but not everything. I think it's time you explained to me what's really going on."

"I will, but I need to get out of this bed and help you find that boy."

"You can't get up, Spencer. Besides, I have practically every man in town, plus half the crew from Jed Wainwright's ranch looking for Teddy. They're checking every building in Settlers Ridge. I have no doubt we'll find him."

"I just hope you find him alive. Minton will have no qualms about killing him if he thinks he'll be able to get away with it."

"Hopefully, we'll find him first." Lance leaned back. "Now start explaining."

For a minute, Lance didn't think Spencer was going to answer him. But finally, the man said, "It started a long time ago. The rulers of this small country, that I'd never heard of, were the Degarmo Family. Shortly after his father's death, Trussnit Degarmo took the throne. After he'd been in power almost twenty years, he brought his wife, Maiabella, and his daughter, Francina to visit this country. It was their law that if anything happened to the ruler, his wife would succeed him. On her death, the oldest child would be in power. Francina was their only child. Since there were no other children, if something happened to Francina, the power would go to a distant cousin, Parquet. In this case, the cousin was a greedy bastard and decided since the family was away, he would make arrangements to make sure they never returned to their country. He and his followers got together and worked up a plan to take over the throne."

Lance didn't say anything and Spencer went on, "A couple of loyal supporters of Degarmo secretly left the country and came to warn him. I'm not sure if this is when our government became involved or not, but it wasn't long until Maribella was murdered and Toussnit had been wounded. It was then I was called in."

"Were you in the military at the time?"

"I was. I had planned to leave the service and head west to start a business, but they enticed me to stay. I felt it was important, so I stayed." Spencer took a deep breath. "Toussnit Degarmo grew weaker every day from his wounds, and it wasn't long until we all knew he wasn't going to make it. As he was dying, he asked me to protect Francina at all cost. I swore to the man I would."

Spencer paused, and Lance said, "I think I have an idea of what you're going to say, but I need for you to tell me everything."

He nodded. "As you have probably guessed, Francina is my so-called mistress. But she goes by Antoinette, which is one of her other names." He looked Lance directly in the eye. "I swear to you, brother-in-law, though we are friends, she is not now, nor has she ever been my mistress."

"I believe you, Spencer. I just don't understand why you can't tell Nelda this."

"Because I don't want my wife murdered, Lance."

"How in the world would her knowing put her in danger?"

"Parquet's men are aware of Francina, but they think she's Antoinette and was my mistress before the Degarmos came to this country. Any other woman in my life is suspect, including Nelda." He shook his head. "I shouldn't have married her while I was involved in this, but I couldn't stop myself. I loved her so much I couldn't stand the thought of her falling for some other man while I was doing this job."

"I guess I can understand that. Still, I think you could tell her about the woman. If you don't want anyone else to know, I'm sure she can keep your secret,"

Spencer changed the subject. "Now that you know this much, I need to tell you something else."

Lance nodded.

"Parquet has two of his known killers in town."

"I assume Con Minton is one of them."

"Right. The other one is Marcel La Gall."

Lance was surprised. "That strange dandy? I know he's rude and aggravating at times, but a killer?"

"It may be hard to believe, but it's true. Con Minton has no conscience and will kill anyone, including children, but he always has a reason to kill. He never kills for the fun of it. On the other hand, La Gall is a thrill seeker. He preys on women and he lives to kill. It excites him to carve up a woman and watch her suffer. It's his trademark."

"Are you sure, Spencer?"

"I'm positive. La Gall has done it before and I'm sure he'll try to do it again. In fact, I believe he's already killed here in your town."

Lance raised an eyebrow. "Are you saying his victim could be the prostitute, Hessie?"

Before Spencer could answer, Nelda knocked on the door and without waiting for someone to respond, she jerked it open. "Lance, there's a man at the back door that says they need you at the livery. They have the man you're after cornered there."

Lance grabbed his hat. "I'll be back. Think about telling Nelda what I suggested."

As soon as Lance was out the door, Nelda whirled toward him. "What did Lance suggest you tell me?"

Spencer avoided her question. "I'm hurting, Nelda. Can I have some more of the medicine the doctor left for pain?"

"No, you can't. It hasn't been long enough for you to have another dose." She closed the door and moved to the chair Lance had vacated. "Quit trying to divert my attention. What did Lance think you should tell me?"

He reached out and took her hand. "He thought I should tell you that Antionette is not my mistress and she never has been."

Nelda jerked her hand from his and jumped up. "Honestly, Spencer. I can't believe you'd lie there and tell me this lie again. I can't wait until you're well enough for me to divorce you."

She went out of the room and slammed the door behind her.

Twenty

Lance eased up behind his deputy who was hunkered down behind a wagon. "Where is he, Bryce?"

"Best we can tell, he's holed up in the hay loft."

"Is he alone?"

"No. He's holding Stokes Stevens and at least one of his kids. Maybe more. That's why we haven't rushed him."

"Do you think he has Teddy, too?"

"Don't know. He could have."

Lance nodded and looked around. "Has he said anything to you?"

"Told us he'd only deal with the sheriff. That's why I sent for you."

"I'm glad you did."

A shout came from inside the livery stable. "Is that damn sheriff here yet?"

A thought hit Lance. "Tell him I'm on my way. I've got an idea I want to try."

Bryce nodded. "I sent for him. I'm sure he'll be here soon."

"What's taking so long?"

"I wasn't sure where he was. They had to find him."

"If he don't show up soon, I'm going to toss one of these people out with a bullet in their head, just to show him I'll not put up with any tricks. I know how devious that bastard can be."

"I tell you, he'll be here."

"I'm giving him ten more minutes."

Lance whispered, "I'm going around to the back. Pass the word that when I yell, start firing to distract him. Just tell everyone to aim high or shoot to the side. I don't want any of the hostages or me, for that matter, to get shot."

Bryce nodded.

Lance returned it, then headed around to the back of the stable. Having used the livery to stable his horse several times, he knew Stokes had a couple of stalls that he could crawl under and get inside without being seen. He only hoped there wouldn't be an animal in the stall he chose. He knew an excited or frightened animal would give his presence away. He also hoped the stalls had been mucked. Grace would want to kill him if he got the clothes he'd put on clean this morning all messed up. She'd had a lot of trouble getting the blood out from the fight he'd broken up. He didn't think she'd be pleased at having to wash out a lot of horse and mule manure.

Grinning at the foolishness of the thought, he eased under the opening. He couldn't help noticing the area wasn't as nasty as it could have been. Once inside the livery, he moved to the edge of the individual stables and eased his way up the corner stairs in the back. He gambled on Minton guarding the stairs that came out on the front of the building.

Taking a deep breath, drawing his gun and rushing into the loft, he shouted, "Now, Bryce."

A confused Con Minton whirled toward Lance as a barrage of shots rang out, going in all directions. He tried to get off a shot, but it went wild. Before he could aim and fire again, Lance sent the gun flying from his hand in one shot.

Stokes Anderson saw the man was disarmed. "Get him, boys!"

His two sons loped toward Con – one grabbed him around the neck and the other yanked his arms to his back.

"That'll teach you to try to take a horse from our livery without paying your bill." Stokes started to join the melee, but Lance stopped him.

"I'll take it from here." he said as he cuffed the man. "Where's the Olsen boy?"

"I don't know what the hell you're talking about."

"Oh, I think you do."

Con said nothing.

"I bet I know where he is," the youngest Anderson boy said.

"Where, Gibby?"

"When he thought I was going to cry, he told me to shut up or he was going to put me in the abandoned barn with another kid and set it on fire. Course, I weren't going to cry."

Con glared at the boy. "That brat ain't there."

"Don't speak to him." Lance turned to Gibby. "Thanks, son. You've been a big help." Looking to Anderson he asked, "Is everyone all right, Stokes?"

"Yeah, Sheriff. We're all right. I just wish you'd let me get my hands on that bastard."

"Don't worry, Stokes. Where he's going, he'll never see daylight again." He pushed Con toward the steps and out the door.

Bryce ran up. "You got him."

"I see your plan worked," Jed Wainwright said.

"Thank the good Lord, it did." He looked at Bryce. "I want you to take Minton to jail, Deputy. I have an idea where Teddy Olsen is and I'm going to take a couple of men with me to get him. The others can go home, if they like."

"It'll be my pleasure to escort him to jail."

Ward Kyler walked up to Bryce. "I'll go with you, Deputy. Just to make sure this rattle snake doesn't try to slither away."

Noticing how Minton kept looking at Jed, Lance said, "Why don't you come with me to get Teddy, Ward? And you, Jed. Will you help Bryce get the prisoner to jail? The way he's eying you, I don't think he'll give either of you any trouble."

"Be happy to, Lance. I'll wait at the jail until you get there."

"Thanks. I appreciate you doing that."

Bryce and Jed walked off—one on either side of Minton.

Lance looked at Ward. "Let's go rescue Teddy. I don't expect any trouble, but it's always good to have a backup."

"Sure."

"The rest of you can wait around here or follow us, if you like. I appreciate all of you taking your time to help search for the boy. As soon as we're positive he's safe, we'll spread the word, but let's make sure before we say anything." He turned and headed to the abandoned barn on the edge of town. He silently prayed they'd find Teddy Olsen alive and in good health.

~ * ~

Marcel Guillaume La Gall came to an abrupt stop at the closed hotel dining room door. Frowning, he jerked the door open and stepped into the empty room. No patrons were inside and the young girl who worked there didn't appear to seat him. This was unusual because it was not long until what these people called the supper hour. He knew instantly, something wasn't right, but he had no idea what. At the moment he didn't care. He only knew he was hungry and he wanted to be served.

"Hello!" he shouted. "Where the hell is everyone?"

Effie came from the kitchen. "What you shouting about?"

"I came to get something to eat."

"As you can see, the dining room is closed."

"Why?"

Effie put her hands on her hips. "Are you the only one in town who don't know the Olsen boy is missing?"

"What's that got to do with the dining room being closed?"

"I guess if the Olsens want to close up 'til their son is found, it's their business."

"But I'm hungry."

"Well, you ain't getting nothing to eat here. Mr. Olsen said close the dining room and close it, I did. Now, if you think you have to have something to eat, go to the Wildcat Saloon."

"Won't they be closed?"

Effie shook her head. "Saloons don't close because a child is missing."

He shrugged. "Then I suppose if I want to eat, I have to go there."

"Looks like it."

He softened his voice. "Couldn't you make me a plate of something, even if it's left over from earlier?"

"No, sir. I couldn't. Now, why don't you get on out of here? I need to lock the door to keep some other hungry straggler for coming in here to eat."

"But..."

She waved her hands at him. "Now, get on with you. I'll have to call Mr. Olsen if you don't hurry up and go."

Though he didn't show it, Marcel seethed inside. If he only had one of his special babies with him, he would show this irritating woman her place. But at the moment, all his lovely knives slept safely in their velvet box. That didn't mean he couldn't return with one of them later, and show her how beautifully they worked on older women. The old worn out woman of ill repute at the saloon was a prime example of the job they could do.

He gave Effie a sinister smile and went out the door, wondering what was being served at the saloon. Planning an event for his special knives always increased his appetite.

~ * ~

A shocked Nelda jumped up from her seat at the table, where she was having tea with Grace and Wilma. She couldn't believe Spencer had walked into the kitchen, dressed and with his gun in the holster hanging at his side. She ran up to him and grabbed his arm. "What do you think you're doing? Get back in that bed."

Wilma and Grace looked surprised to see him, but neither said anything.

He gave them all a crooked smile. "Things are coming to a head and I have to get out there and help Lance."

Nelda frowned. "Don't be ridiculous. Lance can handle anything that happens. He doesn't need you."

"Yes, he does, sweetheart. Now, come lock the door behind me, then join your friends for tea or something. I'll explain everything when I get back."

She was exasperated. "Use your head, Spencer. You're in no shape to be out of the bed, much less trying to catch outlaws."

He turned and looked down at Nelda and took her shoulders into his two hands. "I'm tougher than you think and I'm going. You might as well quit trying to stop me."

"But..."

"No buts." Without warning, he pulled her against him and kissed her passionately without regard to the fact they weren't alone.

Against her better judgment, and in spite of all she could do, she kissed him back. At that moment she wanted nothing more than to continue kissing him.

Abruptly, he let her go and pulled away. Heading out the door, he said, "I'll be back as soon as I can and we'll continue this."

Grace lifted an eyebrow. "Looks like a man with a mission, to me."

"I agree." Wilma got up and moved to lock the door. "Have a seat, Neda. You look like you're going to fall down if you don't."

Nelda moved to her chair at the table. "I can't believe that foolish man got up and walked out of here. He's in no shape to go out there and fight criminals."

"I don't know about that."

She glanced at Wilma. "What do you mean?"

"Well, my friend, the way he kissed you, he looked to me as if he's getting well quickly."

Nelda blushed. "He shouldn't have done that in front of my friends."

"Sometimes when a husband decides to get amorous, they don't stop to see where they are." Grace chuckled. "You don't want know how many times I've had to tell Lance to control himself in public."

Wilma sighed. "I think you're both lucky women. All wives can't say their husbands love them enough to act so romantic in front of other people, I'd be thrilled to have a man like that."

"But Spencer knows I'm going to divorce him."

"Are you sure about that, Nelda?"

"Of course, I'm sure. I've told him over and over, Grace."

"I was talking about you, Nelda."

"Me?"

"Yes, my dear sister-in-law. A woman doesn't kiss a man back the way you kissed your husband unless she loves him and is committed to him for the rest of her life."

"But...but—"

"Don't keep fighting it, Nelda," Wilma said. "I agree with Grace. You're in love with Spencer Barrington, and though you've said you're going to divorce him, if you do, you'll regret it for the rest of your life."

Tears came into Nelda's eyes and she muttered, "But he has a mistress."

~ * ~

Lance was happy when he found a scared Teddy in the barn. When the boy realized Lance was his rescuer, he threw his arms around the sheriff's neck and clung to him. "I'm glad you found me. That man said he was going to leave me here to starve to death."

"We weren't going to give up until we found you, Teddy."

"I was afraid he would kill me for sure."

"We weren't about to let that happen. Your mother and father can't wait for you to get home. They've been awfully worried."

"I want to see them, too. I missed them. I even missed Sophie."

Lance smiled. "Sophie missed you, too. In fact, she wanted to join in the posse looking for you, but her mother and father wouldn't let her."

"I would have wanted to look for her, too."

After Lance made sure the boy wasn't physically hurt, he picked Teddy up and started for the door. He noticed Ward had gone outside. Probably to let everyone know Teddy was safe.

Heading for the stairs, he heard feet climbing the rickety steps to the loft. In an instant, Frank Olsen appeared.

"Pa!" Teddy jumped from Lance's arms and ran to his father.

Frank enfolded the boy in his arms. "Thank the Good Lord, you're safe, son."

"I didn't think I'd ever see you again, Pa." He burst into tears. "I was afraid he would kill me, and I didn't want to die."

"I know it was awful, son. Why don't I hurry and get you home to your mother? She's awfully worried."

Lance butted in. "That's a good idea, Frank. Take your son home to his family. The man who took him is in jail by now. I'll go see what I can get out of him. I'll come by to talk with you folks later."

"Thank you, Lance. You know we'll be eternally grateful to you for finding Teddy for us."

"I'm thankful it turned out so well. Now, go along. I'll take care of dispersing the crowd, who I'm sure want to talk to you. But they can wait until Teddy is back safe with his family."

~ * ~

The jailhouse door opened and Spencer walked in. "Do you mind if I join you fellows?"

The men inside looked around, and Lance said, "We don't mind at all, but I'm surprised to see you out of bed."

"I hate to admit it, but it has taken more out of me than I thought it would. That empty chair over there looks mighty good." He took a seat. "Heard you caught Minton."

"Sure did. Was just going over these papers I got from his room, then we planned to start questioning him."

Spencer nodded and looked around the room. He understood why Bryce was there, but he wondered why Jed Wainwright was. Before he could ask, Lance explained.

"I asked Jed to join us in case Minton is hard to handle." He chuckled. "He acted as if he was a little afraid of Jed when we caught him. Thought it would make him easier to talk to."

"He took one look at me and quieted down immediately." Jed said with a smile. "Must be my Lakota blood."

"I've heard Minton does all he can to avoid Indians," Spencer said. "Some say it's because he lied when he said he saved a young brave's life some time ago and he's afraid Indians can tell he's lying. Others say he did save the boy, but decided to kill the brave when he wouldn't give him that knife he carries. Story goes that the young brave put a curse on him with his last breath. He swore one of his relatives from the tribe would hunt him down and make him pay for his crime if it took a hundred years."

"Interesting. Since Jed seems to intimidate him, I'm glad I decided his presence might make Minton more cooperative."

Bryce grinned. "I wish I could intimidate Lettie like that. Especially when she gets in one of those moods women get in at times."

"Let me assure you it doesn't work on wives," Jed said. "Amelia just shakes her head at me and does what she pleases."

"I think that's true of most wives." Lance held up a sheet of paper. "I'm sure you know what's written on this, Spencer. But would you like to look it over before we bring Con Minton in here?"

Spencer took the paper and quickly read parts of it. It contained no surprises. He handed it back. "You're right, Lance. Nothing I didn't already know here, but there are a few things I can add after you question the man."

"In that case, how about bringing Minton in here, Bryce? We'll see what he has to say for himself."

As soon as Minton entered the room his eyes fell on Spencer. "You're supposed to be dead!"

"As you can see, I'm very much alive."

Bryce led Minton to the chair in front of Lance's desk.

Con's eyes tuned to the other man in the room and there was no way to describe his look, except to say his eyes filled with fright when his sight fell on Jed.

When nobody spoke, Con looked at the sheriff and gave a slight nod toward Jed. "Does he have to be here?"

"Yes, he does." Lance leaned on his elbows and looked the prisoner in the eyes. "Want to tell me why you kidnapped the Olsen boy?"

"I ain't kidnapped nobody."

"Is that right?"

"Yes, that's right."

Lance raised an eyebrow. "Then why were you holding the Stevens man and his sons hostage in the livery stable?"

"I just wanted to get a horse and leave town. No law against that."

"Not unless you had committed a crime and wanted to get out of town before you were caught."

"I didn't commit no crime."

Lance leaned over and opened a drawer in his desk. He took out the carved-handled Indian knife and held it between his two hands. He then turned toward Jed, "Was this the kind of knife you asked me about?"

Con looked terrified. "No! That's not my knife. I found it."

Jed reached for the knife. Turning it over in his hand, he spoke slowly. "It looks as if it is the knife that belonged to the young brave."

Lance couldn't believe the man was falling for their trap. He decided to push him a little further to see if he'd break. "Well, since he says he didn't break any laws in town, I guess I can turn him over to you."

"No!" Con screamed.

"Yes, Mr. Minton. Since you have nothing to say to me, I'm sure you can explain your possession of this knife to this big Indian."

"No! Don't do it, Sheriff. You can't do that. He'll hang me upside down and remove my skin piece by piece just like the brave said."

"I have no reason to hold—"

"Yes, you do. I'll tell you everything." He pointed at Spencer. "Why I shot him and why I took the boy. I'll even tell you about La Gall. He's in this project up to his neck. Just don't let that crazy Indian take me."

"All right, Minton." Lance took the knife from Jed and put it on the desk where Con Minton couldn't help but see it. "Start talking. And your story better be good or the chief there will be waiting to take you away with him."

Twenty-one

Marcel La Gall had only eaten a few bites of his meal when the conversation around the saloon's long wooden table in the dining area caught his attention.

"Hello, fellows," a big cowboy with a long beard came into the room. "Got enough left for a tired and hungry fellow?"

"Shore. Have a seat, Newt," a fellow with a long scar on his face said.

"What you been up to?" the middle-aged, overweight cook asked. "You're later than you usually are."

"Joined the group to hunt for that little Olsen fellow who was kidnapped, Bertha. Caught the son-of-a-bitch that took him, too."

Everyone, including Marcel, stopped eating and looked at the man called Newt.

"Why did he want the Olsen kid? Money?" The cook handed him a cup of coffee.

"Nah. Seems the kid saw him shoot somebody and he wanted to get rid of him."

"Who done it?" the man with s scar asked.

"Con Minton."

"Who's he?"

"You know. He's the fellow who has been around a few weeks."

"He the one who comes in here and shows off with the women?" the scar asked.

"The very one."

Bertha came to the table with a filled plate. "Here you go, Newt."

When he started to get out his money, Bertha chuckled. "Put your money away. It's on the house tonight. You deserve it for going to help that little boy."

"Why, thank you, Bertha. You're a good woman."

"Ah, shoot. I just don't cotton to them who tries to hurt little kids. Now eat up. I got some blackberry cobbler for them that wants dessert."

Marcel took a few more bites and listened. When he was sure he'd heard all that was a help to him, he got up from the table, nodded to the other men and went out.

His mind was reeling. He had known Minton was in Settlers Ridge, and he was sure the man had been sent here to watch him. He knew, too, it was no coincidence that Minton had arrived about the time the old whore left this world, and would have known La Gall had committed that murder.

He wondered if the stupid cowboy would have implicated him in this crime. In Marcel's mind, there was no doubt. Con Minton would tell them anything they wanted to know if they threatened him in any way. Minton might be a ruthless killer, but he was like most of the Western gunmen with whom Marcel had been in contact. When it came to their own life, they'd do or say anything to protect themselves. Minton was no different.

With those thoughts in his mind, he hurried to the hotel. He knew what he had to do before he left town. There was no more time to try to discover which woman was the remaining member of the Dergarmo family. It had to be one of them, or the major wouldn't be here. Though he'd have liked to do away with the right one, his babies would be pleased to rid the world of both of them.

That last thought made Marcel Guillaume Augustus La Gall smile.

~ * ~

"Don't argue with me, Spencer. I'm going to see you back to Nelda's apartment, whether you want me to or not. You look on the verge of passing out and I don't want somebody to find you unconscious on the side of the street."

"But I need to…"

"Look. Bryce is here. Minton is locked up tight and Jed said he'd be in town a little longer if we need him."

"And I know where to get him if we do," Bryce said.

"But, there's La Gall to contend with."

"I'll take care of La Gall." Lance shook his head. "You need to get back in that bed. Do you realize what I'd have to contend with when Nelda realized I was the cause of your relapse?"

"Yes, but…"

"No, buts. Let's head back to the mercantile. I don't want you to get so weak I have to carry you. You're much too big."

"At least let's stop at the telegraph office. I have to send another wire."

"I'll send it for you."

"If you insist, I'll give in. But at least let me write out what I want the wire to say."

"That's no problem." Lance took a sheet of paper from his desk and handed it to him.

After stuffing the note in his pocket, Lance left the office with Spencer. The men didn't talk on the way to the mercantile. Lance realized it was taking all of Spencer's strength just to walk the three blocks to the apartment.

Once inside, he insisted Nelda get Spencer to bed. He then told them about Teddy's rescue and the fact that the kidnapper was in jail.

"Then, can I go home?" Grace asked.

He put his arm around her. "Not yet, sweetheart. I have a couple of more things to do and I don't want you home alone. I'm not convinced that Minton didn't have an accomplice."

Wilma smiled at them. "Then, why don't you come back by here? Nelda and I will cook supper as soon as she gets Spencer settled. You two can join us."

"Sounds good to me." Lance winked at Grace. "My wife needs a night off from cooking."

"You know I'll help them cook if we accept their invitation."

"That's fine." Lance leaned down and kissed her cheek. "I shouldn't be gone long."

As he went out the door, he heard Wilma say, "You're sure a lucky woman, Grace. My hope is that someday I'll find a man to love me as much as Lance loves you."

"I am lucky, Wilma. But I want you to know I love him just as much."

He didn't hear Wilma's reply. He didn't have to because he knew their love was deep and true. He also knew it always would be.

Shaking his head, he took out what Spencer had written on the paper to be sent as a telegraph. It was addressed the same as the other wire he'd sent for the man - CH, whoever that was. The message was confusing, but Spencer had insisted he send it just the way it was written. He would honor the man's wishes, he'd then go to the hotel to confront Marcel Le Gall. Then all he'd have to do is drop by the Wildcat Saloon and let Ned Foster know Hessie's murderer was in jail.

~ * ~

Nelda came back into the room. "I'm glad to see you still here, Grace."

"Lance had a couple of things to do and he didn't want me to be alone."

She laughed. "He can be overprotective at times."

"I think it's wonderful of him, don't you, Nelda."

"I do. It shows how much my brother loves his wife."

"You both know how much I love him," Grace said, then changed the subject. "Did you get Spencer settled?"

"Sure did. Didn't even get his clothes off. He was asleep as soon as his head came into contact with the pillow."

"That's good." Wilma smiled. "I've invited Grace and Lance to supper. You will help me cook, won't you?"

"Of course. What are we cooking?"

"I put that ham you brought up earlier in the oven. We can fix potatoes and beans."

"How about dessert? If I remember correctly, my brother loves his sweets. I bet he still does, doesn't he, Grace?"

"Absolutely."

"What's favorite?" Wilma asked.

"He's partial to cobblers of any kind."

"How about peach?" Nelda suggested. "We got a shipment in the other day. I remember putting them on the shelf."

"He loves peach."

"Then I'll go downstairs and get a couple of cans. Since it'll take the ham a while longer to cook, if you don't mind, I'll do a little work while I'm down there."

"Don't mind at all, Wilma. Grace and I'll call if we need you."

Wilma nodded to her friends and hurried down the stairs.

~ * ~

Lance pushed open the door to the hotel lobby. "Frank, it's great to see you back behind that desk and giving out your friendly greetings."

"It feels good to be here, Lance. Until your baby gets here, you'll never know that what happens to your kids seems to happen to you, too. I learned that lesson well last year when Sophie had the measles. It was brought home again when Teddy went missing."

"I know it had to be upsetting to the boy. Is Teddy doing all right?"

"Seems to be. He hasn't asked to leave the hotel, but I don't expect that to last long. You know how he likes to get out and about."

Lance nodded. "The reason I came in is to check on one of your customers, Frank."

"Which one?"

"Marcel La Gall."

Frank nodded. "He's in room six."

"Do you know if he's in?"

"Sorry. I don't. Shall I send up for him and see?"

Lance shook his head. "If he's in, I think it's best if I surprise him."

Frank nodded and Lance headed up the stairs. After knocking on the door to room six several times, Lance realized the man wasn't there. He'd have to go looking for him.

Back in the lobby he asked, "Did you happen to see La Gall go out, Frank?"

"Sorry. No, I didn't, Lance. I haven't been back in the lobby long. He could have left when we were inside celebrating Teddy's return."

"That was worth celebrating."

"We thought so."

"I'll see if I can find La Gall, but if I don't, and he comes back, don't tell him I'm looking for him."

"I won't say a word, Lance."

Back on the boardwalk, Lance looked up and down the street. Not seeing La Gall in either direction, he decided he'd start his search in the Wildcat. It wouldn't be unheard of for the criminal to return to the scene of his crime.

There were several cowboys in the saloon when Lance walked through the swinging doors. Of course, this didn't surprise him. It was getting close to supper time and the place would become even more crowded as the night wore on.

"Well hello there, you big handsome sheriff," a woman dressed in a yellow and black skimpy dress greeted him.

Lance didn't recognize the woman, but before he could answer, Meggie walked up.

"You're wasting your time with this big fellow, Nell," she said. "He's off the market since he married one of the sweetest women in town. Ain't that right, Mr. Lance?"

"You got it, Meggie."

The woman batted her eyes at him. "I'm sure there are a lot of happily married men who come in here now and then. Variety, is the reason they often give."

"I'm sure the sheriff has a different reason than variety for coming in this evening."

"You're right about that. I need to ask a few questions."

"Move along, Nell. That cowboy in the red shirt has been eying you. See if you can strike up a conversation with him."

Nell hesitated, but finally moved away without saying anything else.

"Don't pay no attention to her, Sheriff. She only came to work here a couple of days ago. She ain't learned the people of this town yet."

"No problem, Meggie. Do you mind if I talk to you a minute?"

"You don't want me to get Ned?"

"He looks pretty busy at the bar, and I think you'll be able to help me."

"Then ask away."

"Has Marcel La Gall been in here in the last few hours?"

Meggie frowned. "Matter of fact he came in early this afternoon. He didn't stop in the bar though. He went to the eating area. Bertha laughed because he'd been complaining about the dining room at the hotel being closed."

"Early this afternoon, you say?"

"Yeah. It was somewhere between three and four."

"And you haven't seen him since?"

She shook he head and looked at him. "Has he done something wrong, Sheriff?"

"Yes, he has, Meggie. I can't say right now what he's done. But if he happens to come back in, I want you and the other girls to be wary of him. Warn that new girl. He looks harmless, but he's not."

She frowned. "Does this have anything to do with Hessie's death?"

Lance shook his head and didn't answer her question. "Just tell Ned to get in touch with me as quickly as he can if the man shows up. If I'm not at the office, my deputy will be."

"I'll go tell him right now."

"Try not to alarm anyone. I don't want any trouble if I can avoid it."

"Don't worry, Mr. Sheriff. A woman like me knows how to keep suspicion down."

"Thanks, Meggie." He tipped his hat to her and went out the door, wondering where he was going to look for the man next.

~ * ~

CH opened the door to the pretty white house in Denver. Taking the telegraph from the delivery boy, he tossed the youngster a coin.

He ripped open the missive, read it and smiled. Then he went into the other room and handed it to the beautiful blonde woman sitting on the comfortable velvet settee.

She took it and read: *Start Move. CM no issue. LG out soon. Business plan in place. Money no problem. MB.*

She looked up at him with a smile on her face. "It seems it's really happening."

"I agree."

"Does this indicate I should pack?"

He smiled back at her. "Yes, Your Highness, it does."

Twenty-two

Marcel La Gall had tried the door to the mercantile and found it locked. Frowning, he stood back and thought about what he should do. He'd watched the place enough to know the women used the stairs from the back alley to come and go when the store was closed. But he had hoped to slip in the front door, wait inside until one or both of them were alone with him. He'd have locked the door and then he and his beautiful knives could have their reward.

But the locked door messed up this plan. Of course, he could use the back stairs, but he knew it would be harder to surprise them going inside that way.

He glanced through the window and saw the one called Wilma come into the store. He almost grinned as he moved back to the door. All he had to do was get her to let him in, then everything he planned would be easy to carry out.

He tapped on the glass section of the front door and waited. When there was no response, he tapped again. On his third tap, the shade over the window went up.

Anticipating what was going to happen, he didn't have to force the smile he gave her. Using his hands, he motioned for her to open the door.

She shook her head, and indicated the CLOSED sign.

He mouthed the word, *please.*

He watched her sigh, then reach down to turn the latch. As the door opened, she said, "I'm sorry, Mr. La Gall, but there's been some trouble in town and the sheriff asked me to keep the store closed until he has it cleared up."

"I'm so sorry to bother you, Miss, but I didn't know where else to go, and I promise not to bother you long."

She frowned. "What did you need?"

"I'm having trouble with my stomach and the doctor is out at a ranch somewhere. Mr. Olsen told me you sold a tonic that would help me." When she said nothing, he added, "If you'll just let me come in a buy a bottle, I'll be on my way."

Wilma hesitated only a moment, then opened the door. "Come in and I'll get it for you, but I need to lock the door behind you. I see the street is getting busy with people and I don't want everyone coming in until Sheriff Gentry says it's all right to open up."

He stepped inside. "I understand."

Wilma turned the latch and moved toward the shelf where the patent medicines were kept. She reached for a bottle. "I'm sure this is the elixir Frank told you about. It's our most popular one for stomach problems."

"That's wonderful. How much do I owe you?"

She told him, took the money and moved from behind the counter to unlock the door to let him out. She didn't make it.

Marcel grabbed her from behind. With his hand over her mouth, he said, "Now, my pretty, head to the storeroom and up those stairs to your quarters. Today, my mission will be complete."

~ * ~

Spencer wasn't sure if he was dreaming as he heard the female voices intermingled with one male voice or if there was someone in the apartment. He frowned as he tried to come out of shadowed land between sleep and wakefulness.

Then one of the female voices said, "I swear, none of us knows what you're talking about."

Somehow, he knew the voice belonged to Nelda. He frowned again. Who could his wife be arguing with here in her apartment? She usually saved her arguments for him.

Then the male voice said, "I don't believe you, so you might as well confess. Which one of you is the princess?"

Spencer knew immediately that voice could only come from one man. Marcel Guillaume Augustus La Gall, the man they often referred to as The Blade.

He knew he didn't have time to wait to hear more. Though his first instinct was to jump out of bed and rush into the room, he knew he had to play it smart. La Gall wouldn't hesitate to stick a knife in either of the women the minute he felt threatened. He'd done it before.

Spencer slid out of bed and noticed someone had put him down with his pants on. Probably Nelda. He shook his head and eased to the dresser where Nelda had laid his gun.

Again, La Gall's voice came to him. "I see you're blonde, like the princess, but you're a new face. So is the one called Wilma."

"You couldn't be more wrong. None of us is a princess, though there were times when we were little that we pretended we were."

This time he recognized Amelia's voice.

"It has to be you, Miss Nelda, as you call yourself now. You could have changed your hair since I know you've been at the fort with him and now you're here with him."

"No!" Nelda screamed.

Spencer threw the door open and his blood ran cold. La Gall had a knife raised to plunge into Nelda's chest. "Drop that knife!"

But the hand was coming down. Spencer didn't hesitate. He fired and the knife flew from the man's hand.

For a second, La Gall looked stunned, but he recovered quickly. "You shot my baby!"

In an instant, he was down on the floor searching for his knife. When he got his hand around it, he stood and stared at Spencer. "You're supposed to be dead."

"As you can see, I'm not. Now, put that knife down."

"You know I have to kill her." He staggered toward Nelda. "She can't ascend to the throne."

Spencer knew he had no choice. He fired a second time.

Marcel Guillaume Augustus La Gall stumbled backward. Blood spouted from his chest and he started shaking his head, as if he couldn't believe he'd been shot.

As he crumpled to the floor, a sobbing Nelda ran to her husband. He folded his arms around her.

Instantly, the handle of the outside door shook vigorously.

~ * ~

When Lance came through the door, chaos reigned for several minutes. But as everyone calmed down, things happened fast. Mayor Hershel Baldwin and Hal Cramer had heard the shots and had followed Lance up the stairs. They took care of getting the undertaker to cart the body away, said they'd sort things out with Lance later, then left.

Over protest, Wilma said since supper was half cooked, she would finish it and they'd all eat. Nelda wanted to send for the doctor for Spencer, but he wouldn't let her. She insisted he go to bed. He finally agreed, if they'd all come in the bedroom and let him explain what the attempted murder of a princess was all about.

When he finished, Nelda stared at him. "Are you saying that woman in Denver was a princess and she was not your mistress?"

He reached for her hand. "Yes, Nelda. No man was allowed to touch her in any way except friendship. She was well chaperoned by some of her loyal subjects. I was one of several men recruited by our government who took turns going to Denver to protect her. In fact, I was the one who would be released from my obligation as soon as Minton and La Gall were taken care of. The next man, who I only know as CH is to take over and see the princess is moved to the area where she will be sent to her country to become its leader as soon as the conspiracy is fully crushed."

"I guess we have to keep our mouths closed about all of this?" Lance said.

"You do, but I'm sure we can come up with a story that will satisfy the people. After all, you have Con Minton on the kidnapping charge. Then when they learn La Gall killed the woman in the saloon, it won't be hard to convince the public that La Gall came in here to rob and murder Nelda and Wilma. People will believe he was surprised to find Amelia visiting."

"You're awfully good at making up stories, husband. Are you sure you don't have a mistress tucked somewhere?"

"I assure you, the princess nor anyone else has ever been my mistress. You can rest assured there has never been any other woman in my bed since the day I married you, and I promise you, here in front of our friends, there never will be."

She smiled at him and squeezed his hand. Her eyes sparkled when she said, "Then, I guess it's a good thing I haven't yet gotten the divorce."

~ * ~

CH stared at the final wire and grinned. "Well, Princess, your ordeal is coming to an end. I'd guess that by spring or early summer, you'll be back in your country and sitting on your throne."

"Are you sure?"

"I am. La Gall is dead and Minton is going to prison until they get the gallows ready. Not only is he having to pay for kidnapping a little boy, but they found him guilty of several murders beginning with the killing of the grandson of an Indian chief that the government had an agreement with."

"What happens now?"

"I'll escort you to Cheyenne. There you will be turned over to ZN. As soon as your cousin's attempt at a takeover is public knowledge, he will be arrested and tried for treason. He may try to leave your country before he's arrested, if someone doesn't kill him first. It will then be safe for you to return. ZN will escort you on the next leg of your journey, but I don't know where he'll take you or who will take over then. Only the government knows that."

"Will I see you and the major or any of my other guards again?"

"No, Your Highness. The other guards were released when we got the first wire. The major will go back to living his former life as soon as I let him know I received this wire. After I make sure things in Cheyenne are safe for you, ZN will take over and I will return to my regular job."

"I will miss all of you, but I'm happy to know I will be going home at last." She turned. "After I give you a hug for your service, I will inform my staff to prepare to move to this place you call Cheyenne."

CH gave her a quick hug, then a bow. He turned to send the wire back to the major. He couldn't help wondering if, when his part in this mission was over, he would be released to pursue the life he wanted to lead, or would he have to return to prison to finish serving his sentence?

Epilogue

Spring came early to Settlers Ridge, and with it came more changes to the town. One of the most noticeable was when the Barrington's Mercantile sign replaced the weathered and worn Brown's. But most people were delighted to see the change. They had grown used to seeing Nelda and Wilma, and soon Spencer, too, in the store. They were also pleased that a stranger wouldn't be buying the place, and since his arrival, Spencer wasn't considered a stranger.

Probably the most surprised about the way things were turning out, was Nelda. Her first shock came when Spencer informed her, he had resigned from the military and planned to move to Settlers Ridge and go into business. He mentioned starting a newspaper, but when she said she'd support him, but would miss working in the mercantile, he surprised her again and bought the store from Mrs. Brown and Stanley. Her second surprise came when he told her he'd also bought the Browns' house. They had been in the house for two months.

Wilma still worked in the store and lived in the apartment upstairs. Though she still hadn't met that special man, she'd made two young fellows in town her ardent admirers when she insisted on presenting them each with a pair of chaps as a reward for helping the sheriff catch the man who shot the major. Since she was so well liked and efficient, this gave Nelda a chance to often go home early and cook supper. It also gave the Barringtons a chance to leave the store together now and then.

They had done so today because Nelda couldn't wait to see Lance and Grace's daughter, who had arrived in the middle of the previous night. Of course, Nelda was thrilled with baby Katherine and Spencer went along because he was happy for the new parents.

The store was closed for the day and Grace had retreated to her apartment. Spencer had come home and was enjoying the supper his wife had prepared.

As they sat at the table, Spencer smiled at Nelda as he reached for another biscuit. "This is really good, sweetheart."

"Though the weather is getting warmer, I didn't think it was too warm to make you a good hearty stew today."

"Never. You know I love it."

She smiled at him. "It's been a good day, hasn't it, honey?"

He winked at her. "Every day is a good day with my wife."

She grinned at him. "And to think, a few months ago, I was willing to get a divorce and throw away everything we have together."

"You know I would have never let you do that."

"So, you said." She laughed. "I'm still sorry I didn't trust you, Spencer. You've always been a wonderful husband."

"I hope you always think so, because I sure like being your husband."

She changed the subject. "Isn't Katherine the cutest little baby ever?"

He raised an eyebrow. "If you say so."

"What do you mean, if I say so?"

"She looked a little wrinkly and red to me."

Nelda laughed. "All babies are wrinkled and red when they're first born."

"What did you think when they said they were going to name her after your mother?"

"I was pleased. Lance had asked me earlier if I'd mind and I told him I didn't mind at all. I know how well Lance looked after mother and me after my father died. He deserved to use her name if he wanted to."

Nelda pushed back her plate and looked at him. "Are you about through eating?"

"Taking my last bite. Why?"

"I feel I want to be cuddled. May I come and sit in your lap a minute?"

He shoved his bowl forward and his chair back from the table. "Of course, you can. Come on, baby."

She sat in his lap and put her arms around his neck. Leaning down to kiss him, she whispered, "I just wanted you to know if we have a little girl someday, we'll name her after your mother if you want to."

He grinned. "If we name a child after my mother, I sure hope we'll have a girl. I certainly don't want a little boy named Cynthia."

She kissed him again, and laughed. "You're right. That'd never work for our son."

"No, it would...." He gave her a sudden frown. "Wait a minute. Are you telling me—?"

She giggled. "I think so. Of course, I could be wrong."

"Oh, Nelda. Are you sure?"

She laughed. "I just suspect."

He stood with her in his arms. "Then what are we waiting for? We need to make sure you more than suspect."

"But the dishes."

"The dishes can wait. This is a much more important mission." He leaned over the table and blew out the lamp. "You should know by now, I never let anything interfere with a mission I'm involved in."

"Yes, Major. I'm very aware of that."

He laughed and kissed her all the way down the hall to their bedroom.

Meet Agnes Alexander

A life-long resident of North Carolina, she counts traveling as one of her passions. She has visited 48 of the 50 states and says Alaska and Hawaii are on her bucket list, but are looking doubtful. Of course, she loves to read, but tries to limit herself to one or two books a week. Besides traveling and reading, Agnes enjoys jewelry making, watching old movies and helping new authors reach their goal of publication. But if you ask her, she'll tell you her most favorite thing to do is to spend time with her family—especially her two grandchildren.

Other Works From The Pen Of
Agnes Alexander

Valissa's Home - Valissa's brother gambled away her home; now she struggles to contend with the cowboy who owns it.

Opal's Faith - When Opal moves to the rundown ranch her father inherited she never dreamed she'd find a half-breed cousin or meet a drifter who became the subject of her secret dreams.

Ulla's Courage - To prevent her conspiring aunt and uncle from stealing her inheritance, Ulla decides to marry a widowed stranger with two children and accompany him on his trek on the Oregon Trail.

Zelda's Guilt - Trying to save the failing ranch, Zelda accepts help of a passing cowboy to foil her bedridden stepmother's vicious plan to force her to marry an unscrupulous neighbor.

Visit Our Website

For The Full Inventory
Of Quality Books:

Wings ePress, Inc

Quality trade paperbacks and downloads
in multiple formats,
in genres ranging from light romantic comedy to general
fiction and horror.
Wings has something for every reader's taste.
Visit the website, then bookmark it.
We add new titles each month!

Wings ePress Inc.
3000 N. Rock Road
Newton, KS 67114

www.ingramcontent.com/pod-product-compliance
Lightning Source LLC
Chambersburg PA
CBHW070629100726
47907CB00007B/1905